Cover Copy

To love and protect…across worlds.

In a world divided by war, a rival prince and princess shall meet…

Here comes a young adult story like no other. First love, epic fantasy, addictive reading.

Faith Stryker never expected her lost father would be a warrior prince from another world, or that she would come into coveted magical skills on her eighteenth birthday. Now, she must take a leap of faith when her father suddenly arrives to claim her. He asks her to leave Earth with him, to give up all she's ever known, and to embrace a new world—her legacy. It's time for her to accept her place as a princess of Dralion, to wield her burgeoning battle skill, and to fight alongside her new nation's fierce band of warriors.

When Prince Davio Loveria discovers he's mated to Faith, the lost daughter from his rival nation, he must either accept his bond with her, or give her up forever. His head tells him to set her aside, that no match can possibly be made between them, but each time he comes into contact with her, his heart still demands he fight for their developing bond.

Is it possible for love to grow as a relentless war rages?

Books by Joanne Wadsworth

The Matheson Brothers Series
Highlander's Desire, Book One
Highlander's Passion, Book Two
Highlander's Seduction, Book Three
Highlander's Kiss, Book Four
Highlander's Heart, Book Five
Highlander's Sword, Book Six
Highlander's Bride, Book Seven
Highlander's Caress, Book Eight
Highlander's Touch, Book Nine
Highlander's Shifter, Book Ten
Highlander's Claim, Book Eleven
Highlander's Courage, Book Twelve
Highlander's Mermaid, Book Thirteen

Highlander Heat Series
Highlander's Castle, Book One
Highlander's Magic, Book Two
Highlander's Charm, Book Three
Highlander's Guardian, Book Four
Highlander's Faerie, Book Five
Highlander's Champion, Book Six
Highlander's Captive (Short Story)

Billionaire Bodyguards Series
Billionaire Bodyguard Attraction, Book One
Billionaire Bodyguard Boss, Book Two
Billionaire Bodyguard Fling, Book Three

Books by Joanne Wadsworth

Regency Brides Series
The Duke's Bride, Book One
The Earl's Bride, Book Two
The Wartime Bride, Book Three
The Earl's Secret Bride, Book Four
The Prince's Bride, Book Five
Her Pirate Prince, Book Six
Chased by the Corsair, Book Seven

Princesses of Myth Series
Protector, Book One
Warrior, Book Two
Hunter (Short Story - Included in Warrior, Book Two)
Enchanter, Book Three
Healer, Book Four
Chaser, Book Five

PROTECTOR

Princesses of Myth, Book One

JOANNE WADSWORTH

Dedication

For my hubby, who cooks dinner while I write and brings home my favorite chocolate.

Acknowledgements

Huge thanks to my hubby, Jason, and kiddies, Marisa, Caleb, Cruise and Rocco. You allow me so much time to write, and I love you for it. With each book I publish, another dream becomes fulfilled. Your incredible support means the world to me.

For my readers, from the depths of my heart, I thank you for joining me, where imagination and magic soar.

Hugs to you all.

Chapter 1

"Faith. Hey, Earth to Faith Stryker." Silvie Carver snapped her fingers and bobbed her head of fiery red-gold hair in front of me.

"Don't you dare say it, Silvie." Her thoughts bombarded me, dropped right into my mind as if I'd conjured them up myself. I shook my head forcefully. "We're in class and there are other students around." Except no one could halt my best friend when she had to get something off her mind, not even me.

"Faith, it's gotta be said." She inhaled sharply. "You need to get laid. You need someone fun to…well, you know what."

Ugh. Elbows on the desk, I dropped my head into my cupped palms. Because there it was—Silvie's answer to the fact we were both now eighteen and still completely single.

I lifted my head, stared her down. "Did you not hear me say we were in class, Silvie? Your timing for that analysis completely sucks. Besides, we should be studying for our end of year exams. A boyfriend comes after exams, which applies to both you and me."

I snuck a look around the classroom, but yeah, I was now the current spectacle because unfortunately for me, Silvie's voice could carry just as blisteringly hot as her stunning, wildfire red hair.

It didn't help that one of our fellow male students now

appeared riveted on our conversation, and giving me the worst slumberous wink I'd ever seen. "She wasn't meaning I should have sex with you, Caleb Stiles. Look the other way." I turned my hostile stare back on Silvie since she was the one who deserved it. "You, Silvie Carver, better sit down before I knock you down. I can't believe you just said that, or why I always put up with you and your big mouth."

She only laughed as she shamelessly scraped one of the blue-gray metal school chairs around next to mine. She plopped herself down on it, dropping her English books, refill pad and pen in front of her onto the desk. Next, she stretched her legs out as far as she could and crossed them idly at her ankles. "Well, this conversation isn't over. I'm sure Belle would agree."

"Don't you dare bring Belle into this." Somehow I'd managed to lower my voice and inflict some kind of control into it.

Silvie scooped her blue pen back up, casually twirled it in mid-air around her first three fingers. This aeronautical pen trick of hers always captivated me, but not right now. Because right now, I was more than peeved. I'd had the worst week ever since my eighteenth birthday, and I mean the— Worst. Week. Ever. No one should have to live through the tribulations I'd just experienced, and was still experiencing, no thanks to Belle Benner still being in town.

Silvie wagged one brow as her gaze rose over my shoulder. "Too late, Faith. Belle's here. She and I have also been talking."

Great. Just grrreat.

Belle pulled out the school chair on the other side of me, her dark locks settling with stunning abandon about her tiny waist as she twirled around and sat. She did everything with such finesse. Even the simple act of her sitting was like watching a moving piece of art. So moving, I had quizzed her about being a ballerina. She just had this way about every precise movement she made. Dainty and delicate.

"So what were you two talking about? I didn't have my ears tuned precisely in," Belle said as she tossed her pad and pen with an artful glide onto her desk. Her slim fingers came around and smoothed her silky mass of dark hair behind one ear.

I snapped my fingers, finally pinpointing exactly who Belle looked like. It was that young star female lead off High School Musical. The one who got the basketball guy and sang and danced with him.

"Focus, Faith. I asked what you two were talking about. I didn't have my hearing turned up."

There Belle went again with that telepathic skill of hers, speaking mind to mind, always trying to draw me into her mysterious world. I sighed and gave in since she knew I would've heard her. *"Silvie thinks I should get laid."* I pushed the words along our newly formed telepathic link, the crazy link we'd created on the night of my eighteenth birthday. We'd been speaking privately like this for the past few days, something Belle called a strength skill, but something I called plain crazy.

Beyond crazy.

Only she seemed to have more insight than me into this odd, spinning frenzy that had become my life these past seven mind-boggling days. She insisted my skills came from the same place as hers, and that place was another planet in this universe—one named after their timeless skills—one she referred to as Magio.

"I can feel your resistance. We are from Magio. I've told you this over and over since we first connected last week. I'm an empath and can feel your emotions."

"I heard you say so the last one-hundred times. It doesn't mean I have to believe you." I sent her a very long eye roll. *"My mother doesn't have any of the skills I've been developing since my birthday. So there simply can't be an alternate planet called Magio. Believe me, I've been scouring the NASA website for any link on this mysterious planet you've been spouting nonsense*

about. There's nothing. Nada. Zilch. Nilch. Got that or do we speak a separate language as well?"

She gave me her own dark eye roll back. *"Obviously, you won't find anything about Magio on the NASA website. Get real. If such a thing happened, the powers that be on Earth would no doubt try to bomb us to smithereens. We live a simple existence, like that of your people hundreds of years ago. We don't harbor advanced technology as you do."*

Quite frankly, I'd had enough of her talk about this other planet and this other country called Peacio. My mother was human. I was human. In fact, for eighteen years I'd been just a regular—or as regular as I could get—New Zealand girl. It was Belle who was the problem. I'd only known her for three short, unnerving months. I couldn't shake her, and on top of that, I had no answer for this telepathy, thought-reading, and other unmentionables.

"Right, let's agree to disagree on this subject." I was getting a headache, just as I always did around her.

Silvie nudged my arm from the other side, winking while a sassy grin tugged at her lips. "Are you two talking privately again? That mind thingy-majigimy you two do?"

"Yes, and it's about Peacio again." Frowning, I pursed my lips. "You've seen those paranormal programs, haven't you? It's not uncommon for some of those weird beasties to speak mind to mind. That's all this is about. I don't believe there's another planet like Earth out there." And I didn't believe I was a weird beastie either, just a weird human being it seemed.

Silvie chuckled and sighed almost dreamily. "You two are so funny. I only wish I could do what you do."

Sheesh. I slapped my forehead, dropping my chin. My best friend needed a mind transplant. No one I knew would want to be this different this early on in life. I sat between two crazy people. I tapped my scratched up desktop, having no idea where to go from here.

"Talk to me." Belle squeezed my shoulder. "What's bothering you the most?"

"Everything, but most of all, I'd really like to know why I put up with either of you." I couldn't shake them if I tried.

Belle smiled, ignoring my rude comment as she had a terrible tendency to do whenever I slung one at her. "You put up with me because you and I share a common trait. Our home planet—whether you believe it or not." She paused to peer past me at Silvie. "And you put up with Silvie because she's like a sister to you. You know I can feel that."

"Oh, would you just quit with the whole empath thing." I threw my arms in the air. "I wasn't exactly asking why I put up with you. I was letting off some steam. I mean really." Still flinging my arms about. "You don't have to over-analyze every single little word I say."

I fell back into my chair, beginning to count, enforcing more than a little necessary timeout to calm down.

"What are you doing now?" Belle nibbled on her lower lip. "I'm getting such a strange reversal of feelings from you."

"That's because I'm trying to ignore your presence. For a blessed moment it worked."

Leaning into me, Silvie chuckled. "Faith's regrouping, Belle. It's her calming thing. Give her a minute to wind down after all your talk of Peacio. You've been infuriating her with it for far too long. Particularly when she's used to only me infuriating her, so getting a double dose lately hasn't been easy for her."

I rolled my shoulders in an effort to release the tension, hating how Silvie was so accepting of Belle's talk of all things Peacio and I was not. But then I was the one hearing Belle's voice in my head along with everyone's random thoughts when they spewed forth. Yeah, that was lucky old me.

I squirmed in my chair and let out a haggard breath. "Let's talk about Peacio later, guys." As Belle would no doubt want to do since she was like a dog with a bone on that subject. "Mrs. Gray's on her way, and I need to focus one-hundred percent on English and not some mystical otherworld."

Belle gave me a strange look with her exotic eyes. "*You can still sense when someone is coming? You're picking up their thoughts?*"

Great. She was back to speaking privately. It seemed like it was her job to constantly remind me of exactly how odd I now was. I moaned with great exaggeration.

"*Only if they're broadcasting strongly. Mrs. Gray is crossing the quad, examining how to prepare us for finals.*" I'd latched onto that. "*So, are you still insisting this grows into forethought, the same thing your supposed King Carlisio has?*" That was like the proverbial nail in the coffin, for Belle mentioning a fictional king had made me completely desert her farfetched notions.

"*Don't flick me off again,*" she growled. "*King Carlisio Loveria is a wise ruler and it's because of his rare skill of forethought. As one of his Peacio protectors, I won't abide my ruler's name being disparaged.*"

Excellent. Now we were back to the whole Peacio protector thing again. I needed to do more than just flick Belle off—I needed to have her locked up in the insane ward. This time I chose to ignore all the impulses to respond, instead busying myself with my workbook. Now was not the time or place for this argument, not when—whoa.

Someone walking with Mrs. Gray released a bombardment of thoughts. They soared right at me. Thoughts belonging to a new student.

A male by the tone in his mind.

Yep, definitely a male. He questioned Mrs. Gray about me, said he knew me.

Mrs. Gray rounded the corner, her salt-and-pepper hair short, straight and styled up higher over her forehead to add volume to the thinning mass. She spoke, although she dimmed into the background as the male stepped forward, his gaze cutting straight to me.

The entire room quietened.

I'd never seen him before, couldn't lower my gaze and break the intense eye contact between us. Such raw power emanated from him, along with a seductive aura that completely fuzzed my mind. My traitorous thoughts spun. He must be at least six foot four, far taller than any of the other boys in our class. His hair held a slight wave and was that teasing shade in between dark blond and brown, the longer length just sweeping his shoulders. His eyes were to die for, their liquid brown speckled with gold, the darker color the same exact shade as his hair.

Oh, yum, yum, yum.

He rolled his shoulders and the white t-shirt he wore stretched tight over rippling muscles. Blue jeans sat low on his hips, the bottoms tucked carelessly into a pair of black ankle-high boots with thick silver buckles.

My mouth dried out and I licked my lips.

His gaze zoomed in on them, and my cheeks heated. Oh heck, maybe Silvie was right, maybe I did need to get laid. Mmm, and he'd surely make the perfect candidate.

Oh, and the way he stared at me in return just melted me. The fire in his eyes set a glow to the golden flecks and lit them brilliantly. In the mere few seconds that had passed, this stranger had disarmed me, his hot gaze running up and down my body.

Hold on. I jerked my head back. Was he really checking me out?

I turned to check who sat behind me, because I was surely wrong, except the last desk in the room remained clear of any student. "Who's he looking at?" I whispered to Belle.

"That's Davio Loveria, the king's grandson, and he's looking at you."

What? Did Belle just say that man, that new male student was the king's grandson?

The fictional king?

From the fictional country of Peacio?

Surely Belle hadn't gone quite so far as to acquire a co-conspirator.

"*Jeez, Belle, and if I ask that new student if he's a prince of Peacio, will he actually confirm it?*" I reverted to our telepathic connection since I didn't need anyone else hearing what I now had to say. "*I mean, do you really think for one second I don't believe you are completely and utterly nuts?*"

Seriously.

I needed to get Belle a straightjacket and lock her up pronto.

She cracked a smile. "*No, silly. With your emerging forethought skill, King Carlisio sent Davio to assess the situation as reinforcement to me as your protector. After Davio turned eighteen earlier this year, even he did not show any signs of the rare skill which his grandfather has. It's sadly skipped two generations in the Loveria family and so far, you are the only one outside of the royal line who shows any signs of it. Why do you think I'm still here and have not returned home?*"

I quirked a suspicious brow and retaliated. "*Because you live to pester me.*"

Easy answer.

I'm afraid the girl was on her way to being institutionalized. There was no hope for her. Not now.

"*No,*" she fired right back at me. "*Because you are too valuable to be left unattended. You need protection.*"

I blew out a harsh breath, right in her face. "*For the millionth, billionth, zillionth time, I am growing very weary of all this Peacio crap.*" Would she never give up?

That was when her declaration sent shockwaves through me. Surprised, my jaw landed somewhere down in my lap. Now why would she feel the need to protect me? And protect me against what?

Okay, it seemed I was actually going to go there. *"Exactly what are you protecting me from?"*

"You can read thoughts, a skill that develops into forethought, and depending on how strong it is, it can't be permitted to go under the radar. I'm a protector. Once your forethought develops, you will need me by your side to instruct you."

Belle was so matter of fact about everything she said. For a brief moment, I felt the first fluttering of belief in her, then it cemented, making me groan out loud. I needed to discover if there was any possible truth in all that she'd told me this past week. I mean, I couldn't exactly deny these skills that had arrived to torment me.

"I want to meet with Davio Loveria. I want to hear from the newcomer"—who was now sitting in his assigned seat at the front of the class—*"what he has to say without any interference from you."*

Belle's lips lifted, and she answered with speed. *"Excellent. Would now be an appropriate time?"*

I observed the princely hunk's side profile, gathering my strength. *"After class. Lunchtime. On the field."* I needed another forty-five minutes to fortify myself. *"You, me and him."*

* * * *

It was the beginning of spring, the first week of September, and I'd chosen an isolated spot under a large, yellow-green umbrella leaf tree on the outskirts of the school's grassy area. Belle waited with me where the sunlight dappled through the loose formation of foliage and warmed the ground. I propped my backpack against the tree, hooked my thumb into the belt loop of my snug blue denim miniskirt and hoped I exuded at least a little confidence.

Belle rubbed her palms down her short, scarlet cotton dress

and stepped forward to greet the newcomer as he crossed the lawn. "Welcome, Davio." Belle turned and extended her hand toward me. "This is Miss Faith Stryker."

"Thank you, Belle. So this is the one Carlisio says has forethought?" Davio narrowed his gaze on me as he stood there, his bearing firm as he clasped Belle's arm, and far too intimately for my liking. Which I really shouldn't have noticed, or should even care about.

Only I couldn't help but frown at the cozy image they made. Exactly how well did these two know each other? And why did the man still look completely edible? Those blue jeans of his molded his long legs and made me drool for a bite.

Frustrated, I ground my teeth together, lifted my chin and stepped forward. "Yes, I'm the one who has forethought, and I'd say nice to meet you, but I'm not sure that's wise." Not wise at all.

Damn. Why was I so irritated? The man had set all my nerves on edge.

"Belle told me you're a prince of Peacio. How do I know that's the truth?" Hungry for more information, I siphoned through his thoughts using the skill Belle kept referring to as my burgeoning forethought. Hopefully I'd find this was all an elaborate and totally explainable ruse.

"I can feel you in my mind." Davio released her arm and stepped closer, touched his forehead then immediately blocked, the same as Belle was able to do when I got too nosy filtering through her mind.

Now there was nothing, although not quite like with Belle. A block existed, yet I still found myself settling into a soft spot within his mind that seemed to be reserved just for me.

I gave him a cocky grin, and he damn well returned it, seriously peeving me further. "So, I guess I have to believe you're the grandson of Peacio's supposed king. David is it?"

One masculine brow quirked. "Davio, not David, but yes,

I'm Carlisio's sole grandson. Who is your father?"

"At present I don't know and quite frankly, I've never cared." I didn't either. I had the world's most fabulous mother, one who'd provided all I'd ever needed in life. While the man who'd irresponsibly provided the other half of my genes to give me that life had never stayed to even say one simple hello.

Davio crossed his arms, frowning as he drew one-step closer. "Father aside, let's concentrate on what you're doing right now. You are lodged within my mind—" He stopped, shook his head as if clearing it, then took another decided step forward. "There's a warmth, like a merging or a similar form of alternate connection, I've never experienced before. What is it you're doing?"

No sooner had he said the words, did I find myself dropping out of that soft spot I'd found and ending the merge he'd noted. Bad move. Ouch. I grabbed my head as my mind demanded to return to his. What the—I jerked, shoved a hand up and tried to halt his sudden advancement. "Stay right there."

A sharp stinging pain took me as he bore down on me. "No. Stop." I clutched my chest, gasping as more pain lanced through me. Somehow Davio's presence caused it.

Against my wishes, my mind pierced back into his and bedded down into that soft place that brought a sense of rightness along with it. I fell against him, grabbed his arm, the closer contact with him somehow now ceasing the pain and my turbulent emotions all at once.

What on earth was going on?

I took a moment, breathing deep, the warmth within his mind rolling through to me. "This is the strangest thing," I murmured, awestruck. "Can you truly feel my mind merged with yours?"

"I can." He pressed his hand over my hand on his arm. "You're in my head. I can feel your presence, but be aware you'll not get a single thought from me since I'm now blocked."

Clearly a set down, putting me in my place.

I gritted my teeth and dropped my hand. I backed up, and the moment I did, the pain returned and all I wanted to do was strike out at him. "I didn't mean to pry, but this is all new to me." Bewitchingly new. Belle had told me bits here and there, yet it would certainly take more evidence to completely sway me to her side.

Annoyance coursed through me as he glowered.

Circling me, his gaze slanted as his enormous body threatened. "Now, aren't you a pesky little enigma."

I curled my fingers inward, nails biting into my palms. "So my mother constantly says, Prince Davio."

He came back around to stand in front. "It's just Davio to you. Don't forget where we are. I hardly need someone from outside of my home world to hear you."

"We're all alone out here in case you missed it." My gut clenched into an awful mess.

"Apart from this skill of mind-merge, you know what I believe is happening between us."

"Well, not if you don't share it."

"You and I are bonded," he said with a hard, defiant tone.

"I'm sorry, we're what?" Please let that not be what it sounded like. The word bonded certainly rang with the term of something rather deep to me, and I didn't want deep with him.

"No, being bonded isn't a *what*, Faith Stryker. Being bonded is a *how*." Then he reared over me, almost toppling me over.

"Hey," I growled, slamming a hand into him. "Attempting to intimidate me will get you nowhere."

"We're somehow bonded, your soul to my soul, although how that could be is beyond my understanding since you're clearly of Earth and I'm not. Who are your parents, and how did you come to have forethought?"

Huh, as if I knew how. I didn't even want the stupid skill

I'd come into the week before. "First, I've always lived on Earth. Second, I have only my mother, who I might add has outdone herself in raising me."

"What of your father? Where exactly is he?"

"I don't know." I had to force myself to hold his very dominant gaze. "Nor do I care." My chest tightened, and not because I spoke of my father, but because of this man's presence. So many emotions battered me, from roaring desire to fierce anger, and all dependent on how close he was.

"Father aside, I feel the deep tension between us. It's too physical."

"I agree, and I've decided I don't want to meet you after all. Let's forget this past morning ever happened and you can wing your way back to your lovely little planet of Magio." However he managed to do that winging. Yeah, curiosity bit me swiftly in the butt. I should have asked Belle before how she'd managed to get here from Magio, only if I had, that would have likely given her too much of an opening in order to push more onto me.

"I don't understand." Belle stepped forward, her lips pinched. "Surely, this is impossible. You two simply can't be mated. She's a Halfling."

"I don't understand either." I gave her a glare. "So let's just forget everything, and you can take him away."

"I can't." Her hands trembled as she pushed them through her dark hair. "I can't interfere in a mated relationship. It is a soul-bound calling, one fixed between the two of you." Her wide gaze begged understanding. "You have to understand. Only half of our population are mated once they come into their adult strength skills at eighteen. The male always senses the bond after he makes direct contact with his female. This is what has happened. It seems you are mated to our prince."

I gulped. Again, not something I wanted to hear, yet if this was all real, then that meant I was likely in a world of trouble. "Okay, so we're mated." I turned on Davio. "Which is clearly all your fault. Why on earth would you allow a soul bond to form between us?"

"The soul bond actually forms of its own accord, and usually not long after birth. Although it's only once a Magioling reaches adulthood that the two become aware of that bond. Until then, little is known." He snagged my hand. "You are not one of my people. I'm not happy about that."

I waited a moment, tortured at his tight hold and at the scowl darkening his face. He clearly detested this moment, and the discovery of our bond, just as much as I did. "Then quit touching me." I jerked my hand free. "If you can't tell, I'm not happy about that."

He winced, the first sign that he wasn't anything other than mad. "I will try. I can see you need some space." He stepped away, propped his back against the wide trunk of the tree.

Now given the opportunity, I too scooted back.

Then it happened.

Once we reached five feet of distance between us, a strange calmness descended over me. I breathed out the last of my tension and closed my eyes, then groaned as Belle tapped at my mind along our telepathic link.

"*Ooo-kay,*" she murmured, "*You need to tell me exactly what's going on with you? First and foremost, I'm your friend.*"

I ignored her, feeling a touch bad, and instead opened my eyes and took in the man who'd dropped into my life and tossed it all about within one single morning. His thoughts blared loud and clear as he eyed me blatantly in return. The light blond color of my hair captivated him, the fine strands catching the sunlight sparkling through the leaves and making the golden hue glow like woven silk.

I grimaced.

He studied my eyes, found the unusual violet color incredibly intriguing.

"Stop it." I crossed my arms with a slap. "Can't you block

again?"

"I don't wish to right now." He tilted his chin and straightened as he pushed off the tree. "It isn't just the color of your eyes I find intriguing, but you as well."

"I'd rather you keep your unhelpful words to yourself too." Damn it. Now he neared. I hated that every time he came so close, I turned aggressive. "Stay there."

My blustery warning was loud and clear, but he didn't break his stride. "I can't stop myself. It's this stupid, stubborn bond. Finding my mate should never have been like this. It obviously shouldn't have been with a Halfling and someone not of my world."

"Amen to that," I grumbled as he ruthlessly closed in.

I threw up a hand against his oncoming assault and tried to halt him. Too late.

My palm hit his chest, his momentum driving me back several steps. Oh boy. I flushed as my aggression instantly dissolved. So strange. When he touched me, the hard emotions promptly disappeared, the pain and anger sliding right away.

"You're more than an enigma." Davio leaned over me, all six foot four of him, his warm honey-brown hair falling forward to curl snugly around his neck, and I longed for him, just as I had during my first sighting of him in the classroom.

"Why do I suddenly want you this close?"

"What's happening is the bond, my mate. It will become difficult for me to keep my distance from you, both physically and emotionally. The same goes for you, unless of course I leave and end this now."

"You really want to leave?" My heart hitched and I swayed closer. "Is that how this bond works? We find each other and then you leave?"

"No, it never happens that way. Those who are mated are bonded for life if we allow our souls their desire, except that would be the most unwise choice for us to take. You are, quite clearly, neither from my country nor from my world, and as such will have no allegiance to me or my people. I have no wish to join with one who doesn't wish to join with me in all ways. With that being the case, I will find another when the time is right. As should you," he added solemnly.

"Hold on." Did he just say he would be joining with another woman?

I bit my tongue. That was good? I should leave it at that, right?

Jeez, what was wrong with me for questioning that choice?

"I'm sorry. We just met, and you're right. Go find your, your—" Strangely, I struggled to get the words out and finally gave up. "Well, have yourself a nice long life, and all that." I patted his chest roughly.

That was better.

The clock ticked and time slowed.

He didn't move.

"Look at me." With one finger sliding under my chin, he tipped my gaze to his. "This would never work."

"I understand. It's been pretty awful meeting you. I certainly don't want to be bonded to you for life." I tried to pull my mind from the soft spot where I'd bedded down, but had no luck. I actually detested the thought of letting go.

Perhaps I'd try physically first. I leaned back, only he moved his hand around to the small of my back and prevented me.

I gripped his arm. "Okay, you were going."

This was going to be the world's fastest breakup—no, non-breakup since we hadn't even been together. "Let go of me so that can happen."

Ultimately, neither of us needed the complication of the other in our life. I didn't want a bonded relationship, not when I had high school to finish and university on my horizon.

Releasing me, he clipped his heels together and inclined his head. "Belle will remain another day, and even though she told me you two have a telepathic connection, you should take the opportunity to learn more about your growing skills while she's here. Afterward, Carlisio will keep an eye on you, and Belle can return as necessary."

A heavy pressure once again pulsed through my blood, and that strange pain when we weren't touching skin-to-skin, rolled through me. "Sure."

I inched closer, closed my fingers around his arm, the necessary and instant relief palpable. I didn't understand this need, although it was definitely real. Tentatively, I spread my fingers wider and blew out a breath. "Can I ask you one last question?"

"Absolutely."

"Did Carlisio's forethought not tell him all that would transpire today? Is that not how this skill he and I both have works?"

"No, any visions he has are mere snapshots and not greatly identifiable. The future is fully changeable as my grandfather doesn't interfere in this way. One must always have free choice."

"Good." That I appreciated hearing. "I guess Carlisio thought it was right to send Belle to me here?"

"Yes." His gaze switched to Belle. "I'll send Sorrell to retrieve you tomorrow." Without warning, he took my hand from his arm and lifted my fingers to his lips, his turbulent gaze returning to mine. "Take peace in the fact that what is between us would never work. We simply don't belong together." His tone, deep and flawless, was filled with firm decision.

Then he released me and shimmered, his form becoming transparent as he disappeared from my sight. He could teleport? Holy moly.

Shock at his fast departure, which in fact answered my question about how he and Belle had gotten here in the first place, roared through me. I tumbled to the ground and sank my fingers deep into the cold grass underneath me. The air tasted stale, as if in that very moment when he'd flashed away, he'd taken whatever fresh air swirled and sucked it away with him.

"He's gone?" Astonishment and a definite spasm of pained grief shook me. "It hurts." Now that shouldn't have happened.

Belle scooted in beside me, and grasped my shoulder. "You wish him back?"

"No-ooo." I shook my head. "Don't get me wrong, but your prince made his choice, and I won't even consider swaying his mind. He is far better back where he belongs, as are you."

I had Silvie.

My mother too.

In fact, men had never been a constant in my life, starting right from my defective father who I'd never known, and now Davio who couldn't have left quicker if I'd been the one to push him away.

I mean, who needed men anyway?

I pulled my knees to my chest and hugged them tightly. Ultimately, Silvie and my mother were the only people in the world who mattered to me. They would always be right by my side.

Chapter 2

Still partially in a daze, I jogged home from school after Davio's departure. I hit the pavement along Centennial Park, my backpack strapped to my back and my PE gear of navy shorts and a white t-shirt and sneakers still on from last period. Best to do what I normally did and not wallow in Davio's leaving anymore. This park was beautiful too, and captured my attention. It consisted of miles of green trees and gardens with a ten-foot wide, meandering blacktop drive, the common ground following a leisurely path as it wove snakelike in and around the town. It linked schools and homes, and delivered a safe pathway for cyclists, runners and schoolchildren, the park's aged trees providing natural coverage against the elements.

I caught up to and passed primary school students walking home. Their home-time bell rang almost a half hour before ours, and my fellow classmates chattered with their younger siblings as they joined them.

Unfortunately, I didn't have any younger siblings. It was just Mum and me, and even though there were occasional times when a real craving to share my life with a sibling struck me, I thankfully had Silvie instead to fill that gap. She was my best friend, she was my sister, the one I'd been raised with since childhood. Baby photos taken of us together in the very beginning showed Silvie with her cute red-gold locks, and me with my pale skin and tufts of blond hair just starting to grow.

I smiled and picked up my pace, fairly flying home.

Along my street, I streamed along, my long hair whipping behind me like a full-blown sail and—whoa. I couldn't slow down. My pace increased even though that was the last thing I wanted.

Oh boy. What was happening now?

I screamed as I almost took out my mother's newly painted gray mailbox, freaked and locked my knees. Bad move. I hurtled, head over feet then skidded across the slippery grass on my backside. Crap! My mother's newly composted vegetable garden loomed. I tumbled and rolled headfirst into the ripest, stinkiest soil on the road.

Swearing at the stupid vegetable garden, I scuttled out and found my feet. Of all the senseless luck. Surely Belle could have warned me about this increased speed skill I'd soon be coming in to, because that's what it surely had to be. A skill her people from Magio held. I'd never moved so fast in my entire life. Not a human speed at all.

After flinging the muck from my butt and my fingers, I tramped inside and marched down the hallway of our two bedroom, brown brick and tile home. I needed a shower. And I needed it pronto.

Snapping up the brass lever in my shower, I dealt with the stench as the burst of water sprayed on me. And why couldn't I get Mr. Royal-pain-in-the-butt Highness out of my head? Every five seconds I thought of him.

Questions raced through my mind. Like where was Magio? And how long had it taken Davio to flash home? Because that hadn't been some nifty little trick.

Shaking my head, I hated that I couldn't disperse these thoughts of him just as easily as he had done with me.

Although I didn't give in. I would attempt to dispel all thoughts of him yet.

I dried off and changed, walked into my violet and cream bedroom and shuffled my homework about on my student desk. I'd try to get my mind into gear and off the man who'd left me before we'd really even met. It was a hard thought to tolerate though, being cast aside so quickly and easily by him.

I sat.

I nibbled on my fingernail and reluctantly closed my eyes.

Then I just couldn't help myself. I needed to see his image.

I pulled it from my memory, and let out a staggered breath as his form crystallized with stunning clarity before me. Damn, he hadn't been so hot looking, surely.

I bit back a sigh.

"Why did you have to make the decision to leave so quickly?" I asked his illusionary image. "I mean, I know you said the bond develops and cements fast but surely we could have had a few more minutes, you know, before you poofed out of there and completely left me without another word. You worthless, worthless—"

Huh, I was acting irrational. I hadn't even liked him.

And of course, the dirt bag didn't bother to answer me. His obstinate form wavered and disappeared, just as the real obnoxious man had so effortlessly done.

Yeah, teleportation. I couldn't deny I'd seen that in action.

I shook my head in frustration. I was such an undecided female. Now, he'd left me with very little persuasion on my part to stay, but that didn't mean he should have.

Still, I had to cease these unnecessary and completely unhelpful thoughts. What was done was done.

I had a future. One I'd already planned.

One which was vitally important to study for, which meant textbook.

I flicked to the right page, gritted my teeth and forced my mind to where it should be.

Several uneventful minutes ticked by.

I heaved a frustrated sigh because there was nothing going through my foolish mind but him.

Stupid, stupid bond. I bet Davio wasn't having these insane thoughts.

After another endless minute, I gave up, pushed away from my desk and walked to my full-length corner mirror.

Reflecting back at me was a pitiful young woman in frayed, blue denim jeans and an overstretched coral t-shirt. My feet were bare and my damp hair messy. I appeared as unraveled and exposed as I currently felt.

Birthdays truly were the pits.

I dropped into a tangled heap onto the violet covers of my bed. "Yeah, birthdays sucked big time."

I crossed my hands behind my head and glared at the ceiling. Turning eighteen had sure been monumental. My hearing was now phenomenal if I turned it up and focused, and my running speed, well, my running speed was world-class spectacular if one actually wanted it that way.

I channeled my superb hearing to the front door as the clear creak of it opening traveled to me.

"Hey, Faith, it's just me." A key jingling and Silvie closed the door with a *thunk*.

Well, at least the precise hearing was a nice bonus. "Bedroom," I called back. "Mum's at work." Where she usually was since apparently I needed to be fed, clothed and housed, as she liked to point out.

"Hey, I brought Belle with me." Silvie blew into the room with her far too cheerful bounce. "I heard all about the prince."

I bolted upright, hooked my knees over the side of the bed and scooted forward. "Come in, guys. I do have one day for all things Peacio to be explained."

Belle followed behind Silvie, a worried expression on her face. She dropped in beside me and muttered, "Clearly the situation today didn't end well. I believe, and I say this with the best of intentions, that Davio should have given you more time than he quite obviously did."

"Ooo-kay." Where was she heading with this?

"Davio never told you about Dralion or about the war that rages between us and our neighboring country. He should have done that."

"Well, then tell me. Davio has left you here for a day. Is this Dralion and this war something of significant importance to me?"

"Hostility has raged between our two nations for centuries. To explain, you must understand that Peacio is rich in raw mineral deposits compared to the neighboring land of Dralion. Dralion is ruled by its monarchy, a King Donaldo Wincrest and his son, Prince Alexo. The tension between Peacio and Dralion is ugly. The Wincrests want what the Loverias have and it's been that way for too many centuries to count. Davio's battle is one that has continued from generation to generation, and you're his mate, his soul match, the one woman who should be standing by his side, not standing unknown a million miles away. Davio should not have turned away from you so easily, not af—"

"Hey, hey, hold on. I'm a Halfling. New Zealand is my country. This is my place of birth. There's no standing by his side. He 'ported away."

"Yes, but Magiolings have strength skills which are imprinted into our DNA and passed on from parent to child. You have forethought—an ability not seen outside of the Loveria family for as long as Peacian history has recorded it." Leaning forward, she continued, "Around ten percent of our people can teleport as Davio can. Most have excellent hearing along with the sharpest eyesight. Then there are our elite protectors who usually hold these skills plus necessary battle skills and fast-healing. Next, are those like me who hold other strength skills, all varied and spread out in some form or another. Although, a stronger lineage denotes stronger skills, as does the resulting mated matches being blessed with higher skilled offspring. How you've come to hold one of the strongest, rarest skills on our planet is shocking, particularly when you're a Halfling."

"Well, don't ask me how I came about that skill." I gritted my teeth, sensing exactly where this conversation was headed. "Let's not forget Davio left and he's not coming back." I wanted to pace the room, but I stayed on the bed, my nerves tied into a knot. "Nothing you say will change that."

Belle twiddled her fingers together, straining the knuckles white. "Yes, but as an empath I'm driven by feelings. I can't leave without giving you all the facts." She gave me a small smile as she paused for breath. "Now you're listening—truly listening, and I need to take advantage of that."

She was right. I needed to hear what she had to say, particularly when my forethought fully came into being. "Go right ahead then."

"Thank you." Belle smiled reassuringly. "One of the most important things you need to know is that our people no longer physically age past the age of eighteen, and we live easily to around one-hundred and twenty."

"I—what?" I coughed raggedly, almost choking on that piece of unheard of news. "Please tell me you're joking. One-hundred and twenty years?" She couldn't be right. "L-looking like this?" I plucked numbly at the tight skin of my cheeks.

"Yes."

I flicked a hand to her temple and double-checked her temperature.

"I know it's a shock, but you'll look just as you are now until the day you die. This is knowledge you should have, particularly when you'll need to deal with the fact that you won't age as other humans do. People will eventually notice that."

I gulped and sent Silvie a very worried "help me" look. Except she inclined her head as if acknowledging Belle's words and agreed. Obviously no aid from that quarter.

Turning back to Belle, I cleared my throat and tried to make her see reason. "O-kay-doe-kay, so you're telling me I won't be getting any gray hair, right?"

"No, not a strand." Her gaze softened, and she squeezed my hand. "Adulthood is reached at eighteen. We come into our strength skills at eighteen. We don't age physically past eighteen, but we do eventually die. Like I said, we live easily to one-hundred and twenty."

My eyes almost rolled to the back of my head. "You seem to forget that I've never paid much attention to your previous ranting and raving of strength skills until I actually showed signs of them myself, and about reaching adulthood at eighteen, well, you've never once said Magiolings never aged." I stuck both hands on my hips. "It sounds impossible."

"Yet it's still true, and provided you have the information that's all that matters. Given time, you'll see the truth for yourself."

I wagged my finger at her, then dropped it. I needed more information, and I needed it now. "Does every Magioling have strength skills?"

"No. Not at all. At times, brothers and sisters born to the same parents differ. One may have multiple skills and the other some, or even none at all. It's simply the luck of the draw as far as we can understand it."

"What else can you tell me? I want details of Magio and the people. Do you not have specialized scientists as we do who can provide this information?"

She shook her head. "I'm not pre-cognitive, and we don't live in an age as advanced as yours is in this scientific field. We don't have such strategic technology, nor do we desire it. Peacians live by a different standard, one of simplicity and selfless giving. Our children are raised within villages by their immediate and extended family and not within bustling concrete cities where one passes another in the street that they do not know. The Loveria royal family lead, and it has been that way since the first male in their line was gifted with the knowledge of forethought and could guide us."

"So is that how Carlisio knew to send you here three months ago? Did he have forewarning I would need our friendship, to believe in a world I can't see?"

"Yes. Now you're beginning to understand the wider picture. Carlisio knew I would be needed here and before you turned eighteen and met Davio for the first time. He saw your image, the image of a young Earth woman who was important to someone close to him, although he didn't know exactly to whom. The king's gift is not as strong as his father's before him, and you heard Davio say his grandfather's visions are like snapshots in time, ones he must decipher to the best of his ability. Our choices are our own and Carlisio doesn't take that away from us. Now it's obvious you are Davio's mate. A mate he has decided not to appreciate when most men are overprotective where their soul-bound one is concerned."

She edged forward. "Nothing can compare to the chemistry and our need of the one our soul is created for, and no mated male does well without his chosen female if he is one of the fortunate ones to receive one. Any feelings for another will be slow in coming, as is for all Magiolings who don't find their soul bound mate."

"What about you? Are you mated?"

"I haven't been found." A simple answer and her tone held sadness. "Yet should you ever wish to make a stand and have Davio return, I will aid you. We have our telepathic connection and it can cross the divide."

"Hold on. Davio isn't returning. You were there and he was pretty adamant about us not working out. Besides," I said and flicked my fingers upward. "I'm quite happy if he stays there. We'll both move on."

Belle heaved a deep sigh. "If you change your mind, you

must tell me." Then a rolling wave of contrasting reassurance and comfort emanated from her, and soaked into me. "Trust me. Davio will be suffering from his decision. The male's emotions regarding his female are all-consuming, and that's part of the bond the males have no control over. Have you noticed your thoughts returning to him? Dwelling on him?"

There was clearly not going to be a simple answer to that question, but I gave it a shot. "A touch. Maybe a bit more." I lifted my chin, stared down my nose at her. "But not in a good way." That was important to point out. "So, say I believe you about all this male-female bonded stuff. Why would I ever want to convince Davio to take on a Halfling when I would only be detrimental to his line? Out of curiosity, of course."

Silvie rested her hand on my back, her quiet touch reminding me of her presence as she said, "Perhaps you need to stop overanalyzing and just go with the flow."

"Nope, I barely know him." Yet a niggling doubt reared its ugly head, one that said I could know him if I wished, one that a brief second later I firmly quashed.

Belle stared at me, a thoughtful look in her eyes. "Faith, you forget I can feel your emotions. You are the soul-bound mate chosen for our prince, which means you have to at least consider the full circle behind the concept."

Frustrated, I dropped my head into my hands. "I don't have to consider it at all. Davio left. His decision stands, and I won't change it." I shrugged my heavy shoulders. There'd be no asking him to come back. What was between us was done. Finished. Over.

Belle knocked my arm with hers. "Hey, even women in Peacio are prone to changing their minds just as often as Earth women do."

I would have laughed if I wasn't feeling so deeply lost inside. "I'll tell you what, should I ever see Davio again"—which according to the man in question wasn't going to happen—"then I'll be sure to mention your concerns." A downright lie. I wasn't the type of woman to consider groveling.

All in all, the current situation wasn't going to change.

With that thought in mind, I lifted my head and forced my brightest smile. "There must be other young and well-connected women for Davio to choose from. Perhaps a noble lady or a princess or two?"

A hard elbow into my ribs from Silvie. "That's outrageous."

"Ow." I glared at her. "What was that for?"

She raised her hands in the air as she quite often did with me. "A noble lady or a princess or two?"

"Well, how would I know? We have a ton of royalty here on Earth. It wasn't that far-fetched of an idea."

As I returned her swat, it made me feel better until she kicked out at me with a low growl. "Quit that, Stryker," she ordered.

I grinned, feeling a little normal again.

"Okay, you two." With a scowl, Belle pushed in between Silvie and me and sat squarely between us. "You two are so odd." She nudged us even farther apart. "Now, we do in fact have other royalty, along with a hierarchal system similar to many cultures right here on Earth. It wasn't an outrageous question."

"See," I gloated, peering around Belle to send Silvie a nasty look. "Davio can set sail and find one of his own kind. We're all good."

Silvie shook her head, although thankfully she kept her mouth shut. Not that she had much of a choice since Belle chatted nonstop about strength skills, their hierarchal system, their culture and almost every other necessary subject I was supposed to become aware of.

It was a weird, wacky and very long day.

Chapter 3

I woke with my brain fuzzy from the fantasy dream I'd had the night before, one which still gently floated around and kept me snuggly happy. Well, that was until I realized said dream was of one infuriating man named Davio Loveria.

Abruptly I dissolved that dream and bolted upright.

I grumbled and shuffled on my bottom toward the headboard. Leaning back, I caught the chirpy sound of a Tui bird outside in the native Pohutakawa tree. At a guess, he had wished me a good morning.

I zeroed in on the Tui bird's pretty call and turned up my receptors to a more satisfactory level. Simultaneously, I turned down the volume of passing traffic, not to mention blocking out my mother's atrocious singing from her adjoining bathroom. Now there was a bonus.

Ah, sublime.

Perfect.

Only the pretty Tui bird's trill left to fill the silence.

Finally, a more fulfilling start to the day.

Especially considering yesterday.

Oh boy, yesterday. Now there was a slice of reality.

Davio Loveria.

Nope, I wasn't going to think about him.

Not worth it.

In fact, I would forcibly thrust him and his dratted recurring image from my mind.

Yeah, that's better.

There's precisely no need to go back there.

He was gone and so soon would Belle be away.

That was the way it should be. Pesky, Peacian people, be gone.

With that thought predominantly in my mind, and as the Tui bird launched from the branch and flew, I pushed back the covers and dropped my feet over the side of the bed and onto the cream carpet. Time to begin my day.

Eagerly, I dressed in a blue stretch t-shirt and shorts so I could go for my regular morning run before school, a run that had become important since my birthday last week. A need that must have something to do with my increased speed.

Racing through to my mother's beloved kitchen, I skidded on the hardwood flooring. I yanked open the white refrigerator door and grabbed a strawberry yogurt and a glass of water.

I made my way down the hallway and tapped on my mother's bathroom door. Mum's rendition of Lady Gaga's "Poker Face" came to a sudden halt at my insistent knocking. "Hey, Mum, I'm taking a run," I yelled through the closed door.

"Be careful."

"Will do."

I cringed as Lady Gaga's song resumed in all Mum's vocal disharmony. Best I leave now.

I took Centennial Park Drive, my sneakers clipping across the pavement as I made the gravel entrance. The early morning sunshine beamed through the treetops, and I glanced left and right before checking my pace and slowing down my sprint so I appeared more like a normal morning jogger. None of this speeding along like a freak.

I half-smirked, half-groaned at the thought, because I really was a freak.

Perhaps I should start a support group of other half-Magiolings. Surely, there were other bizarre by-products like me who'd had an ill-behaved parent who'd spread around unknown DNA as mine had.

Not such a farfetched idea.

One I couldn't help but consider when it seemed I couldn't get a certain man and his country from rolling around in my scrambled mind.

Two, three-mile circuits later, I pounded around the bend and back to my front door. I wiped my sweaty brow, contentment rolling through me as I stretched my muscles. Across the road, Belle exited her house. Three months ago, she, alone, had moved into the street's newest residence, a six-bedroom, L-shaped home. It had been how she'd remained close to me.

Locking the front slider door, she strung her school bag over one shoulder and briskly headed my way. She wore skinny black jeans and a red t-shirt. Once she'd checked for traffic, she dashed across the road.

"Hey, Belle." I hugged her as she joined me. "I think I may actually miss you and your interfering butt after today."

She gave me her sweetest smile. "Well, I'm sure not going to miss you and your colossal temper."

I laughed. "C'mon, let me just get changed for school. I won't be more than five minutes."

As promised, I was back in five and grinned as a rumbling roar echoed down the road. Silvie's beastie turned the corner, it's disturbing and throaty loud engine manufactured somewhere in the late eighties.

But it was such a cute, sporty Mazda RX7, relic that it was.

In her racy, gas guzzler repainted in arctic white, she brought the tiny two-door model to a fast halt by the curb. She opened her car door, hopped out in her short floral skirt and yellow top, folded her arms across the top of her driver's side roof and pulled her sunglasses to the tip of her nose. Peering over the top of them, she eyed first me then Belle. "Well, hop in, girls. This beauty of a car waits for no woman."

I laughed as I shook my head at her.

Silvie gave me an all-knowing eye and impatiently tapped her fingertips on the top of the car's pristine roof. "I know you're internally cussing my car again, Faith Stryker. But it gets us around so stop pussy-footing around and bend yourself in."

My grin widened. "I like your car. It's loud and proud just like you are."

She muttered under her breath as I flipped the lever and the front seat slid forward. "In you go, Belle. The cubbyhole in the back's all yours." I squeezed into my front seat and cast her a glance over my shoulder. "So, I have very little time left to quiz you. Why don't you tell me something interesting about the king's forethought, something naughty," I said with a grin.

With no warning, Silvie squealed out into the traffic. A horn tooted, and Belle gasped as she checked our rear.

"It's okay, we're all good." Belle wiped her brow as she settled back in her seat. "I'm not going to miss these rides, just in case you wanted to know that, Silvie."

"Sure you will." I chuckled. "Now, you've gotten sidetracked. Tell me something wicked about your king."

"Nothing wicked to report." She frowned. "Although you should know that forethought and forewarning are highly sought after skills. Eventually you will be able to focus on someone you know and get an image of what they're doing, or in the same vein, a visual forewarning when something damaging is about to occur. Your forethought is controlled by you, but your forewarning is not. Forewarning will always come when you least expect it, or at least that's the way it is for Carlisio."

Yep, definitely not wicked. It seemed there was no dislodging her loyalty and certainly not when she spoke of her king. Which meant I should take her words more seriously. I was driven to try, because ultimately, the evidence was stacking up. I couldn't deny our telepathic link or my ability to read projected thoughts when I was in the same room as someone. Then there was Davio's sudden disappearance into thin air. Sure, I wasn't convinced on Magio, but if I could work on pressing my forethought and eventually bring forth a visual of his country, perhaps…

"Okay, detail these images for me."

"King Carlisio's forethought appears as one would see a snapshot. Images can be from the present or memories returned from the past, or with forewarning, images of an event yet to occur."

I thumbed my chin, recalling the wavering, illusionary image of Davio from yesterday I'd brought forth after my tumble into Mum's garden. My forethought was developing, but how did I press it harder? "I need more proof."

"You want evidence?" Belle's eyes twinkled. "That'll come soon. Forethought, just like any other skill, is one that develops with practice as it grows into full strength as you reach your rising. So, by all means you should be actively applying yourself to your skill. In fact, King Carlisio reported that his father controlled a much stronger version. The old king could see more than just an image—he monitored a rolling feed of shots more similar to that of an actual event playing out like on one of your televisions."

"Why is Carlisio's forethought not as strong as his father's?" I crooked my head. She'd said yesterday that higher skilled offspring resulted from mated matches, so that might mean... "Oh, Carlisio's parents were not soul-bound."

She nodded. "Yes, and in his case his ability is not at full strength, although the gene carries forward and it will certainly return to its peak in future generations."

"Ah, I understand." I fidgeted. "So explain to me how I can see Peacio."

Silvie's car screamed through the gates of the student car lot, her fast turn catching me off-guard. "Nice one," I groaned, grasping my head before it hit the window. I wasn't sure what was worse at times—her atrocious driving or her throaty car.

She laughed as she found a nice parking space, swerved in with unnecessary force and hauled up the brake. "Gotta love these old RX7's."

"You still alive back there?" I turned and checked on Belle.

Silvie cut the car's engine and snatched out the key. "Hey, what do you mean is Belle all right? There's never any thanks around here."

"Ow, let me out of here," Belle demanded as she pressed the spring lever and bounded out after me. "No offense, Silvie, but I'm more than happy to get out of the back of your terror-ride." She flicked her wealth of brown hair over one shoulder and fixed a smile in place. "You'll be fine once I'm gone, Faith. We have our telepathic connection, remember?"

I scuffed my shoe over the gravel, hating to think I'd actually miss her. My gut churned, tossing into an awful mess. Since Davio had left, my curiosity about him, his family and his country had assaulted me. Sure, there was a need within me to find even more proof Peacio was real, to reason out the emotional rollercoaster ride I was on, but in a way I missed him. The dratted emotion kept stirring, one I had no intention of giving into.

My reality troubled me. Even my mind ached, as if somehow disconnected.

What was with that?

Could one mate feel starved of the other's presence without their wanting it? I shuddered at the thought.

Time to move on.

And it did.

By that afternoon, Belle had gone. Sorrell had taken her away, and I'd watched as she'd shimmered and disappeared so quickly with the large male protector who'd been sent to collect her. Again, another sign Peacio was real—and they were adding up more than I could tear them down.

Even now, I was only partway home and feeling completely moody and seriously lost. Silvie had stayed after school for drama practice—as if she wasn't dramatic enough—and now having no one to pester me was more than a little disturbing.

I kicked at a loose pebble, scuttling it across the path onto the grass as my traitorous mind moved back to Davio.

Always to Davio. Drat him.

How had it been so easy for him to go?

Then there was that moment he'd touched me and now never again.

I blew out a breath, wanting to shake my despair off. Nothing peeved me more than allowing any form of weakness.

Storming down the driveway, I winced as I caught my bag on the spiky gate left unlatched near the road front. I stumbled down the uneven path, wiping my cheeks. Oh hell, I couldn't believe I was now crying.

"I would watch your step if I were you."

My head jolted up as I slammed to a stop.

I inhaled slowly, turning fractionally.

A man.

A stranger.

He had short, light colored hair and was dressed in a night-shaded silk shirt and pressed pants, a thick black leather coat flapping heavily to the ground.

The way he stood, his legs braced wide, his gaze narrowed, brought me to full alert.

Then he moved, twirling around me in the blink of an eye. "Pay attention, Faith."

I would if his speed wasn't inhuman. "Do I know you?"

"No," he stated simply, sharply.

I searched his gaze, shocked to find myself staring into

violet eyes. My violet eyes. "Whoa, okay, who are you?"

The stranger circled me again, the intensity surrounding him as thick and as heavy as the dark trench coat which beat against his legs in the breeze. He crossed his large arms and growled, "I am a warrior, one who is warning you to steer clear of Peacio's protectors. I've seen you with them." His order was arrogant, and far too demanding for my liking.

"Ah—" I drew in a deep breath, making myself find some words. "I don't have much to do with them any longer."

He flipped a hand at me. "They are our natural born enemy." His collar blew up against his thick neck as he spoke, making him appear more than menacing.

"Meaning?"

He speared me with a dark look before looking over his shoulder, his nostrils flaring. "Damn it," he swore. "We'll have to pick this up another time. Carlisio's been forewarned."

"How do you know me? Who are—" I broke off mid-sentence as he raised a heavy baton.

For just a moment, he appeared anguished. "It must be this way. You will not forget me, Faith. I won't allow it."

My head spun, a swirl of gray clouding my vision for a brief moment. Or was it longer? I couldn't tell.

"No, please, there's no need to hurt me." I blinked, stumbling backwards, hands up in instant defense. I was too slow.

My thoughts tangled in a jumbled mess as he brought the weapon down directly over my head.

I slumped heavily to the ground, wanting to hit out at him, but my head splintered with pain and then nothing.

* * * *

Silvie's voice bounced within my fuzzy head. "Did you find anyone or even any sign of anyone?" she asked in a strained tone.

My brows pinched together as I tried to lift my heavy

44

eyelids. Gingerly, I patted the comforter underneath me and found the familiar pattern in the stitching. My covers, which meant my bed.

"No." That someone, an unknown man, answered her. "There's no evidence and nothing to track him from where we found your friend lying, either. Clearly, whoever it was teleported to that exact spot and then left the same way."

"It had to have been the warrior from Carlisio's forewarning, Zac," a female hissed, interrupting the male. "What do you feel, Belle?"

Belle was here? Besides her and Silvie, who were the others?

"There were no residual emotions in the air. I can't give you any additional intel, Viv. I'm sorry." Okay, that was Belle all right, so who were Zac and Viv?

I scraped one eye open as yet another man's low growl in response to that answer rumbled around my bedroom. I tensed, then every drop of blood in my body heated and boiled, followed by a shimmer of pain.

Oh boy. That internal reaction to the one man I'd been thinking constantly of for the past night and two days had returned. He must be close—too close. Still, I couldn't help myself and even with a leadened head, my mind reached out for his. I linked and merged, settled down in that soft spot which was most definitely all mine. Relief rolled through me.

"Davio?" Groggily, I patted the air, needing to physically touch him as well. So wrong. "Come here."

A fast rustle.

"I'm here." The bed beside me dipped.

I pushed my eyelids open the rest of the way just as his hand smoothed over my forehead. I sank into the mattress and released a soft sigh. Oh, skin-to-skin contact was so soothing— like I'd been wrapped in my favorite blanket and tucked into bed by the most caring of hands.

Then I jerked.

"Why is there pain when we don't touch?" It didn't make any sense, but the only relief I ever found from the discomfort came when we touched, or he remained more than five feet distant.

Frustrated, I rubbed the side of my head which had taken the impact of the baton's brutal blow. I expected to find a solid, full-sized lump, only there was nothing—even the ache I'd woken up with had receded. "Okay, do I fast-heal or something?" Because what other possible scenario could explain this?

"Yes, you do. The wound and subsequent bruising is almost gone. You healed within the first twenty minutes you were down."

"I've been out for twenty minutes?" I squeezed my eyes shut, then opened them again. "That's not good."

His gaze captured mine. "No, and it's unacceptable that someone harmed you."

I cleared my throat and edged closer toward him, detesting that I sought more of his comfort. "Okay, how come you're back? Didn't you decide we weren't going to reacquaint ourselves with each other, like ever again?"

"I did." Davio's honey-gold hair fell forward over his wide brow as his gaze heated. "I had to come. Carlisio was forewarned about the danger to you. He couldn't get a complete fix because your attacker used the cloaking strength skill. Do you recall who approached you? Who knocked you out?"

My heart raced, and not from his multiple questions but from the way his hand cupped my shoulder. His touch caused a whole other kind of friction. A friction I was becoming fast fixated with. I stared at his lean fingers. There was only him. He made me feel strangely safe and protected by physically tying me to him. Him!

At no other time in my entire life had a man had that impact on me. Just being surrounded by him somehow soothed me. The reality hit me hard, the truth of my thoughts astounding. For some reason—or for every reason—I no longer felt so lost and alone.

He was back. My soul-bound mate was back.

I couldn't fathom being here without him, and with more certainty than I thought possible.

"Davio," I murmured as I stared straight into his deep-set gaze. Equal determination reflected back in his own. That determination gave me the strength I needed. "Don't leave me again—not like you did before on the field at school." The words slipped out, so easily, so right. Then I spoke my mind again, the second time with striking force. "If we're mated, we should be together. Belle said I could make such a stand and I am." I stood up for my rights, giving him no further choice.

Silvie gasped from across the room. Next to her, Belle smiled softly, relief evident to see on her face. Only they weren't the only ones present.

Beyond them were the other two I'd first heard. A woman with dark brown hair stood to the side of the window, her face half cast in shadow as she scanned the section toward the road front. She was fully armed, a nasty looking blade hooked into her belt on her right. She appeared battle ready, her tight leather vest secured with straps over a ruffled white shirt and inky skintight pants. Wearing knee-high, black leather boots, she was ready for some serious action.

"That's Viv, one of my best protectors," Davio offered as he watched my gaze wander. "Over by the door is Zac, another of our best."

My heart stopped. Zac was huge, a tall, broad-shouldered man whose body rippled with lean muscle, a fighting machine with his sword clasped between both hands and resting point down to the carpeted ground. He was dressed similarly to Viv in dark leathers, but half his chest was bare where his white shirt remained loose and unbuttoned at the front.

I gulped and eyed Davio. More focused now, I couldn't miss that he too was dressed in a similar fashion as Zac and Viv. Dark leathers and a white shirt fluttering underneath a finely made sleeveless leather half-coat made up his attire. Yep, my mate appeared to have stepped out of an ageless time, his clothing nothing like the teenage jeans and shirt he'd worn the day before.

"Well," I said, drawing in a deep breath. "I'm very glad I didn't see you like this yesterday." One look at his combat leathers would have made me freak.

He withdrew his sword, sliding it out of the weighty scabbard belted low on his hips.

"Hey, hold on." I scuttled back, actually cracking my head on the white painted headboard behind me. "Whoa." I held up a placating hand as I rubbed my twice-beaten scalp.

"Would everyone leave the room? It seems it is necessary for me to speak to my mate. Privately." His deep voice resonated with determination.

"Ah, is that a wise idea?" A rush of air left my body at the way he slowly propped his sword beside my headboard.

"It is when you are all I've thought about this past day—when I've been so unsure whether I could've ever kept my word and stayed away. The bond builds fast, and even I have been unable to dismiss it."

The others filed out the door, gently clicking it shut behind them. Davio continued, "As is the way with mates, I need to be close to you, to see to your welfare and quite obviously your protection."

He paused, his large hands gripping my waist as he lifted me. Seating himself, he set me on his lap. "Although I cannot and will not shirk my duties. Not even for you, or for any other. Carlisio has a large country to govern, and he can't do so alone. My father aids him and for the past year I have too."

"Um…okay?" I was on his lap? It felt strangely right. Touching a finger to his bristly jaw, I offered him a slight smile. "Sure, you aid your father, grandfather and your country. Except don't forget me in the vast scheme of things."

"I won't forget you, not after you've haunted my thoughts this past day. Even now, I can sense your connection and the ability you have to merge your mind with mine when we are together. If it weren't for that, I would feel discomfort." His arms banded tighter about me, enforcing a closeness which continued to surprise me.

"So, now what do we do?" I snuggled, discovering my need of him intensifying just as his obviously was. I watched the play of sunlight dancing through the window, dappling across his face and highlighting his strong jaw and his mouth.

"Someone harmed you. Zac, Viv and Belle are just three members of the team I keep quite close to me. No one else will ever get through all of us to you again. But there will be rules. To ensure your safety I want you to—"

"Hold on." I cut off his words by pressing a finger to his lips. Ooo, so soft. And what was with my fascination with his mouth?

His brows drew down, his forehead furrowing deeply. "Are you still not feeling well?"

"Oh, I'm more than well." Then I slowly grinned and leaned in. "It seems I want more than your protection. I want you to kiss me." The complete and honest truth.

That comment stopped him dead cold.

Then he inhaled, slowly, the sound so sweet as his breath stuttered a little. "Kiss you?" he murmured, his eyes now turning a melting hue of delicious brown. "Are you sure?"

"Only if you want to?" I somehow managed to shrug my shoulders like his decision didn't matter either way.

"I want to." Then he closed that last little gap and there was nothing but his warm lips against mine. Every sound around me vanished as my world centered and became only him.

He had come to me at the first sign I was in trouble—no man had done that in my life.

My soul lifted and my heart soared.

Desire flared, and he pushed me back against the soft comforter. He surrounded me, my mind captivated as we shared breath.

Slowly he eased away. "Faith, where you are concerned, my corporal need for you will rally just as greatly as my need to protect you. I believe we need rules." His liquid gaze turned me into a pile of goo.

I inhaled slowly, remembering to breathe. "Yes, I can already tell you could use a few rules. Do you want me to start?"

He grinned and curved a hand around my neck, maintaining our skin-to-skin contact. "I've been raised by my parents and my grandfather, taught to assert myself strongly, and you must do the same with me to ensure you're heard."

I tapped him on the chest with my finger. "Yeah, I've already done that. You need to pay more attention, big fella."

A smile twitched his lips. "Big fella?"

I tilted my head. "That's right, so what else do I need to know about you since we're being all honest?" Because I could sense there was something else, an element of truth below the surface in every word he spoke. I almost had my finger on it.

"You already feel the awareness of it. We cannot lie to one another, or I should say, we can, but the other will always sense it."

Now truth, there was a bonus, because that's what I desired most.

Davio caught my tapping finger and brought it to his lips. Gently, he kissed the tip and made my heart flutter about quite senselessly. "These last few months of your education are important, and I don't wish to take that away from you. Only, I will rarely be here. I will do what I can to give you what you need, but there will be times of separation. It can't be helped."

I stared at him, strangely not liking the idea of this separation he'd spoken of. Ah, and here I thought I was an independent woman. Even my mind cringed at the thought of dropping this mind-merge I had created with him. I loved my soft spot. "There is a place within your mind I'm linked and locked onto, where I'm resting." I looked at my hand in his. "With skin-to-skin contact, our tension dissolves."

"I've felt it too. Touching is important to ensure all is well."

I nodded. "The pain is like a brewing heat coursing through my veins. I merged my mind with yours and with touch, the aching sting disappears." My explanation was real—unnatural and impossibly bizarre—but still real. "Is this normal for mates? Or has it something to do with forethought?"

"Merging your mind with mine has nothing to do with us being soul-bound. Being mated is a relationship, a union of the two souls and is separate to the skills we hold. It's also only you who is forming the mind-merge. It's not my skill." He frowned. "Forethought? Carlisio certainly does not mind-merge like this and bed down in my mind as you are doing. He simply reads others' thoughts when they're near, as they project them, although, it is your father and his line which is unknown. This strange ability may have come from him. We will simply have to work around our unusual pairing."

I could sense the truth he spoke of from our bond—could feel it resonate with unerring accuracy.

"Finding out who your father is will be a priority." Davio stroked my hair, his touch so gentle. We barely knew each other, yet were still bonded so strongly.

"It's never bothered me, to not know of the man who aided in conceiving me. I'm very lucky—I have a wonderful mother who has single-handedly raised me, without even the aid of grandparents or aunts or uncles. There has only ever been Silvie and her mother, Seriah." No one could have asked for a better best friend. I sighed. "I've only ever needed them. My father means nothing to me. No man ever has."

He smiled, giving me a wink. "Ah, but I will."

Then he kissed me deeply, and I kissed him back, overwhelmed by the new emotions stirring within me.

He broke away first, his head coming up. He ducked a look at the door. "Silvie's coming. Down the hallway. I can hear her."

So could I—that precise hearing of ours being immensely helpful.

The door flew open and slammed against the wall. Yeah, that was Silvie, all right.

"Ten minutes is enough you two. Now break it up," she admonished as she stormed toward the bed, red-gold locks flying about her face. "Let's remember we still have a villain to unearth and apprehend." She turned, giving Davio a fierce glower. "What do you think you're doing on my best friend's bed? Get off. Off. Off. Off."

"In the future, Silvie Carver"—he pushed himself to his feet and pulled me up to stand beside him—"you'll remember not to storm into the room the way you just did and disturb us. Correct protocol is that you knock and wait before addressing a prince."

Silvie didn't seem to care as she reached past him and gripped my wrist. She scowled at Davio and tugged me toward her like a mother bear protecting her cub. "Well, lucky for me, Davio Thy-prince Loveria," she shot at him, "I don't have to observe your correct protocol. We are on Earth, you see, not Peacio."

And all this from the girl who'd told me just days ago that I needed to get laid.

I almost smiled. Something was definitely firing up all my friend's cylinders. "Are you all right, Silvie?"

"Well, of course I'm all right. Or I would be if those two sword-wielding fiends of Davio's would stop goading me. Now get your butt out of your bedroom and into your living room and help me control the sudden surge of protectors you are accumulating in this house."

I clapped a hand to my mouth, stifling a laugh. "Mum's not at home is she?"

She better not be. Best I check.

I ran from the room, down the wide carpeted hallway and skidded around the corner into my mother's cozy living room. One of the framed photographs sitting in a place of honor on the mahogany side table rattled.

Davio steadied the frame then curiosity getting the better of him, picked it up. He tapped the image. "Is this picture of your mother and you?"

"Yes."

"You look about six." His eyes twinkled and a humorous grin tugged at his lips. "Nice puddle."

Drat. I hated that print, the one of me plowing down my childhood slide, only to land face first in one almighty, mucky winter puddle. I ignored Davio's light laugh as I continued across to Zac and Viv and smiled politely at them. "I'm so sorry. We haven't been properly introduced. I'm Faith Stryker." I extended my hand.

The female protector shook my hand, while Zac idly stroked the hilt of his sword, his narrowed gaze on me before moving toward Davio with a questioning tilt.

Viv knocked Zac's arm. "Zac," she admonished. "Mind your manners."

He grunted.

"Men." Rolling her eyes, Viv turned her attention back to me. "My apologies. My mate finds your presence unnatural. You are not from our country, and he finds…well, he finds that troubling."

"You two are mated?"

"They are." Davio set the framed photograph back in place and crossed the carpet toward us. He slapped a hand on Zac's shoulder as he drew up to him. "Zac, troubling or not, Faith is still half-Magioling, and whether born here on Earth or in Peacio, she is the other half of my soul. You will speak to her with the respect she's due, and acknowledge her introduction."

"Of course." Zac cleared his throat, dipped his head in a half-bow then shook my hand. "My apologies. I was wary and should not have been. My service extends to you, just as it does, and always will, to my prince."

I scrunched my shoulder blades together, an eerie ripple of discomfort chasing down my spine. This was not a form of formality I was used to, and exactly what service was Zac promising? Hmmm, I also had to remember there was a prince involved. Double eerie. "I don't require anyone's service, Zac, although thanks for the offer all the same."

Edging onto my heels, I backed away from Davio and his protectors as a tense mix of animosity and irritation stirred in my gut. My mate was too close, forcing my tension to build. I reversed, faster, until my back hit the lip of the hearth's upper mantle.

I slowly exhaled.

Relief rolled through me, the pain and frustration dispersing, but only at the five feet mark and no less.

Davio stiffened, a low mutter rumbling from his throat. "Why the distance?"

"It's necessary."

"No, it's not." He stalked toward me. "It's also not your right to decline Zac's offer. As my mate, Peacio's entire contingency of protectors are called to your service. They protect our country and its citizens. You will accept his offer."

With his advancement, I clenched my fists, blood pouring through my veins in a bubbling riot. "Well, you listen here, mister. I'm not a citizen of Peacio, nor have I been to your country." As if that weren't obvious. "Or do I even wish to go there."

At my biting remark, he glared.

My face heated as I continued, "So it's obviously futile for me to accept Zac's offer. I don't know your protector and he doesn't know me."

"Don't." Gaze zeroing in on me, he captured my wrist with one hand, his fingers firm and warm. "Your tension is clearly spiking, as is mine. Exactly how far away do we need to be so we don't suffer these appalling emotions?"

I squinted. "If there's no skin-to-skin contact, then a good five strides away. The irritation is awful if we don't touch."

He dropped my wrist. "Five strides. We'll enforce it again to make certain." He turned and marched across the room the required distance, while Viv, Belle and Silvie all watched with their mouths gaping.

Zac hissed as Davio halted. "Is it possible for you to explain this reasoning? I'm clueless about what's going on."

"One second." Davio pivoted as he reached the far couch, met my gaze and questioned, "This seems good. What about you?"

The release of tension took me instantaneously. "Yes, thank you, that's perfect." Nothing like two mates, destined to be together, standing a good room's width apart. Absolutely perfect.

Turning to Zac and the others, Davio explained our issue, while I resigned myself to what was. We had to be touching and merged for the best outcome, or we had to be apart. Lucky for us, I had the skill to mind-merge and sink into that soft spot within his mind which ensured the pain and frustration dissipated for me.

Beyond the sitting room window, the sun set in brilliant shades of yellow, orange and pink which suffused the horizon beyond the row of houses on the opposite side of the street. A familiar, white four-door Toyota pulled into the driveway and rolled to a stop. The driver's door swung open, and I smiled as my favorite person in all the world stepped out and stood. Mum righted her knee-length, back-slit navy skirt and red blouse then strolled around to the trunk.

"Who's she?" Zac slid in front of me, sword lifted as he blocked my view.

I groaned. Loudly. "That's my mother—Kate Stryker." I slapped a hand against his arm. His strangely immovable arm. Wow, that was one solid piece of muscle. "She'd never harm anyone."

He lowered his weapon and stared at me like I was a pesky bug under his feet. "Your mother—she's young, and her hair, it's chestnut-brown. Yours is so light, so very blond." Next, he looked into my eyes, and not in a good way. "Your eyes are a curious shade of violet. They aren't your mother's color either."

"Well, for starters, my mother was very young when I was born. She was eighteen—and she dyes her hair. Usually she's a blonde." I shrugged my shoulders. "And the eye color—that must come from my father, not that I know him. He disappeared on the day of my birth."

Zac glanced over my head as Davio approached. My mate slid one arm around my waist from behind and I leaned back into him, the contact perfect and preventing any opposing emotions the instant we touched.

Thumbing his chin, Zac watched my mother pull out a couple of eco-green grocery bags from the trunk. "Your mother looks far younger than the possible thirty-six years you say she must be. She could pass for your older sister."

Davio's hold on me tightened, the block in his mind suddenly lifting and his thoughts trickling through to me. He too believed she could pass as my older sister, that she could easily be a Magioling since his people didn't age.

"No." I gripped his forearm tight around my waist and squeezed. "She's of Earth."

"Damn, I mustn't forget you can read my thoughts if I lower my shields." He immediately blocked. "Zac could be right though—your mother appears far younger than her thirty-six years. She may not be from Earth."

"I already said no. My mother has not lied to me for the past eighteen years. You're crazy to think she's not an Earthling. I haven't seen her doing anything magical." I took a deep breath and slowly exhaled. "I'd like to think I'd have noticed that." Which meant my strength skills must have come from my unknown father.

"It's just an observation for now, yet as you said, she was only eighteen when she gave birth to you. She has aged well, although it is disturbing that you have no other known family, that it's only you and her. In Magio, our children are raised within villages by their immediate and extended family. There are always relatives."

Thunk. Mum dropped the trunk and bags in hand, strolled toward the front door. "My mother would never lie to me. She has no family because she's an orphan."

"Your father? Does she ever speak of the man who is your sire?"

"No, and I don't force it. There's too much pain there for her. I only know vague things, like he was eighteen as she was, and that he left her right after my birth."

Davio absently stroked along the inside of my wrist. "Our people don't have this aging disability your people have, but I can't deny that you do have a number of people amongst your population who appear far younger than their years would be. We must seek your unknown father's whereabouts. That is where I'm sure we'll find your lost Peacian heritage."

"And what of Dralion? Could he be from your enemy's country? You don't know exactly where he's from any more than I do." Memories flickered. The man who'd attacked me had said he'd been a warrior, had arrogantly stated that was so. Warriors guarded Dralion, while protectors guarded Peacio. Both nations named their elite fighting forces in that distinct way.

Belle had told me as such during the time she'd enlightened me to all things Magio.

"It's doubtful your father comes from our enemy's land. We allow our fellow Peacians to travel wherever they wish, but in Dralion, circumstances are different. Donaldo Wincrest locks his people down as my grandfather, Carlisio, does not. It is near impossible for Wincrest's people to travel here, unless they're amongst their king's elite fighting force of warriors."

"How does Wincrest lock all but his warriors down?" Belle hadn't covered this.

"Dralion has an energy field which shields their country. It's an energy dome we can't penetrate, yet a dome which has an entry and exit point where only their most highly skilled and trained warriors can come and go from. We can't breach this point since we don't know where it is, or what its physical attributes are for teleporting."

I tried to sift through his mind to understand his reasoning and his obvious hatred of all things Dralion, but the block he had put in place remained immoveable. I resettled my mind into that soft spot and frowned. "I don't like the way you're blocking me."

"It's best this way. All our people can block if they so desire." He gave a little shake of his head. "But you're not to go sneaking about within others' mind when you're not wanted there."

"I had no intention of doing so. Most people channel their thoughts to me, so no sneaking involved, and it's only you I can actually merge my mind with." I also had no intention of trying to merge my mind with anyone else's. Davio was the only one I wanted to connect with in such a private way, and I'd say due to this slightly infuriating soul bond. I let out a long breath and considered the man who had accosted me. He'd definitely said he was a warrior. He'd said the Peacio protectors were his—no, our—natural born enemy. Then he'd demanded I stay away from them.

I cringed, recalling the warrior's last words. "We'll have to pick this up another time. Carlisio's been forewarned."

The front door clicked shut. Mum was here.

I pressed a hand to Davio's chest and pushed him away. "You have to go. Please. I have to help my mother unpack the groceries, and you need to take your people with you. She'll have a heart attack if she sees so many dressed the way you all are."

His expression darkened, his gaze rising over my head to connect with Belle's as she came off the couch and joined us. "Belle, you and Silvie will stay and not leave my mate's side. Contact me on our direct link if you need me to return. I will not be long."

She voiced a quick, "Yes."

Then he turned to me. "I'll be fifteen minutes. I have plenty of Earth clothing since I enjoy the fabrics and styles your people wear. I will return to the castle to collect a bag." He bent forward and lightly kissed my forehead. "Don't find trouble while I'm gone. That's an order."

"Hold on." I grabbed his arm, since he could leave in the blink of an eye and clearly intended to. "You're definitely coming back, right?"

His lips lifted. "I will ensure your safety first before I return to my duties. I have Zac and Viv to aid me, and Belle will now remain for as long as she's required." He glanced at Zac and Viv. "You both need to do a little shopping to blend in with the locals. We'll regroup at Belle's residence across the street in an hour since Carlisio hasn't disposed of it yet. That is where we'll reside until the existing threat to my mate is removed."

Hand on my arm, Belle pulled me clear of the others. "Davio, I take it Faith is to come with us. There are six bedrooms."

I frowned. What was Belle implying?

"She stays with us." He glanced at Silvie. "You too may stay with us if you wish. I've seen how greatly you care for your friend. I welcome any aid you might offer."

I gasped. "Just a second. You can't think to completely reorganize my life. I have a perfectly secure home right here, thank you."

"No." Davio's tone rang with fierce adamancy. "In this decision, you have no choice. When it comes to your safety—my orders take precedence. You will pack a bag and stay at Belle's where the rest of us will be close enough to protect you." To Belle, he ordered, "Stay at her side. Until we remove the threat, a protector will watch over her at every moment."

I opened my mouth to strenuously object, only Davio wavered into thin air and disappeared. I kicked the space where he'd been. "Damn, that's annoying."

Zac and Viv chuckled and followed directly in his wake.

"Annoying, annoying, annoying," I blustered.

"Come on. I'm not missing any of this. I'll stay with you." Silvie jumped to my side and snagged my other arm—the one Belle wasn't fiercely gripping. "We have groceries to unpack."

I scowled at one then the other. "I can walk to the kitchen by myself."

Belle's grip tightened. "Our protectors do not question orders given by our prince, and neither should you."

I tried to jerk my arm free. "What I'm questioning is this sudden imprisonment." Next time I'd make absolutely certain Davio didn't poof away without more time on my side to argue my point. I groaned. Clearly I was going to Belle's place whether I wanted to or not. Swiftly, I twisted free of Belle and shot off into the kitchen.

The large and homey space was my mother's favorite room. The kitchen cabinets were built in, the pale blue doors trimmed with pine to match the varnished wooden floor, and an ultra-wide window ran the entire length of the kitchen, right over the stainless steel bench. Outside, the last of the sun's rays beamed in over top of the tall boundary fence between us and our neighbors. The stunning light pinged off the steel and sent a prism of sparkly pinks, golds, and blues bouncing around the room.

I skidded to a stop, and Belle bumped into my back as she took Davio's protection orders to the very exact point. "Oomph." I caught myself, ignored Belle and smiled at Mum. "Hey, how was work?"

"Endless today." Mum popped out from inside the pantry, her gaze alighting on Belle and Silvie either side of me. "Oh, hello girls. I didn't realize you'd all be here. I thought you were leaving Te Puke, Belle?"

"No, she decided she loves the place." I opened the bags on the counter, removed several packages and passed them across to Mum. "In fact Belle's invited me to stay at her place. Is that all right?"

Mum stacked the goods on the top shelf, half-turned and nodded over her shoulder. "You can sleepover at Belle's place whenever you like. That's never a problem."

"Actually, Kate." Belle breezed into the gap between Mum and me. "I'm hoping to have Faith come over for a few days, not just a single night sleepover. Silvie's coming too, so it'll be just us girls until I have other houseguests arriving. I'd appreciate the female company."

Well, whoever knew Belle could—

Silvie stepped forward, clearing her throat. "My mother knows Belle's houseguests." She scratched her ear. "Ah, Davio Loveria is one of them, and he's very respectable. So are Viv and Zac."

Frowning, I crossed my arms. Okay, was there a conspiracy here? Why would Silvie lie so blatantly? There was no way Seriah Carver knew Davio and his protectors.

Silvie snuck closer, and whispered in my ear. "Sorry, you

got hit on the head, and I want those protectors around."

I squished up my mouth, taking care as I eased past a crowding Belle to pass Mum a bag of vegetables. "Actually, there was talk that Davio and the others may turn up today, but regardless, Silvie and I know the rules around other men. We'll be good." There, that was better, less of a lie.

Mum opened the refrigerator door and stacked the carrots into the lower cooler. "You know the rules, do you?" Standing back with her gaze intent, she continued, "Just run them by me again, hmm."

I rolled my eyes. "Very funny."

Mum tried to hide her smile, but I caught it all the same. "Well, you are eighteen and it's not like I haven't taught you the rules of being responsible."

"That's right." I grinned and snatched an apple, rubbed it against the arm of my shirtsleeve. "I'll just go and pack a bag then." I bit down as I walked out of the kitchen. "Don't worry about dinner for me."

Belle and Silvie joined me in my bedroom as I threw a couple pairs of blue jeans, some comfy t-shirts and my all-time favorite violet-checked shirt into a bag. Belle tossed in two pairs of shoes, and Silvie nabbed my pajamas.

Next came toiletries.

And Belle standing sentry in the doorway of my white-tiled bathroom. Talk about Protection City.

I threw my hands up. "Okay, this is just ridiculous, Belle. It's not like I'm going to be accosted in my own home. Take a step back." I scooped up my toothbrush and toothpaste.

She tapped her head. "Yeah, okay, but only because Davio's on his way."

I checked the time on my watch.

"Faith." A distinct male voice rang out from my bedroom.

"Coming." I dropped the toiletries in my overnighter and slung my bag over my shoulder, then stopped dead in the bathroom doorway at the renewed sight of him in the center of my room. Wow. Talk about a man who could halt traffic with just how good he looked. His blue jeans fit him to perfection, rounding a tight butt I wanted to ogle. His tan t-shirt hugged his broad chest.

Somehow I remembered to breathe. Then I remembered what I should be thinking. Sternly, I crossed my arms. "You can't come and go from my bedroom as you please. We have a front door, and I insist on you using it." Yeah, none of this poofing in and out stuff.

He studied me, his brows slanting down. "I don't care for your antagonistic behavior, so merge your mind with mine now. It's as necessary for you as it is for me."

He drew closer, firing my blood.

I merged, sinking into my soft spot in his mind, and unable to help myself, tried to catch his current thoughts. I hit the jackpot as he remained unblocked. Focusing, I saw that away from me his mind had replayed what had happened—my attack. He wondered why now and could the attack be related to him? He was certain the small and closely tied group who knew about me would never tell another of our bond. Included were his parents, Genevy and Everio, his grandfather and just moments ago, he'd informed his cousin and right-hand man he'd decided not to forego our bond.

My heart hitched. It hurt he'd told so many people when I clearly couldn't tell a soul, not even my own mother.

Stepping up to me, he caught my hand. "Clearly you're reading my thoughts. What concerns you most about them?"

With the slow lifting of my chin, I answered, "A million things."

Not to mention the fact that the one who'd attacked me was a warrior and Davio's enemy, something I needed to tell him now we had more time. Footsteps clacked down the passageway and I swung my gaze to the door. Oh no. Mum was coming.

A whoosh of air, and my hair blew into my face as Davio dived past me and disappeared into my bathroom.

Flinging strands of blond from my gaping mouth, I smiled at Mum as she poked her head in. "Faith, I'm going to take a bath and relax." She glanced at Belle and Silvie who smiled ever so sweetly just as I was. "I'll see you all later."

I lifted a hand. "Yep. Later. Have a nice soak."

"I will." She closed the door.

Belle slid in front of it and firmly pressed her back to the polished wood. "Okay, that was too close. We should all get out of here. I'll go with Silvie and help her collect some belongings. You all right, Faith?"

"I'm good." I was since Davio had reappeared from the bathroom and eased in behind me, his hands gently cupping my waist.

"Thanks, Belle." His deep voice rumbled near my ear, his close touch soothing me as it did when we touched skin-to-skin. "I'll meet you across the road. I'll bring Faith."

"You will?"

"Yes, I will. Hold on." His fingers pressed in firmer and we disappeared within the blink of an eye, then reappeared right inside Belle's open and airy living room, and only a mere moment later.

Such a sprawling, six-bedroom home. The living room was long and angular with soft couches pressed to three of the four walls, which gave the space an even wider appeal. Two stunning pieces of framed artwork hung on the walls, one of a sparkling emerald sea with a striking white lighthouse jutting out over a stony point. The other showcased a rustic cottage teetering on the edge of a magnificent rock cliff-face, with massive white-capped breakers rolling in and slapping hard against the rock. Both pieces of art displayed the force of nature battling against life, and my interest had always been taken by them. "Are those images from Peacio?" I swayed a little as I found my feet.

Davio lent me a steadying hand. "Yes, they are. The second picture is of Belle's family home on the cliffs of Barndon. The Benners have held that piece of land for several generations."

"Really?" My curiosity was piqued. "Tell me about it."

"Barndon is a day's ride from Loveria Castle, although Belle moved away from her parents and younger siblings two years ago. She has a place in the village, some twenty minutes by horse from the castle, as well as a room in the castle for when needed. We prefer our protectors to remain close."

"Did you say two years?" That surprised me. "I take it Belle isn't eighteen?" I'd presumed she was, except of course as I'd recently learnt, no one physically aged. Heck, she could be a hundred for all I knew.

"She's twenty, although Zac and Viv are eighteen just as I am. Let's not talk about them though. Before your mother's untimely arrival, I wished to discuss any recollections you might have had of your attack. Your safety must be secured, so whatever you might remember would be great appreciated."

"Hmm, right." I ambled over to one of the forest green couches, sighed and sank down. Pulling my knees to my chest, I tucked myself into a smaller bundle as Davio dropped in beside me and caught my hand.

Idly, he traced my fingers with his. "You have such soft skin."

I would have smiled, but I couldn't. My mind was on the warrior.

"What worries you?" He ran his fingers over my brow, smoothing out the lines.

Resting my head on his shoulder, I eased into his comforting touch. "There's certain haziness, yet I do recall what he said now I've had time to recover and my mind has cleared." I drew in a deep breath, eased away a touch and looked into his eyes. It was time he knew what I knew. "And by *he*, I mean a warrior. A warrior who seemed aware of you, and who definitely knew you'd been with me. He said the protectors were *our* enemy."

"I see." Davio heaved to his feet and paced across to the window overlooking the road front. After a moment of staring out the window, he faced me again and raked one hand deep into his thick golden-brown hair. "Battles are often fought between Wincrest's elite and ours, and that will never change. But it does make sense that the earlier attack on you is because of me." He inhaled sharply. "Although, I wasn't expecting any warrior attack to be so far from my home shores."

"And now?" I hoisted to my feet.

"It's likely tactical. Dralion's warriors are smart and calculating. Hence his use of including both him and you as my enemy."

I shifted from foot to foot.

A low growl rumbled from him as he watched me. "Or that better be the case, because you are my mate and I won't tolerate any trickery between us."

"There's no deceit. You're not my enemy, and I've never met that warrior before, although you do need to consider the gene pool for my unknown father is now much wider than you first thought. You believe me descended from Peacio, but clearly a warrior from Dralion could be another possibility."

"It could, but it is unlikely." He sounded so certain.

The loud throttle of Silvie's car roared outside and a flash of white showed through the partially turned cream blinds across the ranch slider.

I stepped up to him, for they would soon be inside. "There's more. The warrior threatened he would pick up our disrupted meeting at another time. I've no doubt he'll return."

Davio stiffened, his gaze on me so intent that I retreated a hasty step. "Is there anything else you've conveniently forgotten to tell me?"

"Hey, what else did you expect me to do Mr. Prince I'm-never-returning Davio? Last time I saw you, you were adamantly giving me up. Call me crazy," I blustered on, "but the first thought in my fuzzy head after being struck down by a massive man throwing about an equally colossal baton, was not to blurt out all my rising problems. I happened to need you at that point in time."

Anger surged through me, nothing halting my driven spiel. "As I still seem to do now for some mind-boggling reason." Go figure.

Now, after all that lecturing, he simply cocked one arrogant brow. "As I need you." Then he was there, pulling me against him. "Just so we're both clear, nothing changes between us because of this attack. To that end, I'll have Zac and Viv join you at school for further protection. Belle will also be resuming classes as if she'd never left. This warrior who is coming will not take what is mine. Not all is yet known about him, and until it is, I will do my duty as your mate to protect you from *our* enemy."

Belle slid the living room's glass ranch-slider open and walked in, while Silvie followed with one large suitcase in hand behind. They both spied us at the same time and halted.

I glared at Davio. "Look, for starters, I'm not your duty. I'm strong in my own right and my forethought is developing. Secondly, I'm certainly not used to hearing men spout such words as you're mine, and duty and protection. You see in my country, a girl is not helpless, she's—"

Silvie let out the mother of all sighs. "Oh, puh-lease. Can't we just leave the two of you alone for half an hour without any more arguing?"

I fixed my sight on her. "No, not after the man who attacked me told me that Peacio's protectors were my enemy. He was a warrior, Silvie, from Dralion."

Silvie spluttered and gaped, her face turning white. "I—I beg your pardon? When did he say that?"

Belle stared at me as if I'd grown horns. "Yes, when?"

"It makes no difference when," Davio snarled. "As my mate, her needs fall to me, and her most necessary one of protection still stands—Dralion warrior included."

"Well, now don't I feel all special." I tried to pull myself free of him. "One needful mate instead of one wanted one. Boy," I rallied, "you sure have a ton to learn about Earth relationships, and women in particular, I might add."

I snagged my bag.

"Wait." He inserted himself and nimbly took it from my fingers. "Allow me. This will be going to the twin bedroom you and Silvie will be sharing. For your information, relationships work this way on Magio. After a man gives his promise of protection, it doesn't falter. Ever."

I scowled at him. "You are such a pest."

His chest expanded as he inhaled. "It is not necessary for you to state the obvious, just as this is not a conversation of which the outcome will change." Then he dumbfounded me by placing his palm so gently against my cheek. "Not after you already touch a part of me where your presence is needed. No one will take that away from me, neither you by your harsh words, or due to there being an enemy warrior on the loose. You will therefore accept my aid and give me what no other can."

I gulped and found myself strangely melting at his sincere words. It seemed I secretly liked a "take charge" man. I cleared my throat and found my voice. "Well, when you put it that way..."

"I do. So you will settle yourself in Belle's spare bedroom with Silvie, where you will rest. Fast-healing or not, you still took a very hard blow to the head." He twirled me around, retrieved Silvie's bag from her then directed us both down the hallway. He turned the knob on the third white painted door on the right and strode inside.

Two twin beds with burgundy covers sat either side of an intricately designed iron high-table, the walls painted a pale lemon and the square-cut windows overlooking the road as the lounge windows did.

Silvie claimed one of the two pristinely made beds by dropping down on it. "I hope this means you two have sorted yourselves out." She crossed her legs, set her hands on her knees and arched that knowing brow of hers.

"I have a feeling we've only just begun the sorting out, Silvie." Davio gripped her shoulder. "Regardless though, I would request that you not allow my mate to think too deeply on what has gone down today. If you can, remind her she's important to me. I would greatly appreciate it."

"Hello." I flicked my fingers. "I'm in the room here." Irritated again without his physical touch to soothe me, my blood once again bubbled and brewed with renewed tension. How flippin' annoying. But at least this time I recognized the problem far quicker. I closed the gap and slid my fingers between his fingers, our palms flush together. Such relief poured through me as the pressure melted away. The ups and downs of this new relationship would be a trial.

"I must remember too." Raising my hand, he brought it to his chest. "The strain intensifies for us both if we don't touch, but more so for you of course."

"Are you calling me the grumpy one?" I stared at his chest, at where he now pressed my hand against his heavily beating heart. It seemed we both had a lot to learn. I drew in a deep breath. "This soul match is so strange and difficult. Does it feel that way to—"

My hand, the one he still held pressed to his chest, heated with a shocking swiftness, then my pulse jumped and I swore my heart now beat in time with his, to a rhythm somehow completely in sync. I trembled, fingers shaky in his grasp.

"Don't fear the change, my mate."

"You felt that too?" My skin rippled with goosebumps.

"It's the bond strengthening." His voice was raspy and hard.

Deliciously hard.

I swung my gaze toward Silvie, tried to demand some much needed help with just one shooting look. Only she was no help at all. She grinned broadly, as if ready to laugh her socks off.

Frowning, I struck a look at my mate again. "That better only happen the once."

"Just the once, I promise you." A devilish smile. "The female's heart follows the suit of her male's, aiding him in sensing any distress."

"Honestly?" Huffing, I pushed him away. "Can you tell I'm feeling distressed right now?"

What was I going to do with him?

He was impossible, boundlessly impossible.

Chapter 4

It was impressive all right. One modified 4x4 Holden Colorado in a deep sea-blue color, with a silver sports-bar on the front and a whopping enclosed deck at the rear of the huge cab. In Belle's triple-bay garage, I stood before the muscular-looking vehicle with awe keeping me locked in place.

"What's wrong?" Davio quizzed as he held the front passenger door open. Dressed in casual cargo shorts and a white t-shirt, he waited to take us to school. "You're supposed to jump in. You know. Vehicle. Drives on roads. Uses fuel. Can't teleport this one."

Obviously.

"It's so big. Did you have to buy such a visibly big beast to drive? You were only gone for an hour. No student I know of has a vehicle this"—I tilted my head sideways to take in the width and breadth of the tires, which were definitely enhanced—"size."

"Yeah." He licked his lips as he ogled his new purchase. "I couldn't resist snapping this one up. It seems I'm an impulse buyer." No remorse, not one ounce of it in his tone.

"Well, nice impulse buying," I finally conceded, giving him at least that much.

He turned to Zac and Viv as they approached, pointing out the back two doors for them. "Hop in, otherwise you'll have to squeeze into the back of Silvie's little nugget of a car."

Silvie caught his teasing words as she skipped into the garage and headed toward her own gas-guzzler. "Yeah, yeah, nice wisecrack, Prince Annoying." She attempted to smack him as she passed, clearly aiming for his head but missing since he ducked super quick.

Last night those two seemed to do much of the same, always bantering and joshing with each other like long lost siblings. It was curiously funny to watch how they got on so well.

I laughed at their childlike shenanigans, at how peeved Silvie was that Davio was so quick on his toes.

"Next time I'll make contact with your big head, you towering menace," she threw at him. To Belle, ever so sweetly she said, "Hop in with me since the one with the big head will want to take his mate with him. You can even have the front seat."

"Lovely," Belle groused. "I've always wanted the front seat." She sent Davio a scowl. "I'd also like to point out that there are some things a protector should never be called to do. That includes riding in a car while Silvie's driving it. I expect double pay for risking my life like this."

My heart panged. I hated missing out on riding with Silvie and hearing those two bicker. One got used to squeezing into her ride and dealing with her crazy driving. I'd earnt that front seat spot.

"I agree. Double the pay it is." Davio winked at Belle then slid a hand to the small of my back and guided me toward his beast. "I can see you want to ride with Silvie, but you're coming with me." His tone quickly turned no-nonsense, all sense of earlier play gone. "We can't become complacent. The warrior could return at any time, especially considering his warning to do so."

"Sure," I conceded, taking one last look at Belle sliding into my front seat next to Silvie. I wanted to swap places with her so bad.

So crazy too.

For the first time I had room to stretch my legs. I couldn't even reach the front of the cab. Yeah, now that was some room.

Six and a half minutes later, we arrived at school.

Wearing casual shorts and t-shirts like other typical teenagers, Zac and Viv bounded off to the main office to enroll for what was left of the school year. Thank heavens. I needed to feel the semblance of normality after all the changes of the past few days. Davio wouldn't be here full-time. He had reminded me last night that once the threat to me was gone, he'd be gone. But at present, he was focused on flushing out the warrior, taking his enemy down and all before he could return to his country, his family and his home.

Silvie parked her car and locked it up next to us in the parking lot. She dashed off after Belle along the concrete pathway, both of them disappearing around the high hedging next to the science block.

"You ready to go?" He squeezed my leg as he turned off the key.

"Mmm-hmm."

"Faith?" He cupped my cheek, lightly stroking his fingers over my skin until I turned my head toward him. Alone now, his attention was fully on me. "Did you sleep well last night?"

"Yeah, fine, although I couldn't maintain my mind-merge with you through the walls. The distance was simply too great for me to hold." I breathed in slowly and resettled myself, comforted again as my mind rested in that soft spot, his physical touch calming me even further. "And you?" I asked, since there hadn't been time for any private conversation this morning at Belle's busy breakfast table. "How'd you fare?"

"Not the best." He leaned closer, touched his forehead to mine and whispered, "I find your mind-merge is necessary to provide me with some form of relief. Most mates have bonded telepathically by now. It aids them in staying connected over long distances. Although it is a link of trust, and obviously that confidence hasn't yet built between us."

Well, it wasn't like I hadn't tried to form the link as I had so effortlessly formed it with Belle, except as he'd said there was one simple prerequisite. A telepathic link of this nature was only ever possible if both parties intrinsically trusted the other. So far, I was still dubious.

"I guess it'll happen when it happens." I drew back. We had class, the bell now blasting its first ring.

Passenger door open, I hopped out and met Davio at the rear of the Colorado. I leaned against the enclosed deck. "So, how did you get a driver's license? It's not like you have this kind of transportation in Peacio." Or so I presumed since Belle had spoken of Peacio's seventeenth century vibe of horse and cart prevailing across the land.

"I had private tutors and my education included both your world and mine." He fetched our bags from underneath the heavy black cover and swung both over one shoulder. He clasped my hand and we walked along the grass-trimmed concrete pathway into the school.

Like other high schools or colleges in New Zealand, Te Puke High housed blocks of weatherboard-clad classrooms, many of them two-stories high with anywhere from four to eight classes in a block, along with a wonderful new section of classroom pods. We passed the main school administration building, now remodeled in earth-toned bricks, its aluminum windows colored in a bright trim. Around us, a thousand students made their way to class, arriving by foot, bus or car.

Davio leaned in as students passed us. "Why the frown?"

He seemed to pick up on every little change in my temperament. "I missed my run this morning. I usually jog for an hour or so before school." It dragged at me that I'd missed it. Too much was happening too quickly.

We walked into class together and headed straight down the aisle to the back row. Davio had phoned into the office this morning and confirmed he was taking every one of the classes he'd enrolled in that first day. No surprises there that our timetable matched perfectly. Zac and Viv intended on enrolling in the same classes so they could remain near me too, except as this was their first day, they were required to sign in at the office first. They still hadn't made their way here, but I doubted they'd be long.

I sidled into my regular seat. Davio pulled out what was Silvie's chair and joined me. "That's Silvie's spot, not yours." He couldn't take her seat. "She'll be mad if you sit there."

"I've found I like making her mad, which means this is my seat now, and will remain so until the threat against you is removed." Under the desk, he linked our hands together. "I've also got to get a hold on regulating this temper of yours.

I squeezed my fingernails into his palm, biting into his flesh. "What temper would that be?"

"That vile temper you're always firing at—" His gaze darted toward Silvie as she stormed our way. Zac and Viv marched two steps behind her, Silvie glaring daggers at him.

Clearly she didn't like the loss of her spot any more than I did.

Snapping a chair out behind us, she snarled under her breath. "You shouldn't be this annoying, Prince Annoying."

I laughed, and just managed to slap a hand over my mouth in time to keep it from pealing out too loud, although as Davio held my other hand, I couldn't halt my happiness from spreading. That instant attraction we'd had from the beginning, had now grown into something more. I slid a finger gently along the reddened marks I'd stabbed into his palm. "I'm sorry about these."

"You're forgiven." His hand tightened around mine. "Don't concern yourself with a few small marks. I fast-heal, and you have the right to express yourself freely with me. You're my mate, and there's no one else I'd ever want to connect so deeply with, other than you."

"You've got a way with words too, and the same goes for me. There's no one else I'd ever want to connect so deeply with, other than you."

Our teacher arrived and the room quietened. The lesson began.

Later in the day, once the bell had signaled our lunch break, the six of us walked out to the edge of the field and found a nice spot on the grass in the sunshine. Students sat eating their lunch in small groups around the perimeter of the field.

Content after devouring a chicken salad sandwich, I stretched out on the ground with my hands folded behind my head. I'd settled close to Davio's side, and he played his fingers through my hair as the clouds high above drifted in streaks of white across the vivid expanse of blue.

So peaceful. My mind drifted and eyes closed, my thoughts returned to the warrior.

I truly needed to recollect more, to give Davio something else to go on, something…

Memories swirled, no not a memory, an order.

Somehow and someway, instructions had been left within my mind and I was to follow the path. Bizarre didn't even begin to cover that. Although I was quickly learning that things didn't always appear as they first should.

I searched deeper within my mind and the warrior's image crystallized. He had a strong jaw line with a long narrow nose and light-colored hair, his eyes a piercing violet hue.

That order demanded I unlock more missing memories shrouded in haziness, and there was a way. Go back to the moment and relive it. I did.

Back outside my house near the front door, I stood before the warrior who'd raised the heavy baton as he'd prepared to strike me.

"Hey." In defense, I threw my hands up. "No, please, there's no need to hurt me."

The warrior's violet eyes misted. "I don't wish to hurt you, but you can't recall the truth. Not yet. Loveria will take you. That poses a danger to you which I can't allow."

"Okay, hold on. Obviously your concept of danger differs to mine." I raised a brow at the baton. "Put it down."

He searched my gaze. "I'm your father. Look into my mind and take the image I give you of my safe house. Make it fast."

My skin rippled with goosebumps. Had he just said he was my father?

"Faith, now. There's no more time for thought. You have the ability to block this conversation once you've taken the image. Bring it forth later once you're settled and more at ease."

I didn't hesitate to send my mind flaring into his, his tone urgent and my sudden need to obey him surprising even me. The image was there as he'd said and I grabbed ahold of it, and locked it away just as his arms shook. He squeezed his eyes shut for a brief moment as if detesting what he next had to do. He swung.

I jerked, hands clawing into grass. Grass?

"Faith." Fingers tangled in my hair.

"Davio?" I gasped and shook off the haze that had taken me.

"Your heart's racing too fast. Are you all right?"

Oh my goodness.

I had a father—a father from Dralion. A warrior who was alive and had now made me his co-conspirator because of the impossible information he'd had me withhold.

"No, I'm not." I pulled in a lengthy breath. I had no intention of lying to my mate. "You can't trust me."

"Pardon?" His gaze narrowed. "Why would that be?"

"My father—I'm sorry, but he is the warrior who attacked

me.”

Alert, Zac and Viv moved to their haunches as if preparing to nail me to the ground.

“How do you know this?” Flicking a hand at them to remain back, Davio gritted his teeth.

“He told me.”

Zac scanned each direction. “Does she tell the truth, Davio? You’ll know if she lies. We can’t condone having one of our own enemy among us, the daughter of our enemy included.”

“You understand the bond as well as I do. She speaks the truth. Her father is the warrior who attacked her, but she is an innocent and had no true knowledge of him until just now.”

Zac released a rumbling growl. “There hasn’t been a mated bond in over forty years between the offspring of ours and our enemy, or at least not since the dome containment field came into play. This changes everything if she truly has a warrior for a father. You are Prince Everio’s heir and as your protectors, we can’t allow you to take such a terrible risk by associating yourself with her.”

“I don’t care for your analysis, Zac.” He clasped his hand around mine and drew me to my feet as he stood. “Faith, we’ve already spoken of this. Regardless of your parentage, no one can take you from me, not even a warrior, no matter he’s your father.”

“Did I say he was going to take me from you?” I’d never allow it either.

“You intoned it.”

“I’m sure I didn’t.” I snatched my hand back.

“Hey.” Belle stepped in between us and slapped our hands back together. “As an empath, I don’t appreciate all this simmering tension. I soak in every emotion and right now I’m getting emotional whiplash bouncing off the two of you.”

I tugged on my captured hand again. “He started it.”

The bell peeled out.

Davio turned to his protectors. "This warrior doesn't pose a threat when I have every intention of removing him. As such, none of my existing orders will change. The warrior will die." His eyebrows rose with meaning, and Zac and Viv gave him a quick nod.

Silvie sniffed. "Faith, you need what the protectors can offer. You need all of them and I need you." She swiped her nose. "I know your inquisitiveness will get the better of you. I have a bad feeling about this."

I wanted to reassure her, only class was starting. "Let's pick this up another time."

She drew in a heavy breath and released it. "Yeah, another time."

Students and teachers wandered toward their classes. Life continued, circling and moving all around us. Yet compared to here, Dralion and Peacio were a world away, a world now infringing more and more on mine.

Nothing felt quite right anymore.

I eyed Davio. "I want to go somewhere alone. With you."

"Then let's do that." His agreement came without hesitation.

I strengthened my mind-merge, soaking deeper into that spot I considered my own. It was a mystery, even after all that had played out, that I still felt so as one within his mind.

"I've never played hooky. A prince rarely gets away with that," he whispered in my ear.

I smiled at the thought, but before I could respond, he spoke to the others and tossed his keys to Zac. "I'll meet up with you later in the day. Take care and be on the lookout for the warrior. He could blend in among the other students." Davio paused, raising his brows at me. "Although not if you gave us a suitable description. Now that your full memory has returned, tell me what he looks like."

Every instinct in me screamed not to give a single detail

away. "I'm sorry, I can't tell you. It's not going to happen, not when he's my father. I can't give him up to you that easily. It doesn't seem like a fair fight." And deep inside my heart, defective father or not, my decision had to remain in place. I would never toss anyone into the lion's den, no matter the reason why.

Davio's brown-gold gaze bored into mine. "Please don't tell me you feel an allegiance to your father, not after he abandoned you at birth."

My gut churned. "No, it's hard to explain, only to say my knee-jerk reaction is to protect him."

His thoughts released, distracting me through the merge as they swarmed me. It appeared he didn't care for my so-called intuitive reaction, not when we spoke of a Dralion warrior.

"Class is starting. Let's leave now." Without further warning, his arms banded tighter about me. A small, jerky movement and a belly-rolling displacement assailed me. Through the darkness we 'ported, then before I knew it, we'd arrived, my sandals sinking into crystalline white sand.

The Pacific Ocean rolled in, blue waves topped with a foamy crest of white. I gasped. "Okay, you just can't whip us about so fast. I'm not used to that." My feet sunk deeper, until the grains snuck in underneath my toes and grinning, I lifted my feet and tipped the sandals off. "Except you're off the hook since I love the beach so much."

"We're at Papamoa Domain in case you're wondering." He grinned too.

"I'm aware." Papamoa Domain overlooked the vast ocean on New Zealand's East Coast, this beach a mere ten minutes' drive from my home. Behind us on the grassy land, patrons of a seaside restaurant sat within the outdoor patio area, and a queue of people waited in line at the fish and fries shop next door to it. A busy camping ground sat to the other side, the long rows of colorful tents and caravans, housing holidaymakers. This spot was always a hive of activity, although a little farther along the beach only a few people ambled along. "Let's head to where it's quieter."

"Agreed."

"So, I take it you've been here before?" It appeared my mate was full of surprises, and they just kept coming, one after the other.

"I have. Come, let's walk and talk." He bent and retrieved my sandals and removed his own shoes, tucked them near the rising bank where the sand met the stringy grass and returned to me. Threading our hands together, his fingers firm around mine, he led me down the beach toward the quieter end as I'd requested.

"Tell me whatever you can about, well, about everything." I was eager to learn all I could about him, in particular his likes and dislikes, how he spent his days, what his favorite things to do were.

"If you mean how did I teleport here, then quite simply put, it's impossible for one to teleport without an almost identical image of the requested location. Teleporters store those matching images within our minds so we can travel without any mishap."

As interesting as that information was, it wasn't quite what I meant. I pressed my thumb inside his palm. "The question was actually a private one. I want to know everything about you, although this beach is one of my favorite places. How did you know to come here?" Before us, endless white sand ran in a long line toward the majestic mountain known as Mauao several miles away.

"For the past six months, I've been driven to come here. My father had the same inclination after he turned eighteen and searched for my mother. If one is fortunate enough to have a mate, as around half of our population do, then the male's drive to find his female can become relentless."

Hand to my forehead, I shielded my eyes from the bright

sunshine. "Exactly how did you know I was your mate, when you first arrived and all?" I'd certainly been enamored by him.

Now he truly smiled, like I'd never seen before. "I knew I was getting close as I neared your classroom. Carlisio also chose to send me to where I've been compelled to come. Those two factors combined told me I was close to the one I've been searching for. Then when I first saw you across the classroom full of students, my heart simply stopped beating. My mate sat before me and every part of me zeroed in on you. I knew who you were at first sight. So to answer your question." His lips broke into a delicious grin. "I knew with the most insane urge that the woman before me was my mate, the one who held the other half of my soul, just as you hold mine."

I lowered my hand and heart thumping, barely managed to walk without stumbling. "Oh boy, I think I might have to muzzle you." If pressed, he sure could answer just the right way.

Davio laughed, his eyes twinkling. "I haven't finished yet. Remember after I first left you, I promised to stay away?"

"Uh-huh." I nodded.

"Those of us who are fortunate enough to be gifted with a mate have always found our other half to be completely distracting." He drew in a deep breath and slowly let it out. "We know at adulthood if we are matched because our desires for any other never mature. There can be no other for me, or for you, not unless we force our feelings to be swayed. That in itself is almost impossible."

"I've certainly never desired another man, other than you, and I guess if I'd been raised on Magio as you have, then I would have known I had a mate."

"You would have." His fingers tightened around mine. "And I would have located you that much quicker had you lived on my home soil."

"So, tell me what happens to your unmated people? Do they let their hearts choose as we on Earth do?"

"In a quick answer, yes." His stride slowed and he came to a stop, drew around me in a tight circle and gripped my other hand until we stood facing each other. "Or, if our mate is not found, life moves on and we choose another based on friendship. It's not the same though. The mated bond is one of the soul, and no other can truly satisfy our needs other than the one we're destined for." He turned me by the shoulders to face the sparkling, deep blue sea, then arms wrapped around me from behind, rested his chin on the top of my head. "You're my destiny. I realized that fairly quickly on my return home. Even if you hadn't been hurt by the warrior, I would have been driven to return to you before too long."

The sun continued to warm me, just as his binding hold and his precious words did. I fully relaxed against him, this moment beyond peaceful.

"I can see why you love it here," he said after a minute, softly rubbing his chin in my hair.

"It's a beautiful country, yet also one of the most isolated in the world." Although it wasn't as isolated as I'd first thought, not now I'd learnt so many could teleport here at their own free will. That strange thought sent a gray cloud settling over me. I turned into him. "You can come and go at will, which means you can leave me at any time and I'd never see you again." I didn't want him doing that.

"Our bond grows stronger with each hour we are together." He kissed my forehead. "That bond holds a powerful foundation for us, and one I have seen grow in depth and devotion with my own parents. Separation is difficult, and not something I will ever allow for any long length of time."

I smiled, relief washing through me.

"I have my duties of course, but as you pointed out, I can come and go at will, so in that regard I will never be far away from you."

"Good." My grin widened, and I simply stared into his

beautiful eyes.

I was barely conscious of anything surrounding us. His face filled my vision and set my heartbeat to racing. There was only him.

Chapter 5

Snuggling my cheek against his chest as we stood there gazing out over the Pacific Ocean, such peace rolled through me as he held me tight. Like two halves of the same whole, we were joined together within our bond as if one were indistinguishable from the other, although I still needed to understand exactly how our bond worked, and to learn everything about him. "What's it like for you back home?"

"You mean compared to here?"

"Yes."

"Hmm," he murmured, taking so much time to answer I went to prod him again, only he released me and picked up a washed up stick from the ground. "Let me draw the two countries of Magio for you in the sand."

He moved away, closer to the damp area nearer the water line. I waited patiently as he drew a perfect circle with the craggy end then inside of that, mapped out a large, if somewhat bumpy shape positioned along the central Equator line—an area taking the shape of land.

"Magio compares closely to Earth in size, with the two lands of Peacio and Dralion being one continent in the center. The only continent. Our joined land mass equals twenty-nine percent of the whole of Magio, the remainder seventy-one percent being The Great Orbiting Ocean. No physical breaks lie between us, only a central plateau of desert which separates the two countries as effectively as any divide of ocean could."

He drew a central dividing line right through the large land mass. "We call this desert divide No-Man's Land." He chuckled lightly. "It's aptly named because, clearly no man could possibly live there."

"Okay." I grinned back, enjoying his little lesson.

He rubbed his chin and pointed to the left side of the continent. "This area belongs to Peacio and it's rich in minerals and natural deposits, particularly in the highlands. In the lowlands, we have rivers, lakes, abundant pasture and flat, fertile land. Across the desert of No-Man's Land, Dralion's terrain is much more severe. Their land rises swiftly to snow-capped mountains, before plunging down into deep rainforests and jungles. They have a large central desert area, so it's only on the farthest outreaches that their land is able to sustain actual life."

"So that's why the people of Dralion desire to take what is yours?"

"Yes." He pointed to the central dividing line. "There's a protective energy dome that begins here which ensures we can't return their constant attacks, an enchanted shield, one created some forty years ago under the instruction of the ruling family of Dralion. King Donaldo Wincrest insisted on its creation after his father's early passing, of which he and his son, Alexo, still rule strongly today."

"How exactly was Dralion's protective dome created?" Thumb on my chin, I inclined my head to the side, not even able to imagine an energy field that big that no one could safely teleport or even walk through.

"Forty years ago one of their finest warriors used his skill of enchantment, a man by the name of Gilles Moyer. This ability to enchant takes the form of spell-making, and once he'd spelled the dome into existence, it has forever since remained in place."

"Incredible."

"Agreed, and those with the enchanting skill are sought after, although unfortunately they're few and far between. We've been unable to spell it away. It seems to be governed by an energy source which maintains it." Crouched, he glanced at his scrawled map in the sand and tapped the land area to the right that made up Dralion. "At the time of Moyer's enchantment, we also had spies in Wincrest's country, although they've been lost to us these past forty years."

"That's awful." No one should be kept from their family.

"Worse is the fact that they still have spies on our land." He angled his head upward. "Yet we have no dome to keep them out, and we can't breach their protective field to retrieve our own lost men."

"Have you ever caught any of their spies?"

"When we unearth them on our land, they're removed to a location similar to your prisons. We keep their warriors locked up within steel-lined cells."

"For how long?"

"The rest of their lives."

His words rocked me. Locking someone up for what remained of their entire life seemed extreme, unless of course they'd harmed or killed someone. "Do they get the chance to defend themselves?"

"No." An unwavering answer.

"Why is it you rule so archaically?"

Jerking to his feet, he tossed his stick out into the waves. "My grandfather doesn't rule archaically. The Loveria family rules with precision. I can guarantee you there is no nation on your Earth who'd allow their intruding enemies to go free. Neither do we. The safety of our people and of our land is paramount to our continued survival. If not for the Wincrests, their spies and ensuing espionage, we would not have to defend ourselves to such an extreme. They attack and kill, unmercifully and arrogantly."

"I'm sorry." I sifted through his thoughts with my skill, but he threw up a fast block and halted me. Hands on my hips, I glared at him. "Why do you keep doing that? Are you hiding something from me I'm not to know about?"

"You have disclosed that your father is one of Dralion's warriors. Precautions must be taken." His mouth pinched together, lips turning white and in a flash, he was in front of me, one hand shackling my wrist. "There are thousands of warriors, just as there are thousands of protectors. We protect our borders, our lands and our people."

"I understand." I took in his fierce hold, how he gritted his teeth and stood so ramrod straight. Every inch of his hardened body seemed alert to something. "I'm sorry, but do you think I'm going somewhere right now?"

I tried to break free, only he slanted his brows and shook his head.

"Faith, the Loveria family rules so tenaciously because forethought runs through our line. It can skip a generation, or even two as it has done with me and my father, but regardless it is still acutely a part of our structured DNA."

"That's not what I asked." I tugged again on my imprisoned hand. "You're clearly withholding and I want the truth. I deserve the truth."

"If I left my mind fully open to yours and shared every thought, what might you do with that information if your father arrived and decided instead of hitting you over the head, to take you with him?"

"I would remind him that he left me eighteen years ago and has no right to decide my future." I yanked on my wrist again and groaned. "Come on, let me go."

"I won't give you up."

"We really need to talk about your control issues." He seemed to have quite a few.

"I also can't risk allowing your father near you again, not

when I don't have the ability to travel through their dome. If he took you. I'd never get you"—he stopped so suddenly, his pain clear to see as he grimaced—"back."

"You mean I'd be at his mercy since I have no ability to 'port as you do."

"Yes. You'd be gone. Forever. Do you understand?"

"But I have increased speed, and I mean more than just a fast sprint." I hadn't admitted to anyone that I housed that skill yet, primarily because I sensed it led to teleporting, only I'd yet to ask Belle or him to confirm that.

"When did you notice your increased speed?" A gleam of interest flickered in his eyes.

"A couple of days ago."

"How fast?"

"Superwoman fast."

He frowned "I'm unaware of that terminology."

"That means I struggled to stop at the speed I was going. Likely I was all but a blur to anyone who might have caught sight of me."

"Good, then that means you'll soon be able to teleport, which will give us some more options." He tapped his chin as if deep in thought.

More options were good. Seconds passed and he remained still. A wave crashed onto the shore and rolled with a frothy white-cap right up toward our feet before slowly receding.

His gaze sharpened. "I still can't let you out of my sight."

"I would never risk what we have for a father who has never bothered to hang around."

A low groan escaped him. "If you're attempting to sway my mind, you won't."

I pushed my next point. "No one can keep that close of an eye on another, no matter how many protectors you have."

He half-growled, half-groaned.

I persisted. "What happens when I want to spend time alone

with my mother? When you need to see your family? Attend to your duties back home as you have already stated will take precedence. You can't be watching over me every minute of every day. You'll have to concede at some point. Wouldn't it be best to teach me how to teleport, and then take a step in trusting me? That I'll use it to ensure we're never separated, not by a warrior, or a dome."

He didn't move.

Barely even breathed.

Nothing.

Okay, so I had to try another approach.

"What about my forethought? Surely once it starts to grow and I have visual images as your grandfather does, I'll see the threat the warrior poses to me. Forethought is preemptive, right? So I can get myself out of trouble before it even begins?"

Nice thinking.

Only he didn't think so—his throaty growl deepened even further. "Carlisio's forewarning doesn't apply to himself, so no doubt the same will apply to you. You won't have a hope in hell of seeing any form of trouble before it comes for you."

Dang it! But I wasn't giving up that easily. "Well, there simply must be something I can do. Let's begin with teleporting since I don't have an able parent who can teach me, or I should say one you'll allow me to meet so that he can teach me, or that I even want to meet so he might teach me." I shook my limbs, readying myself. "C'mon. Help me see what I can do?"

I gave him a quick little wink, trying to lighten his mood. "Your girlfriend wants you to teach her how to move through space and time. Don't be an old-fashioned bore."

"You did not just call me old-fashioned." He gave me one of his probing looks I was coming to know well. "I don't like this, but I can see I have no choice."

Ah, I was finally getting somewhere. "That's right you have no choice." I touched the waistband of my soft-pleated, short yellow skirt, grateful I'd slipped my black bike shorts on underneath. I released the top button.

"What are you doing?" Davio snagged my hand and halted me from lowering the zip.

"I have running shorts on underneath, and my tank top's suitable for a run but not the skirt. It's gotta go so we can run super-fast. I want to prove to you I can." I lowered the zipper and the yellow cotton slithered past my hips and pooled on the sand. I snagged and folded it. "Is this small enough to fit in your back pocket?"

"Sure." He held out his hand and I passed it to him. As he pocketed it, he muttered, "Start running before I change my mind. I'll be right behind you every step of the way, and of that you can be certain."

Eyeing the beach toward the more isolated eastern end, I set out, keeping to the wet sand near the waterline as I ran.

"Pick up your pace," Davio instructed from my six.

Without looking behind, I followed his instruction. Swiftly, I directed the energy driving through me straight to my pumping legs.

"Again," he ordered. "Except don't forget to cloak. It's the same as when you block your mind to hide information. Think of blocking your entire body though.

That made sense. I cloaked, blocking my image now for fear of anyone seeing me. I grinned as the increase in power surged through my muscles, my feet barely touching the sand's grainy surface.

For just a moment I needed to appreciate what was about to happen. On my left, I struck a quick glance toward the ocean. It appeared flat and glasslike at this speed. To my right, the dry grassy sand dunes whizzed by no more than a haze of milky-beige. I laughed, such joy flowing through me. "I love this."

There was nothing but me, the wind in my face, the scent of salty ocean air and of course, the rumble of Davio's wicked growl from my rear.

"You're almost there, Faith. Now visualize where you want to go. Aim for somewhere up ahead that you can see yet is still too far away. Bring the image into the forefront of your mind and think only of the jump. I promise I'll be right behind you." His voice almost got whipped away on the wind, yet I sensed him there through the connection of my mind merged with his.

I grinned with abandon, allowing the sheer uninhibited moment to take me, then I centered my sight on the beachside trees half a mile ahead and with a burst of speed, made the staggering jump.

The flash of dark was over before it had barely begun then I was there, that faraway stand of trees no longer half a mile distant, but right in front of me. Wide trunks loomed and I couldn't stop.

Damn. This was gonna hurt.

Davio tackled and rolled me. Sand spat in every direction as we plowed through it. "I've got you," he grated in my ear, taking the brunt of the hit.

We stopped a few meters shy of the trees and I couldn't stop beaming. I flipped my hair out of my face as he lay over top of me. "I did it."

"Yes, you did it." He grinned too, then frowned. "Although the first time is always the hardest. Usually no one can stop running. That's why I tackled you. I apologize if I was too rough."

"Not rough at all, and I'm most grateful. Thank you."

"Let me check you over, ensure you've suffered no injuries." He gripped my hands, extended them back into the sand and ran his fingers over my skin. "Everything appears in order. How do you feel?"

I wriggled on my back, pulled my hands free and wrapped them around his neck. "Like I want to do this again. Where to now? Can I try regular teleporting do you think?"

Still frowning, he lowered his head to mine and rubbed his cheek against my cheek. "Once I get my heart rate back under control, you can."

"C'mon, be happy for me. I can teleport."

"Teleporting means I can't contain you."

"That's right." Although I didn't bother telling him that teleporting or not, he didn't have a chance of containing me anyway. He'd learn that in time. "I promise I'll be good and not go too far astray, but I want to try that again. You don't go running off at high speed before you make a jump, which means you've got a lot more to teach me."

He moaned, kissed my cheek then promptly pulled me to my feet as he stood. "It took me a single speed jump before the knowledge of how to teleport meant I could move to standing motionless. Just remember, instead of using your speed to project the move, use your mind in its place. Bring the exact image of where you want to travel into the forefront of your mind, then push a theoretical speed behind it. Give it a location and coordinates, if necessary."

"Coordinates?" I asked as I brushed the sand off my bottom.

"For example, some outdoor locations change images with the seasons, while some indoor locations change with items being moved. Take your living room for example. If your mother shifts a chair and disrupts the image, then you'll never make the jump. You'll stay right where you are because that location doesn't exist in theory. Everything is always precise, so be sure to make a habit of attaching a location or a coordinate, which is a physical thought of where the image is from, so you can make the jump through space." The frisky sea breeze blew his hair about.

"Got it. Let me try." I caught his hand, linked our fingers together, put into action his words and before I knew it, the beach gave way to a moment of darkness, then my bedroom enclosed us in.

Grinning like a silly two-year-old, I spun around on the tips of my toes and dropped onto my springy bed. Bouncing, I beamed. "This is sooo cool."

"One more rule." Davio pulled me to my feet, tugged me up against him. "You will not be permitted to travel without me by your side. You are my mate and until I'm certain you can teleport without any physical mishap, then you will follow my rules."

I gave him a cute little curtsy. "Rules, sch-mules."

"They exist for a reason, so I won't go insane." He gripped my hips and everything darkened. Mere seconds later, we were back on the beach, right where we'd arrived earlier.

Leaning into him with an amused smile, I delighted in the feel of him and the warmth of the sun as it crossed the sky toward the far horizon. "I like this beach more than ever now, and I like you too. Thank you for the invaluable lesson."

The gorgeous flecks of gold in his brown eyes brightened. "Then it was all worth it for that one comment alone."

I danced over to our shoes. I tossed him his, dropped to the ground and slipped my sandals on. People approached, just over his shoulder. Silvie with her red hair the most obvious, and Belle, Zac and Viv following her. "You told the others to come?"

"Yes, I made the call. Zac was complaining in my head about his hunger and Belle swore the fresh fish and fries at the local shop here are to die for. We'll build a fire as it darkens and have dinner on the beach. Do you like that idea?"

"I do." Zac jogged ahead and led everyone over the sand dunes. I'd enjoy getting to know his protectors a little better.

Silvie giggled and tore past Zac, never to be gotten ahead of. She'd changed into a cute pair of navy blue shorts and a red singlet-tee that contrasted beautifully with its bold colors against her bright hair. Belle too had donned new clothes, putting the rest of us to shame in a long flowing dress of deep crimson. She appeared runway ready, but then she nearly always did.

Beside Belle I looked dowdy, particularly with my plain old discolored bike shorts on. "Throw me my skirt, Davio." I held out my hand for it. "Back pocket."

He fished it out and shrugged his wide shoulders. "It's a tad wrinkled. I may have squished it. Badly."

I frowned, because crumpled and underdressed was not any girl's dream. It didn't help my blood boiled. He was now too close and not touching me, the change firing my anger.

Silvie sprang in beside me, knocking my arm. "Hey, sorry we're late. Zac here couldn't zap us over until Belle had provided a photograph of the beach frontage for him to match an image to. Who knew just how particular teleporting could be?"

"Me. I just 'ported myself."

"What?" Silvie snapped a wide-eyed look at me. "No, no, no. Don't tell me you can move like that too."

"Yep. Let me take you somewhere."

Only Davio gripped my arm and abruptly intervened. "We've already spoken about this. No leaving on your own. I won't concede on that point. Your continued security is imperative."

"You can 'port?" Zac huffed and gripped my shoulders. "You're only a Halfling. You shouldn't be so highly skilled. First came forethought, then fast-healing and now teleporting. Exactly how many strength skills do you hold? You certainly kept your father's status from us for far too long, and now you're obviously keeping more."

"Stand down, Zac." Davio flicked Zac's hands from my shoulders. "No touching my mate unless I give you permission."

Riled, Davio's thoughts swirled, the odd one escaping his tight block and I caught each one.

"Besides," he continued, "just how many skills my mate holds could be anyone's guess considering the Dralion scum who fathered her is clearly one of their most highly skilled. Your job is not to interrogate my mate, but to find and kill our enemy."

My shoulders stiffened. *Kill?* His desire for my unknown father's death irked me. How dare he decide such a thing? What right did he have to take my father away from me? Not that I wanted a father, only I couldn't halt the questions buzzing through my mind. Why would my father suddenly turn up after eighteen years, only to give me a safe location should I wish to use it?

What could he be after?

So many questions.

Endless questions.

And very legitimate concerns too.

I shook off Davio's tight hold. I needed a moment.

Especially considering I now had a mate who wanted to kill my father. I wanted answers from him first, and preferably before he perished.

No, there was simply more to unravel here than what Davio had said.

I poked his pumped up chest with my finger. "You want to kill my father, and I'm afraid I can't let you do that. I'll certainly never forgive you if you do him any harm. I want answers about why he left Mum and me, why he even came to Earth in the first place."

I'd stand up for myself. I always had.

Silvie's mouth gaped open. "Come on, Faith. Your father left your mother the day you were born, and up until he returned, you've never even cared to know a thing about him. He even slammed a baton into you. You're clearly not thinking straight." She gave me that frank look of hers. "Try and argue that point."

"I can't since it's all true, but I still want to know more about him." I nabbed her hand. "Let's talk, just the two of us." A pain stabbed me in the chest. I didn't care to see Silvie turning on me and agreeing with the others. She was the one who'd never wavered from my side, not my entire life.

With the image of my bedroom in my mind, I added the coordinates and flashed us there.

She gasped as we arrived, wobbled and lifted her arms to keep her balance. "Oh no. You have to stay within the protectors' sight. You can't go traveling about willy-nilly wherever you please."

"Since when did we start listening to Davio? Only Mum has the right to boss me around." She'd earnt my undying loyalty, and so had Silvie. "He's not our boss."

"I didn't say he was, but Davio is your mate. He'd never harm a hair on your head."

Davio wavered into sight, frustration clear to see on his face. "Faith Stryker."

"Don't you dare Faith Stryker me." I wasn't letting him have full control over my life.

"You're not to go against a direct order again." He stormed toward me.

"Wait." Silvie halted him with one hand raised, then harrumphed and leaned back against the wall behind her. Crossing her arms, she glared at him. "You have a lot to learn about Earth girls. Stop throwing your weight around and from now on try asking Faith nicely for any request you'd like to make. And nicely means sweetly. Put some sugar into it."

"She's right. I like a lot of sugar with any requests made." I tossed my crumpled skirt onto the bed and stalked to my wardrobe. I needed something more appropriate to wear for dinner on the beach. "You have to turn around," I snapped at him, because changing required stripping first, and I doubted he was leaving any time soon.

He released a harsh breath that whistled between his lips. "Change and then we leave. We need to return to the others. Immediately."

"I just bet we do." I gritted my teeth as I thumbed through the dresses toward the back of the rack, being a little overly rough with the clothes I loved. Could he not move? I gave it one second. "Okay, you're not far enough away. Go and kiss the wall. Five steps."

He remained right where he was, his gaze all fired up. "This erratic temper of yours is completely appalling too. You need to be able to control your emotions better."

"Well, I would, that's if my blood didn't boil whenever you're close and not touching me. You know the rules." I could argue with the best of them. "Touch me, skin-to-skin, or back off. It'd also help it you stopped saying you wanted to kill my father. It's incredibly impolite, no matter what country or world one comes from. Now turn around"—I flicked a finger— "pronto."

He barely managed it before I yanked off my top and pulled out an ankle-length, spaghetti-strap dress. I dropped the indigo cotton over my head, yanked it down and almost tore the innocent fabric.

Davio groaned as he slammed a hand against the wall, his gaze turned away. "I didn't mean you were scum. Just that your despicable father is."

Ignoring his terrible apology—if one could even call it an apology—I took a calming breath and pulled out a pair of silver flats suitable for the beach. I sat on the edge of my bed and jammed them on. "Tell me exactly how you managed to follow me here so quickly. Did you take a wild guess?" I should at least have an answer to that since I wasn't getting any others.

He crossed his arms against the wall and pressed his forehead to the back of his hands. "I simply followed your 'porting airstream. Now are you dressed? I need to see you. I don't deal well with antagonism, and it seems especially not from you."

"Well that's just too bad. Now explain the intricacies of

following my 'porting airstream?" I was all fired up and nowhere near settling down.

He took a deep breath. "Any teleporter can follow another's airstream provided they do so within a second of their leaving. Any longer than that and the scent vanishes on the wind, becoming impossible to trace."

I inched closer toward his broad back.

My mind stirred, demanding the mind-merge.

I snarled and gave in, reached out and locked my mind into his. Soft spot. Ahh, I had it back.

He slumped forward into the wall and held onto his head.

"Faith." He groaned my name, his voice swamped with relief. "I can't explain, but I can feel when you're connected to my mind. I itch for its return."

As much as I detested our argument, at least we'd both gotten what we needed to say out. I also needed him too. "You can turn around."

"I've been a brute. Do you forgive me?" He turned, his striking eyes zeroing in on me, then the door. "Your mother's coming."

My door breezed open and Mum smiled as she peered around the corner. She spotted Silvie first then arched a brow as she caught sight of Davio. "Hello, we have a visitor. I'm Kate, Faith's mother."

All I could manage was a squeak of sound.

I had a man in my room.

Thank goodness, I had Silvie in here too.

"I'm Davio Loveria, Ms. Stryker, a friend of Belle's." Davio bowed so damn politely. Why couldn't he be that polite to me, and preferably all of the time? "Belle sent me to collect the girls."

"Nice to meet you, Davio, and call me Kate. All Faith's friends do." Mum turned her eagle-like gaze on me. "I didn't even hear you come home. Let alone hear anyone else enter.

You're as quiet as a mouse these days."

"I don't mean to be." I kissed her cheek. "I'm still staying at Belle's. I used the back door, but I was coming to see you." Or I would have after I'd finished arguing with Davio. "Anyway, Belle and a few of our other friends are getting together at the Domain. Belle's organized dinner and a fire on the beach." I brushed another kiss against her cheek. "I can't miss that."

"No, you can't." Her answer was a little slow and she squeezed my arms then glanced at Davio again. "Look after my daughter."

"I certainly will." He inclined his head. "Thank you, Kate. We were on our way."

"Yes," Silvie said and hugged my mother. "Belle has Zac and Viv with her. They're new to town and we're showing them the sights."

"Oh right, then you shouldn't keep them waiting."

"Thanks." Silvie hooked her arm through mine and propelled us both out the door. We walked down the front step and marched along the pathway toward Belle's place. "Well," Silvie said once we'd walked far enough so Mum couldn't see or hear us. "Let's get a couple of things straight. You're not alone in all these changes you're going through. I'll always be right here, and there's a reason these protectors are around and even I can see their aid is necessary. We have an unknown Dralion warrior to contend with, one who hurt you."

"You're right." Of course she was, and I understood that this wasn't all about me. I hugged her. "I'm sorry."

"I appreciate the apology, but you also owe someone else an apology too. I agree Davio shouldn't have said that about your father, being scum and all, but honestly he has only your best intentions at heart. He wants to protect you from being hurt again, and you two can surely sort out this issue instead of arguing about it. Just remember we're all fighting on the same side."

"I hate it when you're always right." Flippin' hated it, but still, Davio had said some careless things and even though he followed five steps behind us so my temper wouldn't rise, I still wasn't yet ready to give into him so quickly. It wouldn't hurt him to stew for a bit more, to realize I wasn't going to get straight into line just because he'd commanded it. For our mated bond to work, our relationship needed to be fifty-fifty.

"I can see that look on your face." Silvie groaned. "No giving in yet, huh? 'Port us back to the beach."

"The beach sounds great." Right now I would concede to that much.

With the image fresh in my mind, I took us both there, just twenty feet from where the others had built a fire in a pit. The flames glowed orange and red and chased away the oncoming dark.

A swirl of wind, and Davio 'ported in too.

I stalked around the fire-pit and eased down next to Belle where she sat cross-legged unraveling a large square of heaped newspaper.

"Ooo, that looks good." Viv lifted her nose to the air and sniffed from the sand where she sat. "Smells good too."

"Mmm, there's nothing quite like hot fish and fries on the beach." Silvie smacked her lips together and dropped down next to me.

"'Bout time you guys got back." Zac pulled bottles of water out of a bag and tossed them to us where he sat seated on a log behind Viv.

I caught mine and Silvie's bottles, handed hers to her while Davio took hold of one of the other rounded logs, stepped back a few paces and dropped it with a loud *thunk*, the distance a perfect five feet between us so the pain I endured disappeared. At least he was learning.

Inside, I logged my small win. Sure, I felt a little bad. He'd only been trying to protect me earlier, except those awful words of his kept reverberating through my mind. *Just how many skills my mate holds could be anyone's guess considering the Dralion scum who fathered her is clearly one of their most highly skilled.*

I met his gaze and unscrewed my cap, raised my bottle in a salute of resistance, and he returned the gesture by lifting his own bottle. Then suddenly, with a slow shake of his head, a troubled look flickered in his gaze and he murmured, "I don't want to fight with you. It's not good for mated pairs to be so at odds."

By the drooped set of his shoulders, he clearly meant it.

Silvie bumped my arm and handed me a small paper plate of hot food. "Here, have something to eat, then the two of you can make up afterward."

That was Silvie, forever mothering me. I sighed and pulled the hot fish apart and slipped a morsel between my lips. My taste buds danced at the delight of such fresh fish, which would have been caught that morning by the local fishermen out in the bay.

Within our group, Zac pulled Viv closer into the V between his legs as he settled their joint plate on top of her knees. He encircled his arms around her, warding off the brisk breeze. How cute. They relaxed together, Zac running one hand through her dark locks. He tucked a few flyaway strands between their bodies where his chest was pressed to her back, and she turned her head and smiled at him. Zac tapped his cheek as if requesting a kiss and she giggled, popped a kiss where he'd indicated, then they whispered something to each other which was far too low for me to hear, even with my attuned hearing.

My mother had never had a man to care for her in the way Zac did with Viv. Nope, she'd been a teen mother who'd had to dedicate her life to raising me. Yet witnessing Zac holding Viv touched me. I hadn't exactly seen any real relationships between men and women as I'd grown up, and the obvious dedication in Zac's eyes toward Viv was certainly something special.

Letting out a slow breath, I faced the ocean as the last rays of the day disappeared with the sun dipping below the horizon. The night sky spread out across the heavens, a vast and brilliant midnight-blue with a myriad of twinkling stars blazing within. Somewhere beyond all that blue another world existed, one where my father had been born and now lived. Stunning, and shocking. It was also a world that intrigued me more and more with each passing minute. Davio's drawing in the sand had answered some questions, yet had also opened up a whole lot more.

"This firewood isn't quite dry enough to burn well, although it'll have to do." Zac snagged another log and nipped Viv's ear as he tossed it onto the flames. "You're almost as tasty as this meal, my mate."

Viv laughed and squeezed his leg affectionately, their attention zooming right back in on each other, as if the rest of us weren't even about. For certain Zac and Viv weren't just protectors with the ability to battle and fight—they were close, their mated bond shining through for all to see.

Was that what Davio and I were supposed to have?

Belle spoke up, breaking the tortured train of my thought. "So, Davio, what are our orders now that Faith can teleport?"

He cast his gaze out to sea where the moonlight touched the creamy white surf as it rolled in. The fire crackled and a thin trail of smoke wafted up and swirled away on the wind.

Taking a swig of his drink, he braced his elbows on his knees. "I have to admit I've been sitting here considering my mate's primary concern—that of the warrior who attacked her and perhaps I'm being too harsh with her regarding her security." He turned his gaze to me. "You can teleport and well. I can see that more clearly now, as I didn't before."

"About time." I gnawed on a fry.

With his steely gaze boring into mine, he continued, "I believe that because your father didn't attempt to take you with him after he first attacked you, or for that matter, any time these past eighteen years, he might very well have turned up because of me. I am my father's sole heir."

"Are you saying Dralion's warriors would do anything to ensure your capture?"

"My capture, then my death."

"I won't let my father hurt you." I meant that too, with every fiber of my being.

"Neither would my protectors, but I digress. It's likely not your life on the line, only mine, which means I need you to consider abiding by certain safety precautions I put in place for you, but we'll hash those out together first. Sound good?"

"That depends on what those precautions are."

"Quite simply that you inform me, at all times, of your plans."

"So I can 'port wherever I please?"

"I'd rather you didn't. My earlier request regarding that should still remain in place. No 'porting without a protector."

"That is hardly a concession on your part, or a proper hashing out, but I take it I'm allowed to walk wherever I please?" I frowned and rose to my feet.

"Where you go, I go." He stood too.

"No, that's another bad concession. How about I go for a walk to calm down, and you stay here?" I set my shoulders straight. "You're not allowed to say no."

His jaw flexed.

"I wish to get rid of this foul temper you've heaped on me tonight." I didn't wait any longer. This was my chance for some much-needed space, and I intended on taking it.

Stepping over the log, I strode off. What I needed to do was take control of my life again, because I sure needed some time and space to come to grips with my very new, and very dominant, mate. Davio was in my life now, and I understood that.

I had accepted our bond, and even though we'd fought, I

wanted him and all the bond entailed. I certainly wasn't the sort to just give up simply because we'd yet to sort these niggles out. We would, after I returned. Calming down was imperative.

I walked through the dark, the solitude easing my discomfort and soothing my mind.

So too I wanted what my mother had never had, a man who'd be there to protect me, which Davio clearly wished to do, and sadly I also wanted to know more about the father who'd given me life and then walked away from me. I had a past to put to bed before I could truly embrace my future. Davio was undoubtedly part of that future. He was generous and attentive—obviously too attentive, but I no longer wanted to quibble over that. We could work things out.

Weaving in and around the sand dunes, I continued to set my thoughts in order. I had so few people in my life. There was Mum of course, Silvie and her mother, Seriah, but next to them, that was it. To think I had a father who came from another world still shocked me. He may be a warrior and Davio's enemy, but he'd also left instructions in my mind to recall our conversation, one which wasn't as bad as it had all first appeared. Yes, I definitely wanted to meet him in a secure place and just chat. There was so much I wanted to ask him, so much to learn.

I pressed the small light on my wristwatch and illuminated the time. Seven sharp. I should go now, while the time to make my escape was so easy. I had the image. The safe location. A crunching from back near the fire traveled to me, like the sound of a water bottle being squeezed.

"Faith!" Davio's voice, his tone a tight mix of demand and worry. Footsteps thumped along the sand. He was coming, and I had no intention of allowing him to follow my 'porting airstream.

Swiftly, I brought the image of the safe room the warrior had left embedded in my mind to the forefront then 'ported. Through the dark, I gasped. Oh hell, how had my father known to give me this image? He must have known I'd have the ability to teleport.

Only the treacherous thought came too late.

I had arrived.

Chapter 6

From darkness to darkness, I was here. Wherever here was since I couldn't see a damn thing. My heart thundered. Should I really have come?

"Yes, you should have." A sliver of light chased in under the door, the answer coming from that direction. From someone who'd clearly just read my thoughts.

"Come and join me, Faith. I've been waiting a lifetime for this moment."

I'd always considered myself brave, only right now my legs shook. I tapped my feet on the ground, and fidgeted from side to side. "H-how can I trust you?" I clamped down on my stuttering tongue, the sudden giveaway of nerves not what I wanted him to hear.

"You've always been able to trust me, only you've never known me." His voice was that of a stranger, a man I should have known for eighteen years and hadn't.

This had to be the most defining moment of my life, and somehow I found my courage and set it in place. I could do this. I had to do this. Enough with the indecision. This was my only chance for answers and I intended to get them.

I stepped forward, the sliver of light guiding my direction.

Squinting though the darkness, I clutched the cold steel knob. Get it together. Open the door. "You're clearly reading my thoughts," I muttered to him.

"I am, and I'll explain all you wish to hear if you join me."

I wished to, and I tugged the door open an inch, then stopped as steel scraped loud over steel. The hairs on my neck pinged up. Why such thick steel for a door?

"I'll explain that as well. Your strength skills have come from me. Your ability to read thoughts, and soon the full force of forethought and forewarning will be upon you. I have seen your ability will rise to the same strength and precision as mine." He gripped the door from the other side and the knob slid out of my fingers as he hauled the door open. Standing before me, his violet eyes so like mine, he nodded his approval. "Thank you for coming."

He was real and solid.

"You're truly my father?"

"Yes. Your mother is bound to Earth, whereas I am bound to Dralion, although from what I've seen, Carlisio's grandson has enlightened you to at least that much. Now come out of the dark and stand before me." He lowered his hands to his sides.

"The door is made of steel. You're not leading me into some kind of cell are you? Let's not forget, the last time we met, you hit me on the head."

"It's no cell." He clipped his heels together and walked toward a metal-legged table with two chairs tucked under it, light beaming from the single bulb flaring from a lone lamp in the corner.

Such a sparse room. Gray walls. No furnishings other than what I'd already noted.

"Close the security door after you and ensure you block your mind against the protector known as Belle. It would be unacceptable if she chose to telepath you right now. This time is for us alone."

"Belle can't reach me. I'm already blocked." Yet I still couldn't seem to block him from reading my thoughts, not as

Davio could do with me. I closed the door as requested and got assaulted by the metallic odor of fresh paint. I touched the wall with one finger and came away with a coating of icky gray paint smudged on the tip. "No more harming me. I might fast-heal, but I don't care to keep trialing that new skill out."

Gripping the back lip of the metal chair, he looked at me, his black coat dropping stiffly to the floor over a vivid blue shirt and black leather pants. "I would never harm you." He lifted a brow. "That is again. You are my flesh and blood and the thought of distressing you in any way is abhorrent to me."

He angled his blond head, which I mirrored since I only hoped he meant "again" the same way I'd mean "again."

"I speak only the truth, for you should never fear me." He tugged a chair out and sat.

"I'm staying put for now." Patches of silver reflected here and there within the gray of the paint. "Are these steel walls?"

He scrubbed a hand across his jaw, edged one booted foot out from where he sat and scraped around the second metal chair with his foot. "This entire room is steel reinforced. The walls are freshly painted since I saw your initial distress, and wished to eliminate it."

"Saw? You mean with your forewarning?"

He rubbed his large hands on his knees as he leaned forward. "Sit with me. There's a chair, and I will explain all."

"I can see the chair." I frowned. "Let me read your thoughts first through my forethought." I'd barely made the demand when his thoughts opened fully to mine, the surge of information and images taking my breath away.

I clutched my racing heart.

He'd made the quick decision to try and disguise the steel walls by painting them in the half hour before I'd arrived. He'd been "forewarned" that I'd be upset and he showed me the forewarning.

He saw—so brilliantly, and with crystal clear perfection. It was like nothing Davio and Belle had told me it would be. His forewarning was real, vivid with colors, and like a live feed in real time.

"It's impressive, isn't it? I have to admit I saw Davio explaining Carlisio's forethought to you. His grandfather wasn't born to parents who both held the mated bond, whereas you and I are. The strength of our forethought is unequalled."

I itched to know more, my interest so piqued.

I walked across and sat in the chair he'd offered me. This man was my father. He had passed skills onto me I needed to learn, and I wasn't leaving until I knew more.

He smiled, having followed my movement with his gaze. "Our forethought is strong." He leaned across the small table and gently gripped my forearm. "Your skills grow fast. They are cementing and strengthening just as your powerful lineage demands."

"How do you do that? You're reading my thoughts and I can't seem to block my mind to you."

"We are one and the same. You can block your thoughts from me if you wish to, only you're not currently doing so due to our close ties." His fingers tightened. "Look for yourself within your mind."

I did, and gasped as I saw the truth.

He released me. "It's natural for our blood-bond to direct our motives into complete compliance of one another. In the future if you wish to block from me, you will need to focus more firmly on the task."

So I did, only a second later finding I didn't care for blocking him. I wanted him to know the truth of my thoughts, for now was not the time for any hidden agenda between us. "You can read what you wish."

He watched me closely, inclining his head. "Then let me take you somewhere more comfortable." He eased upright. "We have much to discuss and little time to do so." He strode out the door on the other side of the room from where I'd entered.

"Wait up." I caught up to him, walked side by side down the carpeted passageway, my level of comfort in being around him so strong. Shocking, and fascinating. "Okay, so why exactly do you have a steel room? I know why you painted it, but why have one at all?"

"The steel room is simply to ensure Carlisio can't track you on Davio's behalf. I will not risk any endangerment coming to you while you're with me."

"Uh-huh." We'd see about the endangerment—the jury was still out on that one. "Would you explain why a steel room would stop a forewarner's tracking? There's very little I know."

"Simply put, our cells can't pass through the solidity of steel. They also can't pass through the energy field which protects Dralion. That being the case, this steel room exists for the same reason as the dome. You arrived in the room next to one which holds a large amount of metal. This effectively scatters the initial image of your arrival, and it also allows for a defendable position if one's 'porting airstream is followed."

We rounded a corner, passed two bedrooms with silver thread shimmering in the white carpet under the recessed lights. The walls here were painted a stark gray too.

"Although now, it is quite safe for us to move about the rooms of this apartment. There is no chance Carlisio can gain an accurate visual, not with the natural use of steel contained within this building's construction."

"I see, and I can teleport from any one of these other rooms?"

"The amounts of steel aid in disseminating images, but not in preventing any form of teleportation, only a solid wall can do that."

"So I can leave at any time?" Which I would in an instant, if necessary.

"Yes." He grasped my shoulder. "I see your thoughts, and I

understand your confliction. Yet you are my daughter and tied to me by blood, a bond which our Magioling DNA accepts to a far deeper degree than an Earthling's. As your new relationship with Loveria stands strong, so too does a blood-bond. The two are no different in strength, except he holds your soul."

"My bond with him grows fast."

"So I've seen." A rush of air passed between his lips. We entered a living room.

Ahead, one scalloped wall faced a dark, full-length glass slider, and in the adjoining room, a tidy kitchen in tones of black and white with a marble breakfast bar appeared utilitarian clean.

I moved toward the one and only piece of furniture in the lounge, a two-seater gray leather couch.

"Where are we?" With that precise hearing of mine, I caught the crashing of the surf somewhere close.

"At the Mount."

Which meant we were only a thirty-minute drive from my home.

"Harbor side or ocean side?" I sank down into the leather, ran my hands over the chill of the fabric.

"Ocean, and we're on the top floor of the exclusive towers. This is the penthouse suite."

Oh, he had some fancy digs. "So you just moved in?"

"No." Flinging out the back-tails of his leather coat, he eased in beside me. "I purchased this apartment after the towers were built—eighteen years ago. I needed a base close to your mother and you."

"Really?" I checked out the room again in case I'd missed something that said *eighteen years of occupation*. "So you didn't care to decorate? Some color would be nice." White, black, gray, and silver everywhere.

"This apartment is here for one reason only, and as I've said, I can't be followed. I come here only to check on you and your mother, that's when I can do so without your grandfather becoming aware of my departure from Dralion."

I rubbed my nose. "I have a grandfather?"

Did that mean I had other family as well?

"Yes." He angled his head to one side, that intense violet gaze of his trained on me. "To both questions."

I tapped one foot. Having him reading my thoughts was going to take some time getting used to. "How often do you check up on us?"

"I spend a few short minutes visiting your street, two or three times a week. It's the most I can manage."

"How come I've never seen you before?"

"I'm forced to keep my distance. Your grandfather rules Dralion with a firm hand, an iron grip that doesn't allow me to acknowledge my weakness, my one all-consuming love." He paused for a moment, then continued. "Which is for you and your mother."

I looked at him, trying to find a breath as everything swayed before me.

"Breathe." He rubbed my back.

I inhaled, and vitally important air shuddered back into my lungs. "I—I—" How shocking. "My mother? You love us? And did you say my grandfather rules Dralion?"

He took my suddenly frozen hands in his and rubbed them too. "We have much to discuss, and you have much to learn." Warmth returned, and he continued, "You are a Wincrest and my name is Prince Alexo."

"Oh hell. Hell. Hell. Hell." This couldn't be happening.

My so-called grandfather must be the hated Donaldo who Davio would gladly kill, right along with my father. "You're truly Alexo?"

A small cough as he cleared his throat. "Please, don't call me by my given name. I am your father, and I have waited a lifetime for my daughter to name me as such."

"Right, *Dad*," I exaggerated. "You can't think it's okay to dump this kind of information on me, or at least not this fast after eighteen years of nothing."

Rising to his feet, his jacket flapped out behind him and he crossed the room and pulled the glass slider open. The salty scent of the ocean floated in on the night breeze, and he stood there in the doorway facing me, the moon a golden orb framing him from behind. "Enough with the sarcasm."

"I wasn't being sarcastic."

"I understand you're hurting, but the truth is still the truth no matter which way I present it."

That I understood, was even grateful for considering the kind of week I'd just had. "Sure, you're right about that. So tell me why you've steered clear of my mother and me for my entire life."

"Because of your mixed heritage. Donaldo would only ever see Kate as an Earthling and my weakest link, disposing of her as quickly as possible."

"So why become involved now? With me, that is."

"It is not I who became involved, but the protectors. Your mate is making my life difficult in his claim of you, and that is why we now meet."

"Hold on. Give me a minute to think this through. I'm still coming to grips with the fact I'm standing in the same room as my father. Who, I might add, has been silently watching over me, since my birth."

He rubbed his forehead and moved toward me. "You are safe with me. We are one and the same. Our blood-bond is cemented at birth and that connection is unbreakable. That's why I've never risked coming into contact with you before, for the physical effect of being in each other's presence is the same as you being in Loveria's. I would want you with me in Dralion and you would want the same, but I don't have the heart to take you from your mother. She loves you, and I certainly can't expose her whereabouts to Donaldo, not when I've seen he would harm her. He wants full-blooded heirs, not Halflings, so you've both remained here in New Zealand."

I clutched my head, pressing all ten fingers into my skull. My mind was stretched to capacity, almost ready to explode.

"Take a deep breath," Alexo instructed. "We will get through this."

Oh, I knew I'd get through this, only where would I be at the end? Dropping my hands to my knees, I met his gaze. "Okay, so there's no risk to me because of Donaldo Wincrest, correct?"

"No, he would never harm a child of mine. The risk is to your mother alone. Her death would be a certainty, allowing him to see me married to another to give him full-blooded heirs. But I've never cared that your mother is from Earth, not as he has."

"How does he even know my mother exists?"

"Because I won't take another woman as my wife. I also wasn't careful enough eighteen years ago. I mentioned Kate to him and I shouldn't have. From that moment on, he's been searching for her."

"You've never given us up?"

"No." He took a second, his chest rising and falling as he inhaled. "I see both Donaldo's strengths and weaknesses. He doesn't hold forethought as you and I do since it can skip generations, but he is a great leader. Although by the strength of our familial blood-bond, you too would find yourself called to serve him."

He sat at my side. "I've always wished for you to have choices in your life, for those not to be taken from you as your mother was taken from me. Yet now, Carlisio involves his grandson, and Davio pursues you. This means it won't be long before our spies in Peacio report back to Donaldo that you exist."

"That would be dangerous?"

"Not to you, but you would be forced to leave your mother if you wish to ensure her safety, and for the past eighteen years, I've spent my life ensuring that is so."

I shuddered. "Donaldo has never met me. How will his spies connect me to you?"

"You hold the coveted forethought strength skill. Your eyes are the rare Wincrest violet. Your features are so similar to one of the other females in our family's line. I could go on, but those things alone isolate you directly as mine. No Dralion spy worth his weight in gold will ever withhold that kind of information from Donaldo, not if he saw you."

"I'm not in Peacio, nor do I ever plan to travel there. Dad, I live here in New Zealand." Whoa, and had I just called him Dad? Freaky.

"You called me father?" He grinned and clasped his hand over mine. "Nothing pleases me more than hearing you say so."

Damn it. He'd said the blood-bond was seriously strong, and I surely couldn't deny that. "I hope you realize I'm not enjoying this whole mated relationship, or this whole blood-bond thing that's going on. Someone, who shall remain nameless, tried to convince me it was all going to be a fabulous thing." I stirred my hands in the air. "In fact, she told me I needed to consider the full circle behind the mated concept, although she didn't mention the emotions one would feel for their blood-bonded parent. She should have."

"Let me guess—the empath convinced you. You have to watch them. They're pesky people. All they work on are feelings, and at times feelings can't become involved."

"Well, they are now. Davio is my mate, and I have accepted him. I can't walk away from him any more than he'd ever allow it of me."

A snort. "You make him mad."

"I happen to do that to people, and he's no exception."

He dragged in a stiff pull of air. "I used to make your mother mad too. I miss that."

"You did?" Something more we had in common, and I couldn't help my small smile. "She never speaks of you."

"I'm not surprised considering the way I left her." He clenched his teeth. "Your mother is unaware of everything. Of whom I am. Of where I come from. Of why I left her the day of your birth." Harsh words, yet true.

"How can the mated relationship cross planets? First my mother and now me?"

"That question is one that's always confused me. I'm not aware of Earthlings being mated to our own, but I don't see why it can't happen. It certainly has between your mother and me, and I accepted that before your birth."

I sucked in my bottom lip, nibbled on it. "My mother's very intuitive. Perhaps she has some inkling? Perhaps you let something slip back then?"

"No. Kate has believed me gone, and that ending gives her the least pain, which certainly eases my own."

My legs tingled, and I stood and paced out the prickling. "I have no idea what my mother believed became of you. She said you left us, but I've never asked her for the details. There was never a time that seemed right."

Having not heard his approach, I jumped as he settled an arm over my shoulders. "It's difficult to watch your distress when we don't have long together. There is still much we need to speak of."

"Lay it on me. I might as well have it all."

"I need to explain your boiling blood in the presence of your mate."

"How do you know about that?" Ah, of course, he had forethought.

"The aggression you experience around the direct bloodline of Loveria is a part of our genetic makeup. We've detested our enemy for centuries, as they have done with us."

My mouth opened. "Carry on." Then shut.

"A thousand years ago our family separated from Peacio, taking the lesser opposing land of Dralion. At the time, tremendously bad blood remained between the Wincrests and the Loverias, and that came about because our families alone held the highest skill of forethought. A war raged, and they unfortunately won."

"You can't let bygones be bygones?" A thousand years had passed and they still warred? "It's been millennia."

"Ours is an age-old war, and one that will never end. Over the centuries, information has been passed down within our line, that the Loverias won that battle from long ago, unfairly. Having seen the written evidence, I agree with my father. The Loverias should have left and not us. This means the only way to gain back our stronghold on Peacio is to eliminate, in full, the Loveria line."

"You wish to destroy all three, Carlisio, his son and grandson?" I pulled in a ragged breath. I couldn't condone that.

"I'm not asking you to condone it." He was so proficient in reading my thoughts. Double freaky. "I'm simply explaining why our two lines have so opposed each other. Even though Davio has not yet thought of it, that state of tension is yet another which will prove you are descended from me." He crossed his arms. "You must understand our history has decreed our future, that our blood will always war with theirs."

"Well, isn't that incredibly helpful." And super annoying too.

"I'm sorry." He tilted his head, confusion evident in his gaze. "Perhaps you can explain one thing to me."

"If I can."

"How is it you can stand the presence of your mate? I've personally witnessed you touching. That should be impossible, or at least extremely unpleasant, considering our blood feud."

"Ah, I merge my mind with his, and provided we touch, we cease clashing."

His gaze narrowed. "You merge your mind with his? Don't you mean you read his projected thoughts? There's no merging of the mind with this skill of ours."

"Um, he hardly allows his thoughts to escape. What I mean is, I bed down in his mind, and it's real nice and comfy, but I only do that with him. You must be able to do it. Davio said the skill of mind-merge must come from you."

Frowning, the lines on his forehead deepened. "If it's a part of my forethought, then I've never activated it. I certainly never needed to merge my mind with your mother's as our blood never warred. This is unusual."

To me everything was unusual, but I kept quiet on that front.

"You don't mind touching the darkness of a Loveria's mind?" Confusion chased across his brow. "Is this not aggravating in any way?"

"No, it's not aggravating. The man infinitely is, but not the mind-merge."

"I see. Then perhaps this merging is a necessary extension of your forethought, due to you mating with a Loveria."

Well out of the two of us, he should know.

"Follow my forethought, if you will. I wish to show you more of what will soon be possible for you." He walked out onto the balcony so very far above the ground. "We need the open air for it to fully activate."

I was up for that, and truth be told, my blood-bond with him demanded I please him. Jeez, that was irritating.

Outside under the night sky, we walked to a darkened corner along the balcony that ran the width of the penthouse suite. Far below the glass-railed enclosure, moonlight shimmered over the sandy beach and turned the white-capped waves rolling into shore a stunning silvery hue. A few couples walked hand-in-hand alongside the surf, and seagulls hopped about the rocks near the jutting rise of the mountain so close. That majestic mountain gave this place its name—The Mount as locals affectionately called it.

"This is the perfect spot." He tapped his head. "Look inside my mind."

I focused and examined how he took Davio's image and brought it to the forefront of his mind. As soon as that happened, my mate's image shimmered into vivid life, then a live feed of images rolled through, as if I stood right with him. He paced Belle's living room, Zac and Viv standing to one side, and Belle and Silvie the other. No one spoke, the room eerily quiet.

"They have no idea what to do," my father explained in a whisper. "But as they speak, ensure you listen for you will hear every word they utter."

I waited as Davio continued to walk back and forth, his lips flattened and his eyes darkened to the point where all flecks of gold within the brown were extinguished.

"Carlisio did not see where she went." The words rumbled from Davio's mouth as he ground his teeth together. "She is either near too much metal or beyond Dralion's energy shield. If that's the case and the warrior has taken her..." He paused, his gaze narrowing on Zac's. "Then we kill him, without asking questions."

Silvie pulled a tissue from her pocket and wiped her reddened eyes. "How? Why? I don't get this. After all these years, why take her?" Her voice wobbled, and I cringed. I should never have left her without first speaking to her of my intentions. Not that I'd known of my intentions at the time.

My father squeezed my arm. "Silvie is angry at me, not you. She has always been there for you, and she loves you like a sister. Remember that. Always."

"I know, but they think you took me when it was I who left. Davio wants me back." And our last words had been in anger. I hated that.

"Just look at him. We have yet to meet, and he already wishes me dead."

I stared into my father's eyes. "Hey, you did hit me on the

head. He's been a tad upset over that." I pressed my fingers into the back of my neck, and rubbed. "He's not going to like finding out who you are. Heck, even I couldn't have imagined exactly who you'd be."

With a deep inhalation, I returned to the live feed. Silvie left the room with Belle, and Davio let loose with a string of blasphemous words as Zac and Viv stood with him. Not good.

My cheeks flushed with heat, which was made infinitely worse by the subsequent acts of death and destruction he voiced next.

"Okay, well, I'd say Davio and his protectors aren't people you ever want to meet." I fanned my face. "Which means where to from here, Dad?"

He crossed his arms. "You should return to him, without a doubt."

"Are you sure?"

"Very sure, and Donaldo can't find you on Earth so right here is where you must currently stay. I have to consider what to do about the protectors while ensuring your mother remains safe." He paused, pushed a hand through his hair. "Davio is still your mate and before we met, you'd already chosen him, a choice I'd never take away from you." He sighed. "I wasn't given that option with your mother, and I will not repeat history and take that choice from you, a choice my father took from me. To that end, I'll return to Dralion and attempt to figure out where our lives are headed from here. It will take time, so be prepared to stay under the radar until I can formulate a plan. I have to consider everyone involved, even though I detest the thought of doing so with the Loverias." He shook his head resolutely. "I never saw this mated bond coming."

"Neither did I." Although, I agreed with him. Staying here sounded best, particularly when I too wished only to keep my mother safe. "I'm glad you're not taking my decision to remain mated to him from me."

"When I said I would never harm you, I meant it. You must trust in me and believe I will always choose the best future for you. Which means I need to let you go, so you can return to Davio before he raises all hell. He is preparing to leave Earth and gather more protectors, and should he do that, we will all be in far more trouble than our lives are worth."

"I'll go now."

He touched my arm. "Yes and a word of warning. I want you to inform Loveria of who I am and what he is now going to be up against. Let him know I will never see my daughter harmed, and if he chooses to make you a pawn between our two nations, I will see to his death just as quickly as he's stated he'd like to see to mine."

I screwed up my forehead, feeling a terrible ache. "Righto, that'll be a super nice conversation when I get around to it. Thanks for that."

"I'm sorry to have put you in such a position." Alexo touched my brow. "Do not become distressed. Your forethought is gaining in strength and will soon be here in all its fullness. Don't force it, but when it comes to you, it will be strong." He inhaled sharply and pulled me into his arms. "Ensure you maintain your awareness and take extreme care."

I squeezed him tight in return, the full strength of our blood-bond pulling me toward staying right here with him. "This is strange, but I don't want to leave you." The words spilled out, because I truly didn't. I wanted to learn more about this man who was my father. We hadn't had enough time together yet.

"I don't want you leaving me either." He hugged me even tighter, tucking my head in under his chin. "The familial connection of the blood-bond is both a burden and a privilege, one I could never deny, not with Donaldo, or to my birthplace of Dralion. Although I am soul-bound to your mother and must ensure her safety comes before all else. I understand you will need your mate more than me, so go to him."

I lifted my head. "How can you be so accepting?"

"Carlisio Loveria is a thorn in Donaldo's side, while his son, Everio, and grandson, Davio, are no better. I am their enemy, but for your sake, I'll do whatever it takes to ensure this war doesn't escalate. Certainly the days ahead of us won't be easy, but we'll get through them together." His thoughts flickered with more insight, only he blocked—for the first time. "Now go. I will be in contact again as soon as I am able."

Recalling the last image of where Davio had stood in Belle's living room, I attached the coordinates and made the jump. Although my mate better watch out, for he was about to learn I'd never accept any threat he now made to kill my father, not now I'd met him and spoken to him at length.

The dark ensued, whizzing by then I was there. I toppled against Davio and sent us both to the floor. I landed with an "oomph" on his chest, then jabbed an elbow into his neck to keep him down. Swiftly, I merged my mind with his and bunked down in my soft spot. "If I were you, I'd stay still. I have something very important to say to you."

"Faith?" he tried to grab ahold of me, but I pressed my elbow in firmer as I eased up over him into a crouch.,

"I said stay still."

A low growl rumbled from behind me, and at a guess, coming from Zac.

Definitely Zac. A blade glinted as he slid it up against my neck. Looming over me, clothed in his black battle leathers and his legs braced wide apart, he muttered, "Viv, take the other side."

"I'm here to talk to Davio, not you."

The sharp press of Viv's blade poked into the soft skin of my neck on the other side. Trapped, between two blades.

Zac snarled. "Davio's not thinking clearly and you're holding him forcibly to the ground. That's not going over very well with me."

"Too bad. I happen to like speaking my mind, and I'm not going to stop now." Carefully, I eyed the man I'd flattened to the ground. "So, I heard you were heading out to cause some chaos. You want to explain?"

His eyes reduced to bare slits, his gaze focused on my neck, and he answered not me, but his man. "Damn it, Zac. She's bleeding. Stand back, both you and Viv."

"It's our duty to protect you."

A warm trickle of blood dribbled down my throat. Taking a slow breath, I eyed Davio. "The Dralion warrior. The man we both know as my father." I stopped for this wasn't easy to say. "I'm sorry, but he's Prince Alexo Wincrest, the son of King Donaldo."

Both blades moved, scraping down an inch. More blood, and Davio's eyes closed as he took a shuddering breath. "I have her, Zac. Swords down, now. Both of you."

He had me?

Oh, he did. His hands were firm around my wrists and within a split second, he shoved my elbow in his neck to the side and took full control.

I shook as I slithered from my crouch down fully on top of him. It seemed my life was no longer my own and at every turn, the proof only grew stronger.

I dropped my forehead to his chest, my heart aching at the loss of the life I'd had until so recently. Then I let the burden go and my tears fell. I let it all out. The path I'd chosen in my life had dropped away under my feet and I was in a maelstrom.

"Don't cry. I—" He stopped, twitchy hands sweeping around my back as he rolled me over. He moved to his feet, fluidly lifting me with him. "Faith, no. Don't you dare cry. Here, sit." He pushed me onto the padded couch, and hunkered down in front of me. "These wounds are healing. It's nothing to cry over." He swiped across the sword nicks and directed a murderous look at Zac and Viv as he did.

I wiped the back of my hand across my cheeks. "Did you not hear me? My father is not only your enemy, but your greatest enemy. I met with him, and more than that, I struggled to leave him after he told me I must go. The blood-bond is strong. Why did none of you ever tell me such a thing existed?"

"You were never supposed to bond with your warrior father."

Zac snarled. "Exactly."

Viv came up beside me. "I'm sorry you were not told, but what we feel toward our family is similar to what we feel for our mated one, only our mate holds our soul. You've met Wincrest, which means your allegiance to him will now surely grow."

Lifting his sword, Zac allowed it to hover. "That can't be allowed to happen."

Davio pointed a finger at Zac, his gaze fixed. "Right now, your actions do not aid me in anyway." To me he said, "Don't speak another word in front of my protectors."

I cupped his cheeks, stared into his eyes. "I learnt something else. Wincrest blood battles in my very veins when I'm near you. Everything within me, every cell and tissue is designed to aggressively oppose yours. Surely you already knew of this."

He gritted his teeth. "Damn it, yes. But it didn't cross my mind since we were mated. It's not like a Wincrest and a Loveria meet very often, and when we do, we aren't shaking hands and making friendly. Swords and bloodshed are usually involved."

I glanced at Zac who stood ramrod stiff, my blood coating Davio's fingers. "The same thing's happening now."

Davio wiped the blood on his shirt. "Your bloodshed is my bloodshed, and I need you. I won't be separated from you, ever. It would be a deadly kind of hell—a certain madness if I had to live without you." He leaned in. "For me, who fathered you has never changed how I felt. It only means I must take more care."

"Yes, but how does that happen when Alexo Wincrest is my

father?"

He touched his lips to mine with the softest of kisses. "I will strategize for it."

I pushed him back. "Strategize how?"

A smile, the gold flecks flickering to life in his eyes. "You are the one person I can't tell, not now your blood-bond with your father has come into effect." Then he ducked in, and kissed me proper.

Drat him, but I couldn't leave him anymore than I had wanted to leave my father. Heaven help me, but I had returned to my mate as Alexo had instructed, and now I needed to give my father some time to figure out our future.

I nipped Davio's lips, and broke away. "Alexo told me to come back to you, although he did ask me to stay under the radar. He intends to come up with a plan."

At his groan, I eyed him. "Let me finish. Alexo doesn't wish for Donaldo to know about me, or that I attempt to go near Peacio for fear of Donaldo's spies within your country spotting me." I paused, taking a deep breath. "But he did have a very forthright warning for you. You are never to harm me, and you are never to place me as a pawn between our two nations. If you do, he'll kill you, just as surely as you would kill him."

One brow cocked up. "Wincrest believes I'd be open to giving him any length of time to formulate a so-called plan? The man is an idiot. I'm taking you with me to Peacio as soon as I rid it of Dralion's spies."

"Hey, did you not hear me say I'm not to be a pawn?" I gripped his shirt, and shook him. "I know I mentioned the death and destruction part."

He mumbled, turned sharply on Zac as he closed in on us, swiftly kicked out his leg and toppled Zac to the floor. "Leave my mate alone. She did not mean my death and destruction. Surely, you can see I'm in no mood for trouble from you. Take Viv and leave."

Zac rose, and brushed the back of his pants. "I'm not going anywhere, not when your trouble has just begun."

I caught Davio's hand. "We need privacy."

Without asking, I took us both away.

We arrived a moment later in the bedroom I shared with Silvie.

"Perfect." He smiled. "I should have thought of that."

Zac and Viv shimmered in.

"Enough." Davio opened the door and tugged me down the hallway. "Everyone to bed," he yelled over his shoulder. "There is nothing more we can do this night. We'll have to wait until Dralion's spies have been ferreted out and wholly removed."

I tripped into his back and he swung me into his arms and carried me into his bedroom. He shut the door with his hip, crossed the room to his king-sized bed covered in a royal-blue comforter and sat me down on the end.

Why could I not stay out of trouble?

"Well, this is nice." I jiggled about on the mattress, desperate for some normalcy. Perhaps changing the subject from all the doom and gloom that had just gone on might help. I pointed over his shoulder at a pretty piece of framed artwork. "Is that somewhere in Peacio, like the prints in the lounge?" The painting, a bright and beautiful landscape, one of a fast running river nestled among a forest of trees, captured my attention.

"You're attempting to distract me, but it won't work." He moved to the large bank of windows and pulled the velvet curtains—a shade a mushroom-brown—across. "Although it is late—almost two in the morning."

"It's that late already?" Boy, time had flown with my father. "Then I should go to bed." I jumped to my feet.

With a narrowed gaze, he stepped in front of me, all six foot four of him. "Yes, that bed behind you. Where I can watch you."

"I know you heard the part about my father being Alexo Wincrest. I don't think he'll want me sleeping with you."

"As much as I loathe the Wincrests"—taking my arms, he leaned in—"always have and always will, you are not specifically my enemy. You are my mate, and we are going to sleep together."

"But—"

"No buts." He touched his lips to mine. "I will only concede to the point that Peacio suffers from Dralion's spies breaching our country's tight security. I agree that you shouldn't be permitted to travel to Peacio under those conditions, or as I've said, until any spies are fully removed. So, that means our relationship doesn't change. I want you in my bed. I can no longer deny my feelings toward you. I want you closer to me, right by my side where I can watch over you."

"Spies. Other worlds. Blood-bonds." I flushed, my cheeks heating again. "You want to watch over me—lovely." And here I'd thought my life was all about final exams in a couple of months.

"Go and change for bed. You are sleeping under those covers with me until the morning. Which means you have two minutes in order to ready yourself, for any longer and I'll personally hunt you down."

I could see he wasn't going to give in. "Give me five minutes."

"No. You have two, and just so you're aware, I'm already counting." He turned and headed toward the attached bathroom off his room.

"Hey." I stomped after him. "You can't make those kinds of demands and walk away. On Earth, those involved in a relationship discuss things. You're supposed to come up to three minutes, and then I'll come down to four." The door clicked shut as he closed himself within. I banged the door. "C'mon, you're a prince for heaven's sake. You should know the end deal should have been three and a half." My blood began to boil. "I'm going back to five."

"No," he called through the solid wood. "I don't bargain."

I thumped the door again for good measure, before flashing to my room where I should have been sleeping with Silvie, although where Silvie had gone, I had no idea. I grabbed my clothing from the twin bed and returned.

Davio waited in the doorway.

I stopped, breathing in deeply as I stared at his low slung blue pajama pants.

That was it? That was all he had on?

"I'll need the bathroom," I squeaked as I tried not to focus on the solid wall of his chest. "Where did Silvie and Belle go?"

"They're checking places you might have 'ported to, places where you might seek some time alone. I'll send a message to tell them you're back and to return." He stepped to one side, allowing me to enter.

I puckered my lips and let them pop. "I can't believe I'm sleeping in here with you."

His brow creased, his index finger sliding underneath my chin. "I can't have you several rooms away from me as you were last night. We'll sleep together, and by sleep, I mean sleep." He bent his head, kissed the tip of my nose. "This is not the time for us to strengthen our bonds sexually. In fact, that kind of relationship between mates is generally reserved for marriage, even as old-fashioned as that sounds."

Well, that was an unexpected answer after he'd just demanded we sleep together.

I cleared my throat. "Well, in all honesty, I'm relieved." Because there was the whole glaring issue of my father who had a very long sword instead of a shotgun.

"So, we're in agreement? To abstinence?"

I touched a finger to his chest and tapped it. Oh my, his chest was rock-hard and rippled with muscles. I let out a soft sigh. I liked all that muscle, liked it lots and lots. "Yes. Your idea is solid. We'll go with that."

"Good. Now go and change for bed." He turned me around by the shoulders, gave me a push in the right direction.

Showering in thirty seconds flat was a record for me. I dried off fast, hauled my yellow cami top and pajama shorts on. With a quick whizz of my toothbrush over my teeth, I left the bathroom and halted in the doorway to the bedroom.

Propped up in bed, his back pressed to the headboard, Davio waited for me. He held out a hand and I walked across and scooted in beside him.

Swiftly, I merged my mind with his, and mumbled, "This is a first."

"We'll adapt. Let me turn off the light." He flicked the bedside switch and plunged the room into darkness.

I blinked and adjusted.

"Down. I'll need to touch you, maybe hold your hand since we need skin-to-skin contact so your anger doesn't rise. Is that acceptable?"

"You're actually asking instead of just demanding?" I couldn't help but smile, then shuffled down and settled my head on the pillow. At night, I always wrinkled my cami top up, just enough over my midsection so I could stroke the scar I'd had since birth.

As I did, his fingers bumped into mine. He caught hold of my hand, only the rest of him was too far away, a gaping distance considering the size of the bed.

A minute later, and I still stared upward. "This doesn't feel right. Can you come closer?"

"Sure." His breath hitched as he rolled into me, then he wrapped his arms snugly around my waist and kissed the side of my neck. "Is that better?"

I moaned. "Oh, that is sooo much better." I smiled, threaded my fingers through his, then I caught a stray thought from his mind. He was thinking of his loved ones back home, his grandfather, parents, and someone else named Silas.

Wriggling onto my side, I faced him. "Who's Silas?"

"My cousin. We grew up together at Loveria Castle. Our mothers are sisters."

"If you're as close as you say, why isn't he here?"

"He's my right hand man, and attending to my duties while I'm not there." He touched his head. "He's also knocking telepathically right now, and even though I'm blocked, I can still sense him needing to make contact."

"Oh, if that's the case, go right ahead and speak to him." I traced my fingers along his brow in the near dark. Only a slither of moonlight beamed in through the small gap in the curtains where they hadn't quite been pulled fully across.

"Thank you. I won't be long."

I tugged my pillow more comfortably under my head as he conversed privately with Silas.

Long minutes passed, and I snuggled closer, the sound of his even breathing lulling me.

"I'm sorry. Silas is insistent."

A yawn escaped me. "Insistent about what?"

"Tomorrow afternoon there's a gathering of protectors. We all need to be there. It's very important. But be assured, Belle will stay."

"You're leaving?"

"Not for long, and you will stay put, right here with Belle and Silvie."

"We'll see."

He groaned, and I grinned in the dark.

"So, what's the meeting about?"

"Dralion's spies. That's the one issue I need resolved since I wish to have the freedom to move you there."

"Oh."

"I'm leaving Belle with you."

"So you said."

"And Silvie. I want you to stay close to Silvie."

"Okay, quit that." I flicked his arm. "You're not going to be away for very long. I believe I can look after myself for a couple of hours." I yawned again, clapped a hand over my mouth and murmured, "I'll be fine, truly."

"Promise me you'll be here when I return."

"I promise."

"Good, now sleep. You're yawning and I've clearly kept you up too late. I should be taking more care of your needs."

Great. I could swear the man worried more about me than anyone in my entire life ever had. His innate ability to do so truly sucked.

"I don't want to go to sleep yet. I want to stay up all night talking to you. You're the first man I've ever slept with. This is kind of cool."

"Faith." My name was a warning as he brushed his lips across my forehead. "I know we've had a rough day, especially with what played out earlier with Wincrest, but remember we have a future together. We have an entire lifetime to talk."

I curled up against him, yet another yawn escaping. "Just ignore that," I mumbled, only my eyelids felt like lead. Whether I wanted to or not, I drifted.

"Goodnight." His soft murmur seemed to come from far away, and then I was out, slipping assuredly into my safest haven.

Chapter 7

I awoke and stretched, then stopped at the heavy weight of Davio's arm draped across my waist, his breath warm on the back of my neck. A smidgeon of dawn light sneaked in between the heavy fall of velvet curtaining over the windows and highlighted his features. I smiled. No longer did he have last night's dark shadows under his eyes. They'd gone, and it appeared he'd rested well.

Pushing up onto my elbows, I checked the time. My watch said five-forty. Not much sleep, but I was okay with that. In all honesty, I had to be because my legs ached.

I stroked down my right thigh to my calf, then back up again. The itchy ache felt like coiled energy deep inside needing to be released. I should run.

Swinging my feet to the ground, I checked over my shoulder to make certain I hadn't woken him.

After such a late night, an extra hour of sleep wouldn't hurt him, not when I could look after myself. This outing alone would certainly prove it.

I snuck out of his bedroom, tiptoed down the hallway and peeked in on Silvie.

My lips lifted. She slept so snugly in her bed.

The intricate burgundy quilt was fluffed up around her neck, or it was until I bounced on top of her.

Only she didn't wake.

Didn't even stir.

I took a length of her red-gold hair and yanked. "Wake up, sleepyhead."

She groaned and lifted a wobbly hand. Blindly patting the air, she knocked my hand away. "You're such a pest. Go back to sleep and leave me alone. You disappear, then reappear without even a word to me, then sleep in Davio's room and I'm not happy about that."

"Sorry, Mum, but I promise all we're doing is sleeping. Nothing else." I gripped the top edge of her covers, went to pull but she yanked them right up over her head.

I chuckled, her typical morning moodiness only encouraging me further. "I'm going for a run and didn't want to leave you behind, not like I did last night. I'm sorry I scared you. You wanna run around Centennial Park together?"

"Oh, you're so funny." She whipped a knee into me from underneath the covers. "I don't run and you know it. I'm a sane sleeper, and you're forgiven."

I grinned. "You're such a spoilsport. You won't get fit lying around in a bed."

She pushed the covers down and dragged an eyelid open, one piercing blue eye sending a sharp look at me. "What's wrong with your legs? I can feel the mini earthquake from here. Why are you wriggling about like that?"

She was right. My lower limbs shook. Even clamping a hand on them didn't help. "I don't know. I woke up like this."

She dropped her eyelid as if it weighed too much for her to handle. "Then go for your run and make it a lengthy one. Belle said with your sort of skills accumulating, you'll have an overabundance of energy to expend. Many of their highly skilled people need to run it out a couple of times a month."

"Truly? No one's ever told me that." It made a whole lot of sense though. "In that case, I'll pop home, change and do just that. Run until I've expended my energy."

"Shut the door on your way out." She rolled over and heaved the burgundy quilt back up and over her head.

I smiled for I had been dismissed—Silvie fashion.

One-half second later with the precise image of my bedroom in mind, I flashed there. Oh yeah, I loved that speed.

At my dresser, I pulled out a pair of sky-blue running shorts and a white t-shirt. In the bathroom, I tugged a comb through my hair and secured it in a ponytail. Running socks and lace-up Adidas sneakers on, I dashed to my bathroom and whizzed the toothbrush over my teeth.

At the other end of the hallway, I checked in on my sleeping mother.

With her dark hair tumbled in complete disarray over her pillow, she mumbled in her sleep, so like Silvie I couldn't help but smile. I jiggled from foot to foot, bent and dropped a kiss on her forehead then snuck out without waking her.

Tub of yogurt. Glass of water. Another shake of my legs, and I was off.

I took the pathway, the thicker tree canopy swaying overhead in the breeze. I pounded down Centennial Drive, the hum of chirping sparrows and buzzing bees resounding all around.

Another minute and the sun would rise fully over the eastern horizon. I was in paradise. I adored spring and seeing the roses bloom in a myriad of color over our fence from Mr. Ray's place next door. This park, with its varying shades of breakout green and gold, soothed my very soul. Spring was the most beautiful season.

"Good morning."

I jumped, my heart losing ten very necessary beats as Davio stepped out from behind a tree. "That's not funny." I glared, then half-stumbled at the yum-yum sight of his white sports t-shirt pulling tight across his chest. "Where did you come from?"

"From behind the tree." A devilish grin.

"Obviously." I tugged my ponytail tighter and set out again. "Was Carlisio being nosy?"

"No, this time I shook Silvie out of bed for the information. Stubborn redhead was almost impossible to wake up." He reached for my hand as we ran, and I merged my mind with his. Oh boy. There it was—instant gratification.

Feet pounding the ground, I built up my speed. "Why aren't you asleep like she is? I left you behind for a good reason." I pumped my legs, going faster still.

"Wherever you are"—he grumbled, panting hard—"is where I'll always wish to be."

I glanced at him, laughing. "That didn't sound very wishful."

"That's because we're running like there's no tomorrow. Is there a reason for this?" He clutched his side.

"No idea, other than that I'm just warming up." We neared the isolated end of Centennial Park where the town's perimeter merged with the country. The pavement gave way to an open area of grassy land, and now I truly let loose. "Catch me if you can."

"I'm not letting you get away."

"You appear to be having trouble keeping up with the Halfling."

"I've come to notice you're very feisty in the mornings."

"Only the mornings?"

He smiled and I grinned back.

"Hey, I can't help it. Silvie didn't get all snippy at you for no reason, not after I've trained her so well to be that way. And talking about Silvie, I mentioned to her I woke with lively legs. Apparently, Belle told her it happened a couple of times a month amongst your skilled people. Something about excess energy?"

"Yeah, you have to deal with it and run for a good hour or two like this. But for now, go as fast as you need to. I'll somehow manage to keep up."

With another surge, I did just that.

We wove our way through the bushy lower basin of a gully, the next two hours passing quickly as we tracked away and upward along the Papamoa hills.

Considering our mated bond, I broached the question foremost in my mind as we made the scenic hilltop and stopped. Hands to my knees, I drew in a couple of deep breaths. "Why is it we still haven't created a link, as in a telepathic link? I know it requires trust, but as a mated pair shouldn't that be a given? I have a telepathic link with Belle."

"We should have, and I do trust you." He rubbed my back. "Except we're dealing with more issues than most mated couples. We'll give the telepathic link more time. When it comes, we'll be able to speak to each other no matter where we are—and we'll both need that."

I straightened, looked him in the eye. "I take it there's never been a Wincrest who ever trusted a Loveria?"

He muttered his answer first, then repeated it a second time with more strength. "We are born enemies, but not you and me. Come here." He pulled me into his arms. "We will work this out."

"We better."

His hold tightened. "The people of Peacio are my first priority, but no one, not a soul will be able to drive us apart." He bent his head, pressing every hot inch of himself closer as his lips touched mine.

I grinned as he kissed me. "Are you trying to make me miss school?"

"I wouldn't mind." A second later he 'ported us to my room. "Except one's education is important."

I tilted my head to the side, taking a quick moment to listen for the sound of my mother. Nothing. Everything remained quiet. "Mum's not home, would have gone to work by now, but at some point I'd like you two to have a proper meeting, with a sit-down conversation. Do you want to speak to her?"

"About what exactly?"

"Anything. She doesn't know you, and I'd like her to."

He smoothed his finger along my jaw. "I can't mention Magio, for the obvious reasons, but I'd like that too, to have a sit-down conversation. Now, dress and ready yourself for school. I'll return in two minutes."

I rolled my eyes. "You need to cease with demanding such short spans of time for me to get ready, for either bed or the—"

Chuckling, he shimmered and disappeared before I could finish my argument.

Huh, how annoying.

I stomped to the bathroom, took far longer than the required two minutes as I showered then dressed in my favorite pair of faded, blue denim cutoffs. I pulled on a gray and blue striped hoodie and blow-dried my hair. Minimal makeup and I was done.

Back in my bedroom and low and behold, guess who was back?

He tapped his watch as he frowned. "Fifteen minutes?"

"That's the new standard. Get used to it." I merged my mind with his, stood on his booted toes and kissed his cheek. "You look nice, by the way." I stepped back and circled him. Scrumptious. He was dressed in a black shirt and jeans, his dark hair damp and curling delectably around his neck.

"And you look"—he crooked his finger, beckoning me back to his side—"too far away."

I grabbed my school bag and joined him. "We need to get going."

"We surely do." He firmed his grip on my hand and we made the jump. We arrived behind the trunk of the largest tree at the edge of the field. As we stepped out from behind it, the bell pealed loud and clear. Davio steered me toward the mathematics block.

Viv stood leaning against the wall next to our Calculus classroom door, her dark locks clipped behind her ear as she chewed gum. She blew a purple bubble and popped it, pushed off the wall in skinny black jeans and a white "I-Heart-New Zealand" t-shirt.

"Hey, don't you think I'm starting to look the part?" Viv popped another bubble, acting as if she hadn't just held a blade to my neck the day before. No hard feelings. I certainly didn't have any toward her and Zac, and clearly those were reciprocated.

Davio laughed. "I believe you are. I'm impressed." Then his gaze narrowed. "Where's Zac?"

She touched her hip. "He's not always glued to my side." Then she peered over her shoulder through the window in the door. Zac stood behind his desk, his gaze on Viv, Belle seated farther away at the back of the room. "We're just waiting for you guys and Silvie to show."

"I'm here." Silvie skidded around the corner, her bright yellow tank top and red miniskirt highlighting her pale complexion. She was one of those rare redheads who could wear any color, and the brighter the better. She snatched my wrist and dragged me into class. "We need to be quick. Mr. Houghton is on my six, and I don't care for another detention slip. The one I got last week was enough."

"But, I—"

She yanked out a chair and dumped me in it.

Behind me, Davio groaned.

"Sorry." I squeezed his arm.

"It's all right. Silvie was fast. I'll sit with Belle, and make sure I keep enough distance so there's no pain or anger rising for you."

"Hey." Silvie snapped her fingers in front of me. "Mr. Houghton is here."

In the seat behind me, Zac leaned forward and knocked my chair leg with his foot. "Sorry about yesterday, the sword and all. Did you have a nice sleep?"

"I did, thanks." I frowned as Davio sat next to Belle at the back of class. Belle leaned into him, laid a hand on his forehead and murmured something in his ear. To Zac, I muttered, "How come those two are so chummy?"

Zac glanced back at them. "Not chummy. Belle is relaxing him. He must be stressed, and it only takes her a second to help ease any discomfort. She's an empath, remember?"

Discomfort likely caused by the fact that we sat so far apart. Man, the emotional swings of being mated were definitely crappy, for both of us. I took a deep breath as Mr. Houghton shut the door.

Silvie knocked my arm with her elbow and set a pen in front of me. "You can thank me for that later."

I gave her a nod as Mr. Houghton dropped a pile of papers on his desk and shuffled through the first few. Finding what he wanted, he looked out at the class. "Open your textbooks. I'll put the page number on the board." With a black marker in hand, he scribbled across the board's surface and the lesson began.

I wriggled in my seat. Behind me Zac and Viv whispered, and I extended my acute hearing past them toward Davio at the rear, only I halted as I caught another conversation.

"I seriously can't believe how hot he is. Even the name Loveria is hot." Lauren, one of my classmates, smacked her glossy red lips together, one hand running through her bleached-blond hair.

"Yeah, I'm so gonna get him into my bed." Melanie Steeples pressed one brightly painted pink fingernail against her plump lower lip. Oh boy, Melanie was the worst kind of bragger, not to mention she had a reputation for sleeping with almost every guy she could get her well-manicured fingers on.

I groaned and buried my head in my palms, because I

wasn't going to make it through an hour of Calculus if I had to listen to those two pampered misses talking about how they wanted to get their hands on my boyfriend.

"*Belle.*" I opened our telepathic link. "*We're going to have to swap places. Now if you don't mind.*"

"*Okay, sure.*" Frantic chair scraping from the back of the room. "*Why can I feel your distress so strongly?*"

"*Because you're an empath, and I'm feeling a whole lot jealous right now.*" I snatched my books and squeezed Silvie's shoulder. "I gotta go and sit with my boyfriend before I kill Melanie and Lauren and bury their bodies in my backyard. I'll explain later."

Silvie tapped her pen on my rear. "You are making less sense as every day passes. Go."

I did, breezing to the back as Davio eyed me.

Ah, I could drown in his seriously hot stare.

Only my moment of delight came to a halt as from my left, Melanie and Lauren's chatter continued. Something about me swapping seats with Belle and how dare I? Only Davio stood and reached out, took my hand and steered me into Belle's now vacated seat. I tried hard to ignore the girls' vindictive words as I sat.

He tugged my chair closer to his, swept an arm over my shoulders and nipped my ear. "Don't concern yourself overly much with them."

"I wasn't. I know how you go through withdrawals when not in my company. I couldn't have you getting all explosive in class." At the front of the room, Mr. Houghton continued to write on the board.

Rolling my shoulders, I tried to analyze my feelings. It seemed jealously was a very real emotion for me now.

"Hey, do you see that?" Lauren muttered to Mel in a low hush I easily caught. "You and I should have first dibs on him."

"Faith's a slut. He hasn't been here for long, and she's

already picked him up."

"Take a look at Zac and Viv." Davio squeezed my hand.

Half way down the room, Viv ripped off a sheet of paper, as did Zac. They balled the paper up, and with complete accuracy born of great marksmanship, sent their paper missiles flying. One hit Melanie square in the forehead, and the other hit Lauren.

Beside me, Davio chuckled, and Melanie and Lauren spluttered. Around us, other students laughed at them too. Mr. Houghton, with his head of gray hair and black-smudged fingertips turned around and frowned at the sudden amusement ringing forth.

The room quietened.

Mr. Houghton shook his head, cleared his throat and returned to his cherished whiteboard.

"Zac and Viv did that for me?" I looked into Davio's eyes.

"They are protectors, and none would sit idly by and listen to your name being slurred, no matter you're a Wincrest." He leaned in and nuzzled my cheek. "Just be grateful they didn't bring their daggers into school, otherwise it wouldn't have been paper missiles coming their way."

To Davio it was such a simple explanation. But not to me. And daggers?

"By all rights your esteemed protectors should be slaughtering me." I still felt bad about how I'd tackled him to the floor last night after I returned from my trip to see my father. I had gone a little overboard, only my emotions had been all scattered at that point in time. It wasn't easy having a boyfriend who wanted to kill my father.

His chair scraped a little. "I will hear no more of that. I've made it clear to them you are mine. I adore you." He gripped my hand. "Completely and fully."

"You do?" Because I couldn't help my rising emotions for him from taking me either. I adored him as well.

"Absolutely." Leaning forward, he kissed my cheek. His

lips twitched against my skin. "No one will be able to make me as happy as you will."

"Likely no one will provoke you and be as great of a nuisance, either."

His eyes glittered at that declaration. "Nothing you say will drive me away from you."

"Lucky me." I pulled my hand out of his and picked up my pen. "Stop chatting. I have a Calculus exam in less than three months, and I would appreciate being able to pass it."

He slid his elbows forward on his desk, his voice dropping lower. "Is it possible you feel guilty?"

Not prepared to answer, I busied myself writing down Mr. Houghton's calculations from the board.

"Look at me, my mate."

"I'm not listening to you. Please, try and look busy. If we get caught talking, we'll end up with detention slips, and trust me, you don't need an afterschool detention at a time when you need to leave for Peacio."

He leaned in closer. "Mr. Houghton is practically deaf, otherwise we'd have already scored a handful of them already. What have I said to upset you?"

"Whoa. Mel look," Lauren grumped.

For heaven's sake. It appeared our doings had again captured the attention of the two classroom vixens.

Lauren shoved an elbow into Melanie's side.

"Oomph. I saw, Lauren. He's clearly besotted with her and why, I have no freakin' idea. Faith is too skinny and she has next to no boobs."

I froze at their comment. Sure, I was a B cup, and unlike them, I hadn't had my breasts surgically enhanced to their backbreaking DD's.

Another two missiles of paper zoomed from the front. Melanie and Lauren squeaked as they got hit again.

Davio chuckled. "Just ignore them. Zac and Viv are dealing

with it. My protectors are still wound up after last night and those girls..." He snuggled an arm around my waist. "They clearly have no idea what they speak of. You're perfect just the way you are, as well as feisty and strong-willed, which is exactly how I like you. No one else could ever stand so strongly at my side, other than you."

"Thank you." I wanted to smother him in kisses. "I adore you too." I tapped his nose with my blue pen. "You're perfect for me as well. Hopefully you'll be able to stand just as firmly at my side too. This relationship goes two ways, and I'm going to make sure it all works out."

The corner of his lips lifted and his eyes crinkled. I wanted to keep on staring at him, only Mr. Houghton's voice droned on and I tipped up my textbook. Page one-hundred and one. Paragraph four.

I sighed. Calculus. Oh how boring.

Chapter 8

I made my way down the hallway, then halted as Davio's low growl resounded toward me, right from the direction of Belle's dining room. Zac and Viv were supposedly with him while Belle had told me she and Silvie would be collecting supplies for the weekend.

As my forewarning activated, I stilled. A wavering vision of Davio seated at the large oak table across from his two protectors shimmered into life before my eyes. Shocked, I squeezed my eyes shut and gasped as I caught another protector seated at Davio's right side. He wore battle leathers studded with bits of steel, and a sword glinted at his side, his hair short and springy and the same stunning red-gold shade as Silvie's.

Slowly the vision of the four of them in discussion melted away.

Wow. My forewarning, my ability to see what was to come had definitely advanced, but why had I been forewarned about there being a new protector in the house? He was with Davio, so they clearly knew each other, and no one around Davio would harm him or now me, not since he'd made that abundantly clear to one and all that such a thing wasn't permitted. No more swords being bandied about near my neck.

I waited, hoping for more as I recalled Alexo's solemn words. *Your skills grow fast. They are cementing and strengthening just as your powerful lineage demands.*

For certain, the more I used them, the stronger they became. A thrilling thought, and I was eager to experience for myself even more of what Alexo had shown me of his skill.

Loud complaints came from up ahead, then Viv scraped back a chair and strode down the hallway toward me. "There you are. We need to be away, including Davio. Silvie called and said she and Belle are on their way back. We'll leave the moment they've returned."

"I was coming, but just had a vision, one of forewarning. There's another protector here with Davio. Who is he?"

"Ah, that's Silas."

Davio had spoken telepathically to Silas last night, his cousin a man I actually couldn't wait to meet since Davio had said they were close. He'd called Silas his right-hand man. "You're all leaving for this all-important meeting in Peacio now?"

"We are, and Silas is here to ensure Davio's return. The protectors in Peacio have already been called together and are awaiting us. We have spies to find." Viv clasped my arm. "Making certain Peacio is safe should you venture there is imperative."

"Of course." Not that I wanted to visit Peacio right now, not when my father was sorting through a plan as well, but still, I could understand Davio's need to ensure his country remained safe for me to visit, for whenever that might happen.

"Make your goodbyes fast. Silas has never been one to dawdle."

"Sure thing."

We walked together into the dining room, and Davio's gaze veered immediately to mine. He pushed back his high-backed leather chair and stood.

"Faith, come and meet Silas." He motioned to his redheaded cousin. "Silas, this is my mate, Faith."

"It's a pleasure to meet you." Silas pushed back his chair and extended his hand to me. "Davio has spoken of you and your bond, of your father and your meeting with him. I'm aware of all."

"Nice to meet you too." I shook Silas's hand. His cousin was tall, the same immense height as Davio. He towered over me, his hand firm around mine. Memories surged as I looked into his eyes. Images formed and—oh wow. A vision.

My knees buckled and I dropped to the floor under the heavy weight of a pressing feed so similar to Alexo's in all its full and absolute glory.

"What's happening?" Davio knelt beside me, his face stricken.

"It's a vision, and a staggering one at that. Don't touch me." If he did, I might lose my shaky hold on the images, and the last thing I needed was for them to flitter away.

Carefully, he eased back, only an inch, but it was enough.

Eyes closed, I followed the images, those actually mimicking a memory from back in the summer and not a vision in itself.

I'd bounced into Silvie's lounge with its bright burgundy couches and blue carpet, the framed photo of Silvie and her mum hanging prominently on the wall facing the fireplace. Silvie and Silas had been chatting, both deeply immersed in their conversation, then as they'd hugged, I'd cleared my throat from the doorway. *"Sorry, am I interrupting an important conversation?"*

"No, not at all." Silvie had jerked back and clutched her chest. *"This is Silas, a friend of a friend. He was just leaving."*

"Yes, I was." Silas had whizzed right past me and when I'd turned to say goodbye, he'd already disappeared out the front door. Gone, within the blink of an eye.

Huh? A friend of a friend? Silvie must have blatantly lied to me that day.

No wonder that memory had soared forth, a forewarning as such from the past.

Hot tears burned behind my eyes and I opened them and stared at Davio. "Silvie's hiding something from me."

"What?"

"I've met Silas before, several months ago now, and my vision was of a memory from that time. He'd popped around to visit Silvie and they'd been chatting in the sitting room when I turned up. Neither heard me walk in, then Silvie mumbled something about Silas being a friend of a friend. He left before I could even utter one word to him, bolted straight out the door as if the hounds of hell were on his tail. And now he's here." Only how had Silvie known Silas back then? He was a protector, Davio's cousin and a Peacian, and we'd only learnt of them recently.

"Silas." Davio eyed his cousin. "What's this about?"

"Damn," Silas muttered, his gaze wide with shock. "Faith is right. We met several months ago in the summer. I'd been visiting Silvie as I often do, and hadn't heard her arrival. I got out of there as quick as I could though."

"Yet clearly not quick enough." Davio scooped me off my knees.

"Wait. You visit Silvie often?" I squeaked. My ears buzzed.

"I'm so sorry, Faith." Davio scrubbed one hand through his hair. He slashed a hard look at Silas. "How could you not have told me you'd met my mate while visiting your sister?"

"His sister?" I know I screeched, right before I lost all breath.

Davio gripped my arms, his gaze searching mine. "Clearly we need to speak. Silvie and Silas are twins, both born prematurely in Peacio eighteen years and two months ago to my mother's beloved older sister, Seriah. Silvie was going to talk to you about it all this weekend, although I had no idea you'd already met Silas, otherwise I wouldn't have just introduced you."

"You're saying Silvie isn't from Earth?"

My heart bumped out of rhythm. Such deceit and lies, and all coming from my best friend no less. The magnitude of her dishonesty broke through me, shattered my heart into a million pieces.

I closed my eyes and shoved Davio away. I glared at Silas and the last straw snapped. "How did I not guess? You have the same hair, the same blue eyes, the same damn freckles even."

It hurt to even look at him.

Silvie had been by my side my entire life, and this deceit had gone back eighteen shocking years. Silvie was no friend at all. "Why is Silvie here?"

All I'd ever shared or known with her had been the worst kind of a lie.

Shame rolled through me, and anger…so cutting and painfully deep.

From behind me, a wracked gasp rent the air.

Silvie stood frozen in the doorway, hands to her mouth and her eyes bugged wide while Belle stood next to her. "Silas." Silvie stared at her brother. "W-what are you doing here?" Her tormented gaze swung to me. "Faith, don't move. I can explain."

I sucked in a fast breath and stormed across to her. "Lies, Silvie." I shoved her shoulders and she jerked back a step. "Since we were children," I ground out, never more furious in my entire life. "We've known each other since we were babies and not once in all these years did you ever tell me you're a blasted Peacian, from another world entirely. What kind of a friend lies to that extreme?"

"I'm so sorry, Faith." She grabbed my arms, her fingers pinching in razor tight. "I didn't know how to tell you I had a twin brother, not with everything that's gone down since your strength skills came into being, but I was going to tell you now the weekend is here. I promise I was going to tell you."

Fury blew through me. "What about the past eighteen years? You didn't think I deserved the truth sometime then?"

Tears streamed down her cheeks. "Please, let me explain."

"Explain?" I was losing it, and I knew I was, but I couldn't halt the pain wracking through me. "How about saying I have a damn brother I've never told you about, Faith! How about saying I was born in Peacio. How about saying I'm from the same place as Belle?"

Belle had never lied to me about where she'd come from, and whether I'd believed her or not in the very beginning, I'd still listened, right from the start. Surely Silvie could have spoken up then.

My pain doubled, so explosive. This was the worst kind of betrayal.

I turned my back on her and everyone else in the room. There was no way I was willing to listen to any one of these so-called Peacio protectors. This information had been withheld by all of them. I stormed through the living room, my hair flying around my face. I hauled the ranch slider open.

"Where are you going?" Davio caught me around the waist and swung me back inside before I could step out.

Everyone stood behind him.

"I'm leaving." I didn't want to see him at all, not for another moment, not since he too had most certainly been a part of this subterfuge. "You have a country to return to, or have you forgotten, just as you forgot to enlighten me of Silvie's connection to you?"

"No, I'm not leaving you this upset. You haven't heard Silvie out. Listen to her. She had a very good reason for remaining quiet."

"You mean dodging the truth, tricking and deceiving me, and not just for a few months, but eighteen long years." I staked him with one very venomous glare, one that should have slain him on the spot. "You're no better than Silvie, and who knows just how many more secrets both you and she have left untold, and likely all for my own supposed good too. My best friend isn't my best friend at all, and it appears nothing I have in this world is real anymore."

Nothing, and my heart broke at the thought.

Goodness, Silvie had to have been planted here since what other reason or purpose served such a lifetime of lies. Carlisio was my father's enemy, held the forethought skill, could so easily be behind this huge farce. For certain he had sent Belle and Davio.

I couldn't focus. It was all too much. Like torture to consider how very badly I'd been used. Such heartache swarmed through me.

"Just go away. All of you. Leave me alone." I desperately needed space.

"No. Nobody shall leave this room until you've listened to Silvie's full explanation, just as she wishes for you to." Davio gritted his teeth at Silvie. "Here's your chance. Explain now," he snapped at her.

In my worked up state I had no intention of listening. "Silvie's had long enough to tell me the truth, and you and your black heart have had enough time too, but no, everyone has to wait until poor Faith finds out on her own, and before the truth can fully emerge."

"Zac, block off the door." Davio swished a finger in that direction. "I won't have my mate this distressed without me. She comes with us, warrior spies on the loose or not."

Zac slid in behind me and cut off my path to the outside and sure freedom. Silas and Silvie circled to the left of me, while Belle and Viv swept around the other side. Six against one. They all corralled me in, and the hairs on the back of my neck stood on end as everything within me rose for the fight to come. I would defend myself, not give them an inch.

"Bring it on," I snarled, so beyond caring of the choices

they'd all enforced on me.

"*Faith! It's your father.*" Dad's voice resounded through my head.

"*Dad?*" Even more shock coursed through me at the instant formation of our telepathic connection.

"*Tell Davio and his protectors to stand down. If they attempt to take you against your will to Peacio, then I will intervene.*" A snarly order. "*Right now they're placing your very life in danger, and I won't stand for it.*"

"*Danger?*" I firmed my stance. "*No, they'll never take me.*" Of that, I would make absolutely certain.

"Who are you speaking to?" Davio accused from two steps in front of me.

"Your enemy and my father." Yeah, I said that with deliberate purpose and gloating.

Davio glowered. "No. That can't happen."

"Well obviously it has."

"*Faith, if they don't do as I say, I'll make my presence known with several of my best warriors in tow. I do not make that threat lightly. They will not be allowed to take you with them, not in any way, shape or form.*"

Oh yeah, now look who had the upper hand. It seemed I had a force on my own side. Bitingly, I answered Davio, "Alexo's riled by your threat. He said he'll bring in a contingency of his warriors if you don't stand down and leave. You don't have a choice. You're the one going, not me."

He shook his head with arrogant stubbornness. "Not when you trust your father enough to create a link and we've been squabbling like small children. My leaving you right now would be more dangerous than you can ever imagine."

"*Tell Silas and Zac to force Davio's removal. You've got five seconds or I'm coming in. No one takes my daughter against her will.*" Alexo Wincrest meant business.

I set my gaze on Silas. "Prince Alexo is coming with armed

warriors. You've got five seconds to get Davio out of here." I was more than happy to give Silvie's brother that warning.

"*Four*," my father shouted along our newly created link.

Proudly I held my head high, my gaze directed right at Silas. "That would now be four seconds."

Silas motioned for Zac and Viv to step forward and take Davio.

"Don't even try it," Davio spat at his protectors. "Faith is my mate and I won't leave her behind. We take her with us."

"*Three.*"

"Three, Silas." I planted my hands on my hips. The tables had well and truly been turned.

Silas, Zac and Viv pounced on Davio. They took him down, and Silas mumbled between clenched teeth, "I'm sorry, cousin, but as our prince, your welfare comes before all else, and right now we aren't well enough armed to take on several warriors."

Davio bellowed and kicked out at his imprisonment. The four of them slowly shimmered and disappeared from my sight, him screaming for me not to leave him, not to ever turn him away.

"*Out of there now, Faith. Neither Belle nor Silvie can teleport and I want to see you immediately. My apartment. This second.*"

"*I'm coming.*" I didn't spare Silvie or Belle another glance. I left, glad to be done with my back-stabbing best friend and an empath who could surely sense my wounded emotions.

* * * *

Saturday—the next morning—I studied the incoming rain as I sat on a bar stool at my father's breakfast counter in his penthouse suite overlooking the ocean. The gusty wind blew against the windows and I swayed to the beat of its blow. The stormy waves rolled in heavy and hard, white foam patterned within the deep blue for as far as the eye could see, the wide expanse of windows before me opening up the entire skyline.

The skies were a mass of angry, bubbling gray clouds and rain sheeted down and drenched the deserted beach below.

It was a storm of the likes I'd not seen in many years, a storm that ricocheted within my heart as well. Deep inside me, a storm of dark emotions brewed and suffocated every good memory I'd ever had of Silvie.

I was alone.

With no one.

Even my father, after my arrival here yesterday, hadn't been able to stay with me for more than a few minutes to calm me down, not when he'd been on duty during his forewarning and his threat to bring in warriors with him had been the absolute truth. In order not to raise too much suspicion, he'd told me to remain hidden within his apartment and that he'd return as soon as he'd sorted out any and all issues back on Dralion. Thank goodness Mum still believed I was staying at Belle's place, so I hadn't had to leave my sanctuary and burden her with my heavy heart, not that I'd have been able to tell her why I was so down. I still had to keep the truth from her, for her own safety's sake.

This was all such a mess, although at least I had a sanctuary now that not even Davio could locate. Not through Carlisio or by any other means. My relief was tangible.

Yet I was still alone.

I'd always hated being alone.

I thumped my legs, frustrated with the fierce ache that pushed through my muscles and limbs.

Another lie.

Silvie and Davio had inferred that my need to expend my excess energy would be once or twice a month, but that need clearly drove me again today.

Sighing with vicious frustration, I pushed off the bar stool and slipped outside onto the balcony. I pulled the image of my bedroom into my mind, caught sight of the unwavering form of Zac standing in one darkened corner, his face half cast in shadows, although not his glinting blade belted to his hip. The fine steel shone, reflecting the Peacian protectors' insignia.

Davio had clearly set Zac there in order to catch me when I returned.

Not happening, not even for a fresh set of clothes, which I desperately needed.

I focused my forethought on my mother and sagged with relief as she lay tucked up safe in her big bed. Zac wouldn't go near her, would certainly never harm her. At least in that I had no doubt.

Next, I focused on Davio. He came to me crystal clear, very strong and determined as he opened the entrance gate to what appeared to be a massive open-aired arena, one rather reminiscent in structure to one of our ancient Greek arenas with its circular dusty floor sprinkled with sand. Blocked seats were layered back and up, to at least three stories in height. Thousands of spectators could pack the arena's closed-in seating.

Awestruck, I panned out and took in more. Men practiced with their swords and spears and axes, with shields and headgear worn for protection. The battle fierce men wore ancient leathers, their red tunics and leather-flapped skirts from an era on Earth so far gone. The men in battle-practice were huge, emanating great strength and accuracy as they wielded their brutally sharp weapons.

I cringed as one's blade struck flesh and bone, blood spurting as the injured man groaned and fell to the sandy ground. His partner—the one who'd maimed him—bent to one knee at his side and checked on him, applied pressure to the terrible pumping arm wound then tossed him over one shoulder, wavered and disappeared.

Ouch. That blow had to have hurt, although the man could likely fast-heal. All Davio's protectors could, possibly a prerequisite for being amongst the elite band of his country's finest.

Davio closed the gate behind him then jogged across the arena. Wearing black jeans and a midnight blue shirt with chunky boots, he fisted the hilt of his belted sword. He slowed then stopped next to Silas. Once he reached his cousin, he muttered, "Zac has reported there's still no sight of Faith. I've instructed him not to leave his post, not unless it's to bring her immediately to me."

Silas inhaled and slowly nodded. "At least we did one thing right this past night and have captured and contained one of Dralion's spies which Wincrest told her of. The warrior is now in the cells with the other imprisoned warriors, another threat thankfully taken care of. If there are any other spies about, they're not anywhere within this group, or even close to the castle. Everyone here is well known to each other. All background searches have been completed."

Oh my. Davio had ferreted out one of the spies already, although I hadn't doubted he would.

"Well done." Davio eyed his battling men, his gaze narrowed. "Belle and Silvie have searched for Faith in all her favorite places, but there's been no sighting of her, either by them or any of the protectors I have searching for her. No one's seen my mate in fifteen hours." His voice broke at the end, his pain quickly becoming my own, which had me rolling my eyes in disgust. Stupid bond.

Silas pulled out his sword and rested it between two hands, blade flat. "Let's battle, cousin. That'll get your mind of her. Everio and Carlisio will be down from the castle soon and it won't go over well if they see you weeping over your girl." He knocked Davio's arm with his elbow, a smirk on his face.

My goodness, Silas was as much of a tormenter as Silvie was. My heart panged. I missed Silvie, and I hated that I missed her.

Davio sent Silas a sharp glare. "I don't weep, although I am steaming mad. I didn't care for the way Faith enforced my leaving, or the way she took her anger at Silvie's deceit out on me."

"Ah, but think of Faith's betrayal. That kind creates the worst damage." Silas arched a brow. "It's also not really Silvie's fault she couldn't come clean with the information sooner, not when your grandfather wouldn't allow it. There were extenuating circumstances."

Davio met his cousin's stare and briefly nodded "Agreed."

"The girls have always been close and with Faith finding out about Silvie's heritage the way she did, it clearly broke her heart, Silvie's too."

"Yes, there's been substantial damage, which can only mean finding Faith has become even more imperative."

A haggard sigh from Silas. "That woman is so much trouble. My comment wasn't meant to make finding her more imperative, but simply to explain matters."

Davio yanked out his sword in one very precise motion. "Take care how you speak about Faith."

His cousin only grinned. "I am attempting to aggravate you into battling with me, and it's working. I need the old Davio back, the one who can focus on the here and now and therefore keep his concentration in a good healthy fight, one which I'm currently spoiling for."

"That's it." Davio glowered and sheathed his sword, but only for long enough to pull his shirt over his head without any hinder. He threw his top over the arena's safety barrier, where it landed with a soft swish on one of the benches, then he hauled his blade free and tapped it against Silas's weapon. "Let's battle, right now."

Oh boy, so impressive. His chest muscles rippled with strength, and no wonder since he clearly trained hard with his weapon while on home soil.

"I'm going to send your overinflated butt straight into the dirt." Firm words, and I didn't doubt he'd follow through on them.

Silas's grin widened with complete satisfaction. "Now that's better. I've had no one of your strength to battle with all week, and I desperately need the distraction."

So did I, and it seemed Davio wasn't going to disappoint either of us.

He lifted his booted foot and kicked said butt. "Get over there now and stop irritating me. You've got two hours to train with me before we head out again in search of my missing mate. That's all the time I can give you."

"I'll take those two hours, but don't forget the Dunbarn project which must be overseen. We are expected out there by nine this morning."

I checked my watch. It was six now. I'd go for my own early morning run then be back here to hide out from eight to nine. Thank you, Silas, for that information.

Rubbing my aching lower limbs, I closed my forethought and opened my link with my father. "*Dad, it's me.*"

"*Good morning, my daughter. I've cleared an hour and will be with you soon.*"

My relief at not being left alone any longer swept through me. "*My forethought is strengthening and I've noticed Davio has stationed one of his protectors, Zac, in my bedroom so I can't return to collect any clothing. Mum will be fine, but I wish I could tell her what's going on.*"

"*You can't, not if we wish to continue ensuring her safety, and don't forget, should any harm be about to befall your mother, our forewarning will activate, yours as well as mine. I would go to her in an instant if I thought her in any danger, as I'm sure you would. Secondly, there's an ATM card in a metal box in the hallway cupboard. Go to the mall and spend whatever you need and then drop the card back in the same spot. Just remember to keep a low profile.*"

Wise advice if Davio was accurate in saying Silvie and

Belle were keeping an eye on my favorite places.

"Okay, thanks. I'll just grab some stuff. I've gotta run, literally."

He chuckled along our link. *"I'll join you in your run. I'll meet you at the base of the Mount."* The Mount's walking tracks made the perfect spot for a run, either around the base, or to the peak which usually allowed one to take in the stunning view from the top once they reached it.

"Thanks. See you soon." I closed our link, found the card and 'ported to the sports shop in nearby Tauranga harbor, cloaking to make sure I wasn't seen. Silvie had never come with me on these particular trips, not since she considered that if one owned sports clothing then one would probably need to use it, which she had no intention of doing. Morning sleep-ins were precious to her.

I wandered around the shop, grinned when I found the perfect pair of Nike running pants and a matching gray-hooded t-shirt. Socks and sneakers next, then I paid for the items and buzzed next door.

This shop sold casual clothing and lingerie. I took a quick minute to choose underwear, nightwear and a couple of lightweight shirts and jeans so I was covered for the next couple of days. Walking to a safe spot at the side of the building, I cloaked to hide my departure and flashed back to the apartment. Once in the bedroom, one which Dad had said was mine, and thankfully far better furnished than any other room in this penthouse suite, I dropped my purchases onto the bed and dressed in my new training clothes. Yep, this room had an oak dresser with a pretty oval mirror, a large chest at the end of the bed with an array of bedding stored in it, two side tables and a tall corner lamp with a fringed edge. The view was to die for as well, the wide window overlooking the ocean and the Mount rising high to the side.

With the ATM card back in the metal box, I winged my

way to the base of the cone-shaped mountain.

The rain still pounded down, but there wasn't anything I could do about that. A river of water was gouged into the sandy base track, making it muddy, which forced me to veer off the regular route, but to compensate I instead jogged up the more sheltered bushy path snaking upward along the western side to the summit. Every step soothed me, bit by bit draining away the sharp press of excess energy.

Up ahead, a familiar form wavered into sight and I joined my father who looked so incredibly youthful in his black running shorts and white t-shirt. Running on the spot, I smiled at him. "Sorry about the atrocious weather we're putting on for you today."

"I'm glad of it since it'll cloud Carlisio's forethought." He hugged me then adjusted a white Adidas cap on his now drenched head. "With this bad weather though, I should have suggested we run in Dralion."

"I don't mind where we run, rain or shine."

"Neither do I." He reached out a hand and tenderly wiped the water coursing down my cheeks. He popped a kiss on the top of my head and murmured, "Particularly since it means I get to spend more time with you. This is like a dream come true for me, although I'm sorry you've been dragged into this age-old war."

"I'm only sorry we've missed the last eighteen years getting to know each other." But I intended to make up for it now. "We'll deal with the war and everything else, somehow." I rubbed my still achy thighs and jogged faster on the spot. "You said we could have run in Dralion though. Isn't Dralion dangerous for me to visit? You said so only a few days ago."

Alexo took my elbow, his hand gentle as he steered me up the track. "Let's keep you running since we're both already soaked, and yes, taking you to Dralion is still dangerous since the dome room is located within an underground chamber of the palace and I don't want you stumbling across your grandfather by chance."

Oh, that he hadn't told me before. "I take it that information needs to remain between us, where the dome room is?"

"Yes, you'll need to guard that information with your life, Faith. But don't worry that you'll slip up and allow that information out." He grinned, so charmingly. "Your faithful Wincrest blood alone will ensure you'll never tell a soul of the location."

"Cool. That's good to know."

He ran in a fast pace beside me. "Now that we finally have a chance to talk, tell me about your decision regarding Silvie. Will you speak with her? And when?"

In other words, I should speak to her.

I let out a long sigh. "At the moment, I'm still too angry with her." That anger hurt so bad even though I knew I would have to come out of hiding sooner or later and speak to Silvie. I couldn't go ignoring her and her deceit for the rest of my life.

"And your mate? He'll be searching for you again come eight o'clock."

"How'd you know that?" I bounded over a snaking tree root pushing up out of the hard-packed soil right across the track. White shell remains were littered around the area to both highlight the obstacle and to aid in keeping feet on the steep track.

"Through my forethought. I watched him and Silas in the arena and caught their conversation earlier this morning."

"I caught their conversation too." I chanced a glance over my shoulder at him since he'd fallen behind as the track had thinned to single file in the denser, bushier area. "Do you follow the protectors and their actions often?" I was so curious about him and all that he did.

Tree branches snagged at his white t-shirt and pulled at his cap. He adjusted the peak down lower over his face to shield himself from the pelting rain. "Not usually since I neither have the time nor the inclination to do so, but your grandfather does by keeping spies close in their camp."

Which reminded me of what Silas had said in my forethought. "Did you catch the part where Silas referred to the capture of one of Donaldo's spies last night? They've locked him in their cells with the other imprisoned warriors."

"I did, and with great interest since I was made aware that the man did not check in this morning with Donaldo's security team. He was the only spy we had right within the protectors' barracks stationed closest to Loveria Castle. Your grandfather has decided he isn't sending any more warriors out for another few weeks. He detests losing good men."

Which meant it would in fact be safe for me in Peacio should Davio or one of his protectors find me and take me there. I opened up my thoughts to my father, rather than voicing them.

"That is true, and should there be any imminent danger, my forewarning would also activate. I imagine it'll be some months before another warrior is sent to infiltrate Peacio's tight inner circle again. There are thousands of protectors, and unfortunately all are known to one another within their close-knit groups, so a new warrior must be sent in at their lowest level where he will first be accepted without too much questioning."

Relief poured through me just as the rain lightened to a drizzle. We jogged out from underneath the dense bush line and hit the grassy hilltop. Powering on, I kept my sights on the peak so close. "It's a good thing Peacio is safe even if Dralion is not."

Dad jogged in beside me, his expression grim. "Parts of Dralion will be safe for you." He pushed his damp cap back. "We're almost at the top. We'll speak more there, for I have a plan."

"I like plans." I ran, keeping one foot in front of the other as we hit the uppermost track. The drizzle lessened even further to a fine mist and the wind eased, the breeze now lifting with the fresh scent of pine and the sweet tease of the salty ocean air. Once we reached the upper plateau, we hiked it over to the picnicking area and sat at one of the tables with its wide bench on either side.

Dad faced me from across the other side of the table. "Well at least with all this rain we've been assured of complete privacy up here."

"No crowds for sure."

"Yes, it appears only the lunatic Wincrests came running today." Smiling, he glanced about the area devoid of any tourists and other runners, the wide panorama of the ocean stretching out along the eastern coastline in a haze of blue.

"Puh-lease." I mock-frowned. "I'm no lunatic."

"No, but you are a Wincrest." His smile drifted away.

"Come on, tell me everything. Tell me exactly why you and my mother aren't together. Davio has always insisted that mates are rarely parted."

His eyebrows squeezed together, the color as golden as his hair was. "That is the case, but Donaldo would never have accepted Kate as my wife or as the mother of my children."

"So you've said before, but Mum is your mate." I tapped the tabletop. "Could you not have swayed Donaldo in some way?"

"No, which is why after she gave birth to you, I was left with no choice but to leave her in peace with the one thing she'd ever asked of me."

"And that was?" I asked, surprised by that answer.

"You, Faith. Kate had no parents, no siblings, no family whatsoever when I found her. She'd always desired children of her own, and even though I could never tell her of Dralion, I could in the short time we were together give her a child, one which she'd so earnestly desired."

"So that's why you left her straight after my birth?"

"That and other things." Alexo stared off into the distance.

"I could also no longer continue to hide my repeated trips out of Dralion to be with her. I had told Donaldo of her and his reaction made me fear greatly for her safety. Everything was compounding, each constant coming and going so difficult on your mother since I had no choice but to hide my origins. In the end she believed there was an affair—" The break in his voice echoed with terrible pain, and after several drawn out moments he continued, "I allowed her to believe such a thing so she would hate me and not become destroyed by my decision to leave."

Hot tears streaked down my cheeks, his pain suddenly becoming my pain. "Still, you continue to protect her by staying away."

"I do, and never could I have imagined how strong you would become. It's true that children of mated pairs carry their skills to the fullest degree, but due to your Halfling blood, I couldn't possibly be sure. When I initially told your grandfather about Kate, he didn't wish to risk waiting eighteen years to discover what skills you might come into. Now look at what you can do. He would be honored to have such a granddaughter as you."

"I'm not weak at all. I have all your skills, including the coveted forethought and forewarning, and even though I'm not full-blooded, surely my being so highly skilled is enough to secure my mother's safety?"

"That's my plan. I thought of it when we first met at my apartment, but I had to be certain of the outcome. Having Donaldo see your skills is proof the mated bond prevails over any mixed heritage. Now I'm also assured any future children Kate and I might have could also carry such strong skills. Kate being an Earthling no longer comes into play. Donaldo has no argument about our line being weakened by such a match." His brow rose. "Our family should no longer be torn apart. I want, and need, to have you both where you belong."

And by "belong" I had no doubt he meant in Dralion. My

heart plummeted. What of Davio and my relationship with him? I might be angry at him, but I missed him. So how did I build on our bonded link from within enemy territory? Because regardless of our fight, I didn't want to leave him, certainly not forever.

I eased out from behind the wooden-slatted picnic table and stood, my feet soggy in my sneakers and the pressure of Dad's words rocking through me. "What if Mum won't forgive you for leaving her? She never even speaks of you."

Alexo edged to his feet as well, gently took my arm and flashed us back to his apartment. He gave me a tender smile. "But I have every intention of trying…once I can *see* that the time is right in which to approach her."

It seemed the decision was made.

"It would be impossible to deny me, Faith. Your blood, like mine, is the same. Even Donaldo's constant demands for skilled grandchildren are ultimately dictating how I react."

"I'm so sorry." I felt for him, for the tortuous position he was constantly in. I wrapped my arms around his neck and hugged him. "As you said, the Wincrest blood that flows through our veins is both a burden and a privilege."

It was a burden that had kept my father from his family for eighteen years, a weight I had no desire to continue inflicting on him. Truly, I had so very few options left.

Dad held me, as lost in his thoughts as I was in mine, until finally we broke apart.

"Go and warm up. Take a bath and change into dry clothes." He urged me toward the bathroom.

I shut the door on the lavish room with its gorgeous marble bathtub, vanity and sparkling brass fixtures and fittings. The hot water ran clear as I poured in bath oils scented with vanilla and jasmine.

One decision-making bath coming up.

I had an uncertain future ahead of me, but not an uncertain mate. Changes would be afoot, changes my mate would need to accept. Changes I needed to soon tell him about.

Chapter 9

It was barely six in the morning, and on top of that, Monday had now rolled around. I scrubbed a hand up and down my thighs and slapped them. My legs were throbbing, for the umpteenth day in a row. And to think I used to like my runs.

I stumbled out of bed and yanked on my Nike running pants and t-shirt, tried to lift my heavy eyelids past halfway as I shoved a brush through my hair. As I did, I unblocked and opened up my link to Dad. *"Hey-ya."*

"You sound exhausted."

"My legs are on fire. What's with this daily two-hour run?"

"I'm not sure. I only experience excess energy three to four times a month, and then that's entirely dependent on how often I use my skills. Perhaps you should increase your usage and teleport around more."

I groaned and pushed my tired muscles to the kitchen. *"I'm coming out of quarantine today. Did I tell you my head hurts just as bad?"* I was sure I had.

"Yes. Your fast-healing should have dealt with that. Perhaps take a rest after your run. Will it matter if you're late to school?"

"You'd have to ring. Only a parent can lodge—" I stopped mid-step down the hallway, cracking my first smile in days. *"Ah, that sounded odd didn't it?"*

He chuckled. *"It does since I don't own a telephone. Those contraptions are out of date when one can use free telepathic communication."*

"No worries." I continued around the corner. *"I'll head in. I'm going to have to talk to Silvie sooner or later."* That much I'd come to accept over the weekend.

He cleared his throat. *"Your separation from Loveria is likely the cause for your headache. I recall suffering many after leaving your mother. Oh, and a word of warning—watch out for the birds."* He signed off.

"The birds?" I mumbled to myself, frowning as I opened the fridge. Strange message. I grabbed a yogurt, drank a glass of water and pocketed a muesli bar for later.

Sneakers laced, I lowered and stretched my legs then jogged down the building's internal stairwell rather than taking the elevator. At the front security door, I checked both directions and zipped across the road, hit the boardwalk and followed it around to the base of the mountain. Around me, a flock of seagulls screeched. There were a few about, clearly after a free feed from me.

I ran through the throng of them lining the walkway. "No, you're not having my muesli bar," I snapped. "Go and get your own food."

A flap of my hands and they flew off.

Up ahead, the rocky mountain base track appeared. On one side, the mountain rose high, and on the other the harbor water lapped in over the rocks.

Taking care, I scaled the entrance gate, hooked my hands on the top rung and bounded over. I wobbled as I landed on the other side, while above a flap and rush resounded. Half a dozen white-feathered seagulls zoomed in fast.

The birds opened their beaks and the Pipis I couldn't miss spotting dropped from their mouths like missiles. I ducked as shellfish splattered like bullets on the rocks at my feet. Harbor ducks cackled and the seagulls hissed at their meal being stolen.

I stumbled back as birds everywhere dived in on the smelly treat.

"Rover, stop!"

A single bark, and one golden Labrador on a length of blue leash rapping on the pathway, pounded toward me. Yelping, his jaws open and drool flying, the dog sprang overtop of me as I dropped low.

What had I done to the universe today?

I flattened myself to the ground as the dog's owner tripped over the rocks, his sneakers skidding on the crushed shellfish, his arms flapping as he lost his balance.

Birds took wing over the water, the dog chased and an almighty bellow resounded as the man went flying into the water. A shower of salty sea-spray coated me and I wiped my face and heaved to my feet.

The man trudged out of the water with one equally wet dog hanging off his heels. He wrung out the dripping ends of his blue shirt, his dark hair plastered to his skull as he mumbled under his breath, "Sorry about that. Didn't mean to get you wet. My dog has a mind of his own some mornings."

"The birds didn't help either." I bit my lower lip to stop from giggling, because I'd never taken myself too seriously. "At least the day can only get better, right?"

"Yeah, so true." He chuckled, and his dog rolled his torso in preparation for a fast dry.

Or maybe not. Dropping my head into my palms, I waited for the inevitable next spray.

I got hit with the wash, giggled some more.

Although my legs ached even greater.

Time to get moving.

I brushed the sticky gravel off my backside, slapped my sore legs and muttered under my breath as I set out, "Yeah, Dad, thanks for the warning and all. Watch out for the birds? Jeez, just you wait until I get a forewarning about you. I'm going to give you minimal information."

Every part of my body ached, but still I ran.

I circled the mountain's perimeter then took the track looping to the summit, each grooved and planked step along this track different to the route I'd taken with Dad. A sheep-gate appeared ahead, but my legs gave way before I made it there. Mind fuzzy, I dropped to the grassy patch of ground. A wrenching pull from within assailed me, as if my mind sought the merged link I could create with Davio, yet with him nowhere close, I couldn't make the connection.

I groaned, my need to sink into my soft spot doubling.

Yep, my mind definitely needed the physical connection of the merge, this skill one my father didn't seem to have yet I did. So annoying.

The summit loomed so close. I had to get there.

I flashed to the top, slumped back to the ground, my legs a dead weight.

For the first time in close to three days, I unblocked my link with Belle.

I dragged in a deep breath and called out to her. "*Hey, long time, no hear.*"

"*Faith Stryker. How dare you ignore me. I've been sooo worried. I haven't—*"

Okay, she wasn't in the best of spirits. "*I'm sorry. I didn't realize empaths got so upset.*"

"*They do when the boss—I mean—gee, I've been in your company too much.*"

"*It's okay. I get it.*" I tried to raise my hand to my head, but my arms shook badly. The thumping continued in my head, tripling in severity. "*I'm at the summit of the Mount. Something's wrong. Tell Davio I need him. We don't have a telepathic link yet, so I have to go through you.*"

"*I can feel your pain through our link. What's going on?*"

I dragged in a deep breath. "*I'm going to pass out.*"

"*But you're a fast-healer. Fast-healers are rarely sick. The summit. Give me a minute.*"

I took several deep breaths, each one stuttering in and out.

"*I'm back. What have you done to yourself?*"

"*Is he coming?*" Tears leaked out and ran down my cheeks. "*I can't move, and it's all hit me so suddenly. It's as if my mind is crying out for his.*"

"*He's on his way.*"

The air stirred, just the gentlest of breezes, then another whoosh.

He was close.

My mind soared and I lay blinking, my head swimming as his thoughts flew right at me—most not so good.

My mind rolled around within his, and I soaked in everything and let out a long sigh of satisfaction. My headache eased back, although my legs still felt like jelly. Oh yum. I now had what I wanted, the merged link returned.

I rolled onto my side, lifted my head as I tried to push to my feet. I staggered.

There he was, just along the rise.

Pushing one foot in front of the other, I yelled, "Davio!"

He spun around, gaze narrowed on me then he flashed in front of me, dug his hands into my waist and held me upright. "Where the hell have you been for three days?"

I tried to lift my arms, only they flopped uselessly at my sides, my legs barely holding me up.

"Around." I lost my balance.

A grumble as he caught me. "You look so pale. Why can't you stand? What have you done to yourself?"

"Everything's spinning. I feel—"

I hiccupped.

"Ooo, Ieee." My tongue got stuck over tingly lips. I tried again. "Ooo, Ieee." I giggled at the silly words.

"Are you drunk?" With his hands under my arms, he lifted me higher, his fingers tickling.

I laughed. "Stoppy." I wobbled, wagging my head at him. "Nooo be wonky and angreee," His eyes were darkening in that way he got right before his temper exploded. Definitely getting angry.

Which meant I had to find my feet. I glanced down. Where were my feet? I sniggered as I saw them. No wonder they didn't want to work. They were spinning, or was that still my head now I'd finally reconnected our merge?

He growled. "Silas and Zac have arrived."

I looked up, and oh hello, they had arrived. One big smile for them. "Howwwdy."

Davio lifted me higher, until we were nose to nose and I dangled several inches from the ground. "What's happened to you?"

"Oh, I'm just a hangin'. Wha' 'bout you?" What was wrong with me? I laughed again, impossibly giddy.

Staring into my eyes, he took a deep whiff. "Are you under the influence?"

"Noopey." Hand to mouth, I burped. Good grief. I certainly sounded intoxicated. "But I am high." I tittered as I clutched his shirtfront. "See, high, high, higheee. Way up high in the sky."

I couldn't think straight. It was as if I'd guzzled a whole bottle of vodka, not that I'd guzzled vodka before, but if I had, I'm certain this would be how I felt.

Silas grumbled. "I think your mate's been drinking."

"Sounds and looks like it to me too," Zac added unhelpfully.

I tilted forward, banging my head into Davio's. "Nooo"—*hiccup*—"sloshy." Dumbfounded, I scratched my tummy.

Setting me on my feet, my mate gripped my chin with his forefinger and thumb, tipped my head back and looked into my eyes. "Your pupils are dilated and your skin is flushed." He turned to Zac. "Ask Viv to meet us at Belle's place. Tell her I want our personal physician brought to me, immediately."

I heard Zac's answer seconds later. "It's done."

I swayed and smiled, drinking in the heady sight of my returned mate. "Goodness, but you are sooooooo gorrgeeous. Misssy yooou."

"I've missed you too." He scooped me up in his arms, held me close to his chest and stuck his nose in my hair. Breathing deep, he sighed. "Really missed you. Let's get you back to Belle's and find out what's wrong with you."

"She's clearly drunk." Silas stepped up. "And at seven in the morning no less."

"Not drunk." I slapped Silas's chest and giggled some more. "You're annoying."

"He can be at times." Davio tucked my head under his chin. "Close your eyes. I don't want you being sick while we teleport."

"Oh no. No-noooo sicky," I slurred as I tried to catch my fingers in his beige button-down shirt. My eyelids slid shut.

The jump was swift as he flashed us back to Belle's, and my stomach rolled once we'd arrived. I gulped great mouthfuls of air and tried to clear my foggy head.

Gee, maybe I was wrong. Maybe I had been drinking. It certainly felt like I had.

Ooo, yee-ah, that unreal bottle of vodka had a lot to answer for.

Carefully, Davio propped me on the couch and held my shoulders as he crouched before me. Over his shoulder, he called out, "Belle, some water, please."

Belle appeared with a glass and I grinned sloppily at her. "I misss—"

She frowned, tut-tutting under her breath. "I can't believe this. You're drunk?" She edged in, kneeling and taking my chin in her hand. "I'll just tap into your—oh—oh no. She's so drunk she's making me feel drunk."

Then Belle slipped onto her bottom and belched.

I clutched my stomach, giggles rolling through me.

Silas rolled his eyes as he lifted Belle, her limbs flopping around as he propped her beside me. He glared at me. "Belle can channel reactions along with emotions so if she says you're drunk, then you're drunk. You gotta wee alcohol problem there, Blondie?"

I half-snickered half-giggled, my chest bumping up and down. "Silas is funnee."

He snorted and set his hands on his head.

"Faith." Davio arched a brow at me. "What did you drink?"

I blinked, lifting my finger and jabbing it at him. "Nothin'."

"Excuse me, Your Highness."

I jumped, albeit sloppily, having not seen Viv arrive. I blinked and brought a far too young-looking doctor into sight. He'd arrived with Viv.

Oh right, duh, they all looked young.

Davio stepped over to speak to him and the moment he let go of me, I fell sideways into Belle.

Grinning at her, I mumbled, "Soooo misss"—*hiccup*—"d'you."

Belle squinted at me through half-closed eyes. "Shh, tirrred." She fell flat on her face.

I laughed as I lost my head rest and slumped on top of her.

We were a pathetic pair.

"Miss?" The doctor hunkered down before me, lifted one of my eyelids and sent a bright beam of light flying.

I recoiled, shoved my eyes shut and sank my anxious mind even deeper into Davio's. "Go away." I tried to flap my hands at him, but they went nowhere. "You're not allowed to hurt me. Davio will kill you if you do."

The doctor checked my temperature, his hand moving over my forehead. "She's most definitely drunk, Your Highness.

Allow her to rest for an hour or two. Her fast-healing will deal with the excess of alcohol quicker than any drug I could ever prescribe might. Do you need me to stay?"

"Yes. I need you to take every precaution with her health."

I snuggled into Belle's back, my friend's gentle snoring so comforting, although the sound partially muffled by the cushions in her face.

"Here, let me take her somewhere more comfortable." Silas grumbled something loud.

I cranked one eye open as he picked Belle up and set her gently down on the opposite couch. With my anchor gone, I slithered into Belle's spot headfirst and ate a mouthful of fluff as I did.

Davio turned me over, swept clinging strands of my hair from my face, his gaze so concerned. "Try and sleep, okay? Belle isn't appreciating your current state of inebriation since she can't fast-heal. You have to do it for her by healing first since she's tapped into you. And why do you smell like you've swum in the ocean?" He pinched his nose.

"Birdees."

He frowned. "You're seeing birdees?" He rubbed his forehead. "I guess you will if you're drunk."

I didn't bother to defend myself. No one believed me and quite frankly, I barely did either. I yawned and burped, the noise hammering the nail into the coffin of everyone's current assessment of me. "Lie sidee. Mindy thingummy."

"You mean your mind-merge?"

"Nooo loozy."

He groaned, but bedded down beside me, wrapped one arm around me to hold me in place.

Like I was going anywhere.

Sighing, I burrowed, the world around me darkening before it disappeared.

* * * *

"Mmm." I stretched and uncurled, and oh boy, my body felt like my own again.

"Go back to sleep. It's only been five minutes." Davio's voice rumbled under my cheek.

"I feel so much better." I elbowed up.

"So do I." Belle straightened on the other couch, stood and blinked. "We're better already?"

"I think we are." I tried to wriggle up higher.

"Wait." Pressing the back of his hand to my cheek, Davio frowned. "The doctor said an hour or two, but you feel cool and your words aren't slurred anymore."

"I was never drunk." I rolled my shoulders, really wanting to move. "If it's of any help, I may have imbibed on too much seawater, but that's it. I promise."

He scrubbed his stubbly jaw. "If you weren't drunk, then what happened?"

"I need to move." I squished up my mouth. "Please, let me up."

I got a look in return that said a definite no.

I slumped back. "Okay, so my mind might have missed yours. And I got a touch tipsy when we reconnected. Now that my head is clear, that's what I believe happened."

Across the room, Silas doubled over in laughter and it was impossible to tune him out. I threw a scowl at him before catching sight of Silvie fidgeting from foot to foot near his side. Great. I needed to speak with Silvie, and clearly waiting any longer wasn't an option.

Davio squeezed my arms. "Are you sure that's all it was?"

"Yeah, I'm sure. It seems you can send me spinning out, in all sorts of different directions, even when only seconds back in your company."

Silas scoffed. "There had to be alcohol involved. The blonde was definitely drunk."

I narrowed my gaze on him. "I don't like you much, and I

should know since I watched you rambling on about me all weekend."

"And it seems you're nosy too."

Davio scratched his head. "If you were watching, why didn't you come?"

"Because you need to learn who the actual boss is."

His lips lifted. "That would be me."

The doctor cleared his throat, reminding us all of his presence. "Excuse me, Your Highness, but is she saying she watched others, as in with the coveted forethought skill?"

Davio turned sharply to Viv. "Take the doctor back, and have Stavros Sequeria wipe his memory of the past quarter hour to the point of when you collected him. I'll not have him recall Faith or what she's spoken of."

"You have a protector with the skill to wipe memories?" Wow, that was a new one.

Viv disappeared with the doctor, and Davio ran his hand over the back of my head. "Are you sure you're okay?"

"Ah, I'm thinking it could be a recurring problem, depending on how angry you are."

"Right now, you're back. I can't be angry about that." He touched his lips to mine. "Except in the future, you can't run as you did. If we have an issue, we address it."

He was right. "Yeah, we'll see."

He raised an eyebrow. "We'll see?"

"I'll start with Silvie. I need some practice on dealing with issues." Because eventually I would have to enlighten Davio of my father's decision, and I wasn't looking forward to that. "Let me up."

He did, and I faced Silvie. This wasn't easy to do with her wearing her favorite pink and white striped pajamas, her red locks a messy tumble sticking everywhere. I crossed my arms.

"Begin," I issued.

Tears swam in her eyes. "I—I'm not sure where to start. I

can't remember the early years, only from the time I was about six or seven."

"Then start there."

She wrung her hands together. "Mum made it pretty clear Peacio was a secret. She said Carlisio had sent us, that he saw enough in his forewarning to interpret that you would have a soul mated bond with someone close to him. He presumed Davio, but he wasn't one-hundred percent certain."

She paused, her voice strained. "I don't know if Carlisio ever imagined us being here this long, but with your father keeping his distance, there was no way Carlisio could accurately identify if he was from Dralion or Peacio. And since Carlisio simply couldn't risk Davio losing his future mate if you disappeared as your father had, we stayed and I remained close to you, something that was never a hardship, not when we were the closest of friends."

I inhaled, taking all her words in. "I considered you a sister, much more than a friend and you know it. I've been betrayed by you."

Her lower lip trembled. "I know and you've every right to feel that way, but I couldn't speak of it. Yet one day I knew you would be mated, and quite possibly to my own cousin. Please, you have to know that I'll do anything to make this up to you. I never wanted the lies that have been there between us."

I sighed and shook my head. This was so hard because in the beginning when we'd been so young as she'd said, she surely had been an innocent. Carlisio it appeared was the one at fault, and her explanation tugged at my heart. "I've always told you everything. Do you have other siblings? A father? Because now I know you have a brother, a cousin, and an aunt and uncle."

She caught a hand to her chest, tears streaking down her cheeks. "Yes, I have a father. He has brothers and sisters. I have other cousins and family unrelated to Davio. I'm so sorry, but you have to forgive me for never telling you. In my heart, you are my sister, and I know I've hurt you. Trust me, I'll do whatever it takes to repair the damage." She crossed the small gap and took my hands. "I'll make sure you meet them all. Please, you have to forgive me."

I'd never in our entire eighteen years been able to handle seeing her in pain, and I couldn't now. "I'll never forget."

She wiped her nose. "Can you forgive?"

Davio bumped me forward from behind. "You'll hurt more if you don't move past this."

Releasing a new wave of tears, Silvie hugged me. I squirmed, hating not just her pain but also whenever she got this upset. It wasn't like her. She was the stronger of the two of us, always the first to mock and banter.

I patted her back. "Okay, okay, you're forgiven."

"Thank you."

"But you'll still need to make things up to me." Since I wanted her to calm down and relax, that meant she needed to cook. Cooking always relaxed her. "Chocolate chip cupcakes would be a good start in making things up."

She sniffed and sucked in a deep breath. "Are you asking me to cook you some cupcakes?"

I gave her a nod. "That's just the beginning of this whole forgiveness thing. I'll be after rocky road tomorrow."

"Okay, but we'll talk more later. I need that."

"We will when there's time. Right now, I have one very determined father who wants his own forgiveness from my mother. Alexo intends to right the wrongs of these past eighteen years and admit to his lies and what he's withheld. Which means way too much on my mind."

"Are you saying Alexo wants Kate back?" She frowned.

"That's pretty much it, but with her, comes me."

Davio froze, then his gaze bored into mine. "Are you saying you intend to travel to Dralion?"

Around us, his protectors drew closer, including Viv who

had returned.

My heartbeat raced. "Yes, and what am I supposed to do? I have an actual family, one I've never known. You try turning away from that."

His hands pinched into my arms, his breath blowing out. "It's that damn blood-bond." Then he unblocked, his thoughts churning in a whirlwind toward me through the merged link.

I fell back a step at seeing his need. He wanted me to choose him over Alexo, to decide on embracing Peacio over Dralion. For him, there was no other choice.

"Look at me." He was so focused. "I'm already falling in love with you. I can't allow you to leave me, not even for a day, or three in the case which has just passed. If you were gone forever beyond Dralion's dome, it would kill me."

I held my breath. Why did he have to say that?

"I understand what you're saying, but—" I lifted my arms and wrapped them around his neck, squeezed my hands together so there was no letting go. I cried, thoroughly wetting his shirt.

"Shush, don't cry. We'll work this out." His tone rang softly in my ear.

"I can't fix this." If I couldn't, he couldn't. "I don't know what to do. It's all so hard." I sucked in a stiff breath. "If you make me give up my family, I'll hate you. You're my enemy, and perhaps that's the way you should stay. Maybe we shouldn't tamper with history."

His jaw twitched, his fists bunching. "Wincrest is brainwashing you."

"No, he's not."

"Stay right here." He turned on his heel, snarling at Silas. "I won't be gone long. Don't allow Faith to leave this room or your sight. I need to consider what should be done."

He flashed away.

And there was nothing but silence.

Endless minutes ticked by.

"I can't believe you said that." Silvie came around in front of me. "He's my cousin. I've spent as much time with him as I have with you, and he's in pain. What you said—"

"I only spoke the truth." How on earth were we to make this work? "Our relationship is impossible. Dralion and Peacio are at war. I can't—" I shook my head. "You and Silas have to take him home, to his family and to his people. It's where he should be, not here with me."

Her mouth pinched into a tight line. "You haven't seen mates who are bound to each other attempt to regain their lives after one has passed away or become lost to the other. If you left him for Dralion, it'd be like suffering a death. He's been in a great deal of pain this past weekend, and I don't want to see him suffer such a loss again."

"Silas." I looked at him. "You and Davio are close. Surely, you can see this won't work between us. Will you take him away?"

"You would agree to remain out of his sight, beyond Dralion's shield if I did? No moving back and forth and giving him hope where they'd be none."

"I'll do my best. My father deserves this time to have his wife and family back."

"That was a trick question." Silas crossed his arms and glared. "Like my sister, I'd never do as you ask. As much as I hate to say it, he wants you, and I'd never begrudge him the mated bond, even if it's with you. If you left him to live within the protective boundary of the dome, he'd suffer greatly. That kind of pain I'd never allow."

I ground my heel into the floor.

"Dad."

"Yes, I've been watching."

"How do I get out of here without one of the protectors following my teleporting airstream?"

"You have to mask it. You must use a water source to

teleport through, meaning you leave your current location and use a pool of water, the sea, a river or a pond. Once you're submerged in water, provided no one has taken hold of you, you teleport to the next safe location. No teleporter can follow you through the water's natural airstream masking."

"Got it."

Silas gripped my arm. "Are you speaking telepathically to Alexo Wincrest?"

"Yes." I slanted my head. "What of it?"

"Zac, call Davio and tell him Faith appears ready to do a runner. And you." His hold on me tightened. "You will stay right where you are."

"You can't—"

Without warning, he took me straight to the floor. "When I say stay put, I mean stay put." Shoving me onto my front, he thrust his knee into my back.

I bucked against him, locking and kicking my legs. "See, Silas," I panted. "This is exactly why I don't trust you. You're mean and nasty."

"No, what I am is loyal, and that would be to Davio."

Belle knelt at my head. "Not so rough, Silas. You're hurting her."

I rolled my eyes at the carpet. "What's actually hurting is his trunk-sized knee knifing me in the back."

"Get over it," Silas muttered. "My knee will soon be the least of your problems."

I kicked out at him again, but nothing worked. I barely moved an inch.

The air stirred, lifting strands of my hair, and a deep growl echoed through the room. "I return and this is what I see?" Davio, definitely Davio, and a very mad Davio.

"Yes. It. Is." Silas snarled in my ear. A second later, I lost my breath as my arms were wrenched behind my back and he jerked me upright onto my feet, his grip punishing from behind.

"She is nothing but trouble."

I glared at Davio. "It's crazy for a Loveria and a Wincrest to be mated."

Stepping forward, he tipped up my chin, his fingers stroking down my neck. "I still want you."

I yanked on my arms, but Silas continued to hold me militarily firm. "My father deserves to have what he gave up eighteen years ago. He's earned his family back, and I can't keep that from him. The blood-bond is too strong. It trumps what we have."

His hands moved to cup my face. "It can't. We hold each other's souls. What you're feeling is the familial loyalty behind the blood-bond."

I wanted to kick him. "You are a terrible listener. I can't fall for you, and I can't change what's between us." I tugged, still trying to free myself from the loaf holding me. "Jeez, you need to let me kill Silas before I can continue yelling at you. This being restrained is not working for me."

Silas snarled in my ear. "Show some respect."

I kicked back at him, managed to thump him somewhere good since he grunted hard. "I hope you mate with your enemy. In fact, I'll pray for it, Silas Carver."

"Like that would ever happen." He laughed and released me, handed me to Davio and said, "She's all yours. Congratulations and all that."

I snorted, then bit back a smile, somehow seeing the funny side of this terrible situation. "This is so impossible."

Davio took my hands. "No one takes you from me. Work with me on this. I can see it will be difficult to keep you tied to one location. I'll have to allow you to come and go from Dralion, just as your father and his warriors do. Speak to your father now and discuss your need for free access."

"I said—"

He pressed a finger to my lips, shaking his head. "Just do it.

For this is an argument you'll never win."

I sighed. "I think we need counseling. You're too uncompromising, a—" Again with the finger to the lips.

"For both our sakes, give me this."

I rolled my eyes. "*Dad.*"

"*I'm here.*"

"*Is there any way I can come and go from Dralion as you have done over the years?*"

"*The dome room—even with its limited knowledge by others—is naturally available to every Wincrest and our most elite warriors, so in answer to your question, yes. Although you would have to ensure each reason you have for coming and going was legitimate in case you were ever questioned.*"

"*I need to complete my education. I've always intended to go to university.*" It was a start.

"*That would work. Donaldo has always encouraged education amongst his people, and yours would be a given.*"

I looked at Davio. "Free access is available to all Wincrests and warriors. If I use my education as a reason to come and go, I simply have to take care."

He ran his hands down my sides. "See, who needs counseling?"

I sighed. "You are insufferable, you know that?"

"It's one of my finest charms." He grinned, then crooked his head. "Which you'll come to appreciate in time."

"That'll nev—" His lips touched mine.

Oh, he did not fight fair.

I was so hungry for him, so intent to dull the past three days from my mind until only the peace of his thoughts spread out through the merge. Even as that blanket of warmth wrapped around me, I didn't stop kissing him. I didn't want to give his mouth up for even a second. I was drowning in him, literally losing myself in a sea of craving.

"Hey, excuse me. There are still people in the room," Silas

snapped.

I moaned and whispered against Davio's lips. "What shall we do about Silas?"

"Silas is family. Come with me. We still have much to speak about."

I grabbed his shirt. "Hold on. I do have to get to school and first period will already have started. Education, remember?"

"We'll go after we speak."

He flashed us to his bedroom and he tightened his hold on me, his mouth moving along my neck, nibbling in a way that had me right back in that pool of craving.

I grinned. "I thought we were going to speak?"

He nipped the soft skin of my throat. "We will." His mouth traveled upward and he took my mouth in another hot, hot kiss. "You have my heart." His gaze softened, and my heart pounded. "What we have will not be torn apart by another, Faith. Give me your promise, from your heart to mine, that you will uphold the same vow."

"What I'll promise is to annoy and pester you for all time. Will that suffice?" And by the strength of my blood-bond, I was going to abide by my father's will as well. I'd never had a family and I desperately wanted one now that the possibility was within my reach.

"It'll do, but we'll need to work on how you deliver your words."

I rubbed my nose against his. "We should be in class."

He smoothed his hands down my back. "I've never told you, but I undertook my studies six days a week, jamming twenty-one years of education into as few years as possible, just so I could be done at eighteen."

"You did?" That was impressive. "You never took a holiday?"

"Rarely. Silas and I were tutored together, and now the two of us have the freedom to do what we've always enjoyed."

I laughed. "Yeah, like returning to school with me?"

He tweaked my nose. "I like to think of it as spending as much time as I can with my mate. But what I was referring to was being with my people and defending my country alongside Carlisio and Everio."

"Ah, you mean aiding your grandfather and father into continuing the war against Dralion, against my own newly found family."

"There's that." He quirked a brow. "You said school. Let's get you there so we can make second period."

"Before we go." I ran my finger down the front of his shirt. "You said you would speak to my mother."

"I did. Will this afternoon suit?" He wrapped his arms around me and flashed us to my bedroom.

I was home again, after almost three days away. "My mother means everything to me, so yes."

"As you do to me." His words were a vow, and I stepped away from him even though I didn't want to.

"You're so serious all the time. We need to work that out of you." I rummaged through my wardrobe, seeking the dress I wanted to wear. It was a short white number bought for my eighteenth. I took it from the hanger at the back. This was the perfect dress for Mr. Serious. "Turn around."

He crossed the room, braced one hand on the windowsill and stared out across the road.

I pulled off my training gear, tugged the glove-like white dress over my head and down my body then adjusted it into place.

"Are you okay? You're suddenly quiet." I stepped in behind him and rested my cheek against his broad back.

He turned, his brow shooting up. "I was scared to look. Now I know why. I insist you change."

"You insist?" I couldn't help but smile. "My mother bought this for me." I stepped back, reached over my desk at just the right angle to retrieve my schoolbooks, and dropped them into my bag.

"Please." A choking sound. Only his heated thoughts escaping his block cemented my decision.

"No." I snuck my hand into his and zipped us straight to the field.

Ha. I was right to stand my ground. I loved the way he looked at me in this clingy number, particularly after so many days spent apart. Then after school he met with my mother and we sat over hot drinks and cream cake. Having raised me single-handedly, Mum knew me better than anyone. She was so inquisitive, but who wouldn't be when their daughter brought home her first man.

At a knock on the front door some hours later, I stayed on the couch while Mum walked out to answer it.

I eyed my man, squeezed his hand idly stroking mine. "My mother likes you."

"She is much like my own mother."

"Tell me about her. It's Genevy, right?"

"Yes, she's soft hearted, and yet one of the strongest women I know. She can't wait to meet you."

I looked into his golden-brown eyes. "I can't promise when."

"It'll happen when it's time." He stood and pulled me to my feet. "Yet right now, I must leave. I have a training session with Silas. His mistreatment of you must be dealt with."

"By deal, you mean…" I sidled closer. "Make him sweat it out, kick his butt over and over, right? You need to take him down, because I'd be super excited if you did that."

"Silas is still family. All I need to make certain is that he's never so rough with you again."

"Then butt-kicking is necessary." I pursed my lips. "We have to have a talk about you leaving me out of all the fun stuff as well. I wish I could see the butt-kicking going down."

"I'm sure you would." He raised my hand to his mouth, lightly kissing my fingers then turned and pulled me along behind him. "Walk me to the front door since I'd best leave the regular way."

"Walk me to the front door?" Repeating his words, I smiled and mock gasped. "Gosh, now I just have to get you to arrive in the same regular way too."

We neared my mother who spoke to a door-to-door salesman. The salesman ceased speaking and Davio took the opportunity to thank Kate for her hospitality.

She gave him a bright smile. "Anytime."

I squeezed my mother's arm. "I'll be back in a minute." I stepped through the front door and walked down the steps.

Behind me, the salesman said something about taking a yearlong subscription to the New Zealand Horse and Country magazine. I frowned. Now, why would a salesman sell a townie a rural magazine? Who didn't own a horse?

Ooo-kay, something was wrong with all that.

Davio set a hand at my waist, guided me along the path to the road and I snuck a look over my shoulder.

Oh no.

My breath caught. Thick sunglasses hid my father's eyes and a dark cap covered his blond head. He wore brown felt pants, a brown checked shirt and knee-high riding boots as if attempting to look the part of a countryman, but I wasn't fooled any longer.

The sight of him meant Davio had to go, pronto.

With jittery legs, I picked up my speed.

"You look suddenly nervous." He opened the front gate.

I stopped my fidgeting. "It's just that you're leaving. I'm used to having an argument, and then you leave. Don't make anything out of it."

His lips lifted. "You want an argument before I go?"

I tapped my watch, glaring. "Not right now." I harrumphed.

"I'll see you at Belle's at eight."

"You will." Then chuckling, he shimmered and disappeared from my sight.

Phew.

Wiping my hand across my brow, I ran back to the house, for I had more important issues at hand. I had an all-too-familiar salesman that needed locking firmly inside and a mother who was about to freak out. What I wouldn't give for a regular-old day.

Chapter 10

Never had I seen a man looking so uncertain of what he should do.

I stepped up to Dad, yanked off his black cap and exposed his head full of short, light hair. Next, I pulled off his darkened sunglasses and those remarkable violet eyes of his were clear to see. "This is for your own good," I scolded. "Tell Mum you still love her and be quick about—"

The Horse and Country magazine fell from my mother's hand, flapped to the entryway floor and she swayed—not breathing—then knees caving in, crumpled.

Dad grabbed her. "I was getting around to revealing myself once Loveria left." Scooping her up, his gaze flitted over Mum's face. He dragged in a deep breath, then stuttered as he released it.

"Are you all right?"

"I'm holding my wife." A single tear slipped from the corner of his eye, his voice dropping to a whisper. "I could never get this close before, not in all these years. Ever."

I strained to listen to his words. "You're not going to faint too are you?"

"No, I'm good." He reeled back a step, then caught himself.

"Mum's okay." I pressed the back of my hand to her cheek, found it clammy, which was totally expected in these circumstances. "I'd say fainting is the right reaction to have after seeing your husband eighteen years after he last disappeared."

He gazed at Mum, his throat working. "I—where can I take her?"

"Her bedroom. You'll have the most privacy there since it looks out over the backyard. I'll be in my room if you need me."

He lifted her higher in his arms, brushed a kiss against her lips, the hopeful look in his eyes tearing at my heart. "I can't believe I'm holding her."

"Bedroom's at the end of the hallway. And yes you are holding her. Now go and make up."

"I'll try, but I doubt our coming conversation will be easy." Clutching her closer, his knuckles whitening, he murmured, "If you hear or have any forewarning that my discussion with her is too difficult for her to handle, then interrupt. Also, keep the protectors away."

"I'll be on guard."

My mother moaned, her eyelids flickering.

"Down the hallway, at the end," I urged, pointing the way.

Dad set off with her and rounded the corner, and the *click* of her bedroom door shutting both eased a touch of my nerves, and set them to rising all over again. I leaned back against the wall. My hands shook, and so did my legs. So nervous. This was the strangest feeling, knowing that my parents were about to have such a monumental talk. Right now would be one of those times I'd call Silvie, but that wasn't happening. She would let the information slip.

I fidgeted as the house became super quiet.

Theirs was a private conversation, and I had no intention of listening in.

I flashed to my bedroom and sat at my desk, rocked back and forth and when that didn't help, I pulled around a textbook. I would read, although whether I took much in was another matter.

Three hours passed with only the occasional higher-toned

words drifting to me from Mum.

This was killing me.

Eight o'clock now loomed, and with no signal from beyond, I changed into my favorite faded jeans and a violet stretch t-shirt, brushed my hair until I could brush it no more, then braced myself.

I had to leave, otherwise Davio would turn up here wondering where I was.

Flashing fast, I bumped down in the area just off Belle's kitchen. The heavenly aroma of roast beef wafted through the air. Steam plumed from the oven as Silvie, her hands gloved, slid out a deep blue dish holding tonight's meal.

My mouth watered.

"Can I help?" I stepped into the kitchen, not that I had ever been very helpful in a kitchen.

"Hey, there you are." She popped the dish on a wooden board and looked over her shoulder at me. "I'm all good." She wiped her hands on the white apron tied at her waist. "You can set the table though. How's your mother?"

"What do you mean?" The hairs on my neck rose.

"You know." She shrugged while poking a fork into the meat. "She met with Davio. What did she think of him?"

"Oh, that." I wiped my brow.

"Yes, that. You're acting strange."

"She liked him."

"That's it?"

"Yep. Is your brother joining us for dinner?" I pulled plates from the crockery cupboard and set them on the table, came back and collected cutlery and glasses. "Because he and I seem to be getting along so well, if you didn't notice."

She laughed. "He and Davio aren't back yet, and I didn't think to ask." She returned the roasting dish to the oven. "This meat needs another ten minutes. Tell the others in the family room for me that's dinner will be real soon."

"Will do." With the table set, I walked down the passageway to the family room at the other end of the house. Zac and Viv's hushed voices drifted to me, as well as the action going on with the TV. A staccato round of gunfire. They must be watching something gruesome.

"Hey." I rounded the plush, brown-gold corner couch that seated eight. Zac lay sprawled on his side in a forest-green t-shirt and jeans with Viv tucked in front of him wearing a miniskirt and emerald tank top.

Zac played with Viv's dark hair, then elbowed up and smiled at me. "Davio's with Silas in the castle's training room. Sword practice. Do you need me to seek his return?"

I plopped down beside Belle sitting to the right of the others. "No, but Silvie said dinner's in ten. Is Silas coming?" Silas was the one I'd have to keep an eye on, particularly as my father relied on me right now to ensure all remained safe at home.

Belle knocked my arm with hers. "He'll be here now that all things Silvie are sorted."

Zac's brow rose, a grin taking over his face. "I can't wait to see how much of a mess he's in. He outdid my sword pricks on you, ten times over."

Viv squeezed his arm. "We really shouldn't have poked her."

"No, you shouldn't have." I flicked Viv's leg since she sat so close. "No doing that again. I really can't believe you both wanted to slice and dice me when all I did was nail him to the ground. Jeez, how does Davio manage to put up with you lot?"

Belle smiled. "We're loyal, and we've been friends a long time."

I looked at her, for I certainly saw the loyalty and friendship she spoke of. I nodded. It would be great if I could form such strong friendships in Dralion to such a degree. It would be nice to meet new people, and at the very least, I had a new family.

That counted for so much already.

"What's going through your mind?" Belle rested her hand on my shoulder. "Your emotions are bombarding me.

I rubbed my hand on my jeans. "I'm glad Davio has all of you. I'm looking forward to forming the same kind of bonds with others in my father's country." As an empath, I hoped she'd understand my words.

Belle let out a close-mouthed hmm.

"I get what you're saying." Zac twined another lock of Viv's hair around one finger. "I wouldn't care to live in another country and not form new friendships either, but a word of warning, don't align yourself too strongly with any of the warriors there."

"Well, my father's a warrior, so what does that matter who I align myself with?" I flexed my fingers along my thighs, my thoughts zipping back to my father and mother. Mum was incredibly independent, had to be to raise me all on her own, and I was much the same as her. Thinking of Mum had my worry for her rising again, and even though I really wanted to check in on her and Dad, they needed this time alone. No spying for me.

I heaved to my feet to find something better to watch rather than the mindless killing spree going on with the current movie. "Here let me find you guys something better, more appropriate for visitors to my, ah, world." I rifled through Belle's DVD collection in the cabinet, spotted the ever classic Braveheart movie. I swapped it out. "This, Zac, will suit you. Lots of swords." Killing and battling too, but with some all-important historical information about Earth gathered along with it. A good choice. Over my shoulder, I grinned at him, then my mouth dropped open.

Behind Zac, bare-chested and looking so gorgeous, Davio stood in his dark leather pants hanging low on his hips with the weight of a very wicked sword belted at his side.

Licking my lips, I stood. "Ooo, look at that. I have my very own Braveheart right here in this room, just minus the kilt." Merging my mind with his, I skipped across the room and plowed into him. "I missed you." I ran my hands over his broad shoulders and tipped into him. "You're late."

"I listened to your conversation regarding Dralion from the passageway. It is as Zac said." Davio bent his head, rubbed his cheek against mine. "You'll need to take care. I won't have you around other warriors."

"I'll take your request under consideration." I wrapped my arms around his neck. "Kiss me."

He swept his arms around me, his lips on mine, his skin pressing hot and oh so close. Now this was the kind of *under consideration* I wanted.

Because in two seconds flat, I was delirious.

Belle coughed. "Okay, you two. I have to put an end to this. It's dangerous for an empath to be saturated in your overabundant kinds of feelings. It makes me get all mushy when I don't have a mate to get mushy with."

I stared into Davio's eyes. "You want to tell me how you slaughtered Silas then?"

"I did no such thing." He grinned and it was such a telling lie.

Drat. I should have been watching him with my forethought. No scrub that, perhaps I should have been watching my adult parents. Maybe I should zip home for a moment and check on Mum. Argh, I couldn't do that. I needed to fight the urge and leave them be for a bit longer. I clamped my teeth together.

"Hey." Davio ran his finger under my chin. "Why the sour look?"

"Ah, nothing." Couldn't exactly delve into any of that. I wrinkled my nose. "I can smell dinner. Silvie did say ten minutes and that time's about up."

"I'll take a quick shower first. Tell her I won't be long, and behave while I'm gone." He swatted my backside and turned, orders once again dispersed.

Only I followed him and I couldn't stop myself.

Belle snatched my arm as she caught up. "The dining room's this way."

I looked in the direction I wanted to go, toward Davio's room and that shower. Grumbling at Belle, I muttered, "Davio needs to send you back to Peacio. Pronto. I can't see what use you are here anymore."

She laughed as she yanked me behind her.

At the kitchen bench, Silas lifted his head, arrowing a look at me.

I smiled. "Ah, Silas. It's a shame you fast-heal." I just couldn't help myself.

A grunt. "I'm also sneaky so watch out."

Silvie pursed her lips and flicked him in the arm with a tea towel. "Go and sit down." She walked up to me. "And you, you promised me this morning we'd talk."

I took the seat next to hers, inhaling the smell of cooked beef plated right under my nose. "This looks wonderful."

"I made cupcakes for desert."

I grinned. "No wonder I haven't seen you all afternoon. I've been busy studying by the way."

"Cooking is my form of study." She was right, for her grades were already there, and her acceptance a given for the university's food technology course.

"There's no change in your plans for next year?" We'd always talked about studying at the same campus, just different courses.

"Nope."

"I apologize for keeping everyone waiting." Davio eased into the leather-backed seat at the head, then he arched a brow and looked down the table at me. With his jaw smooth and shaved, his white button-down shirt pressed to perfection, he looked better than cupcakes. "Is there a reason you're seated so far away from me?"

"Ah." I tapped my fingers on the varnished tabletop. "Silvie and I are catching up."

He folded his arms and gave a quick nod. "Then let's eat."

Lifting the fork to my lips, the scent of spiced pumpkin and baby potatoes with rich dark gravy drizzled over the roast beef, made my mouth water.

"*We're leaving.*"

"*Dad?*" I held my fork steady. "*You have the worst timing. How's Mum? And leave for where?*" Oh, my father couldn't mean Dralion? Surely not so soon.

Belle squeezed my hand from beside me. "What's wrong?" she whispered in my ear.

"Give me a minute."

She shrugged and picked up her water glass.

"*I asked about Mum.*" I straightened in my chair. "*Is she okay?*"

"*Kate's fine or at least as fine as can be in these trying circumstances. But as I said, we're leaving.*"

"*Mum's agreed to go? Like right now?*"

"*She's wary, but I've assured her she can speak to you first. We'll meet in my apartment. Don't be long.*"

"I can tell when someone's chatting telepathically with another." Silvie set her cutlery down with a glare. "That had to be your father since he's the only one, other than Belle, who you've created a link with. What does Wincrest want now?"

I scrunched up my face as everyone around the table stared at me.

I hated this.

"C'mon, speak to me," she urged.

"It's not so bad." I looked at my food, and my stomach did a slow dive.

I'd known this moment would come, but having it arrive so

quickly, well, I wasn't quite ready for it. I dragged in a deep breath. "My mother's agreed to go. She needs to speak to me."

The chair at the head of the table scraped and I closed my eyes as Davio gripped my shoulders from behind. "To Dralion. When?"

Holding on with every fiber of my soul, I spread my mind deeper through my mate's. "You knew this was going to happen, just as you know I can return. My father promised that would be so."

"A damn Wincrest's promise." He pulled out my chair, all four legs gouging into the wooden floorboards.

Once on my feet, I spun and met his darkened gaze. "You were okay with this all earlier today. We compromised."

"I realize that." His jaw clenched, his mind a turbulent storm of thoughts and all coming directly at me. "We haven't had enough time to speak of the finer details, of you knowing exactly where the dome's entry point is before Wincrest takes you and to make certain you don't allow the man to blindfold you. I have to know you'll have access to the image and can safety return. I can't risk allowing you to leave otherwise."

"I've already been told where the location is."

He slid one hand around the back of my neck, and drew me closer. "Then where is it?"

Palming his chest, his heartbeat racing under my palm, I answered, "I won't allow any blindfolding. I promise you."

"I asked where it was." His fingers tightened. "Damn, if only I held the skill of forethought or mind-merge as you do. I need to be able to read your thoughts."

"I'd still block as you usually do with me." I tapped his chest. "Besides, the dome protects Dralion for a reason. Peacians can't know the image of where to get in."

He snorted. "I can't stand this."

Shaking my head, I pushed up onto my toes. "Stop freaking out, just this once."

Silas snuck around the table, and motioned for Zac to take Davio's other side. He eyed me. "I know the signs. My cousin is preparing to take you from here."

Fingers biting even deeper into my skin, Davio glared at Silas. "One day you'll have a mate and feel what I feel." With a low growl, he pulled me back toward the solid pine wall behind us, although with Silas on one side and Zac on the other, there was no escape.

"I need to go," I urged him. "Please."

"I can't let you go yet. I want more time with you."

Silas narrowed his gaze on me. "We're going with your plan of making it in and out of Dralion on your own steam." He released a thought. *Duck. Now.*

I dropped, scrambled back as Silas and Zac slammed Davio into the wall.

"Get off me," Davio bellowed, both his shoulders pinned. "You bull-headed protectors derive far too much pleasure from this." He appealed to Zac. "I hunger for her, as you do for Viv. Give me more time with her. I'm not leaving yet."

Zac didn't move, not one muscle. "Your protection comes first."

"I don't care about my damned protection right now, only being with her. She holds the other half of my soul."

"Which proves you're not thinking clearly. She needs to go, and you need to go, but in different directions."

"Don't even try to force me back to Peacio against my will again." Davio shoved into Zac.

Silas tightened his hold on his cousin, feet planted wide. "We hardly need a contingency of warriors hard after your hide, Davio. Your mate already has a workable plan that's the best I've heard. Remember, the plan where King Donaldo need never know of your relationship with his granddaughter? Do you not think an all-out war should be evaded when tensions between our two countries are already so inflamed? Because that is what will happen if you don't let her go. Donaldo Wincrest wouldn't rest if he knew a Loveria cavorted with one of his own. We need to take every precaution, which means taking you back to Peacio where there is a larger safety net of protectors in place."

The air seemed to crackle and snap, and Davio narrowed his gaze on me. "Come here and ignore them."

I inched forward, needing to touch him one last time.

Silas snarled. "Stay there, Faith."

"I can't." Not when Davio needed me the same way I needed him.

Davio grunted, hooked one foot out and snagged it around my knees. I toppled forward, hit his chest, and he wrenched one arm free of Zac and wrapped it around me. Silas forced him back to the wall, and Zac pulled at me, shoved me clear.

Viv joined the fray, snatching Davio's legs. She twisted and sent them all careening to the floor, only before they hit the ground, they were gone—all four of them, gone.

Blinking, I stared at the spot where they'd been.

No. This wasn't happening. I needed to say goodbye to him properly. I dropped my head into my palms and sobbed. Pushing my forethought forward, I brought his image into my mind. He was on his back, pinned to the ground within an indoor training hall with steel-bladed weapons lining the block walls. He bucked and Silas and Zac held him tight, Viv still on his legs.

"He's not happy, but that's to be expected," Belle murmured in my ear. "They've taken him to the castle where he's safest, so you can leave without issue."

"You're saying I can't go to him?" I locked down the training hall's image for 'porting, my fingernails biting into my palms. Davio's pain right now ricocheted through me as if it were my own, only Belle was right. I needed to leave for Dralion and I couldn't forget that, or my mother.

"Silas protects him. That's his job. Don't make it harder for him," Belle urged.

Silvie wrapped an arm around my shoulders. "You can see he's safe. Go now. The moment you do, Silas will release him."

The vision melted away, and I wiped my cheeks. "Take notes for me in class." I hugged her. "And tell Davio that I appreciate the fight."

Her lips lifted a smidgeon. "You'll have more than a fight on your hands if you don't keep your word and return to him. Try not to take three days next time."

"I'll be back before you know it." I looked at Belle and drew in a long breath. "Look after him for me."

She squeezed my hand. "Silas is in my head and telling me you better hurry. I'm the only one who can keep in contact with you, and also calm Davio. I'm needed there now."

"I'm going to speak to my mother first, before we leave. I'll let you know when." I stood back, raised my hand in farewell and flashed away.

Seconds later, I arrived in the dark of Alexo's safe room and opened the connecting door to the suite. The familiar screeching sound of metal on metal assaulted my ears.

"I'll get the light." Dad flipped the switch and beckoned me in. He'd changed and now wore dark leather pants and a silver threaded loose shirt, a leather jacket slung over his arm.

"My mother?"

"In the living room." He steered me down the hallway. "I've been gone for hours and Donaldo and several warriors are tapping at my head to be heard. I need to make contact with Donaldo soon."

"Are you sure everything will be all right?"

"Yes." He set a hand on my shoulder. "Donaldo will want you, and he'll accept Kate since she's given birth to a highly skilled daughter. There's no more hiding." He paused. "Although there is one more thing I need to mention before we leave."

I let out a breath, preparing myself. "I'm listening."

"During my time on Earth, I went by the name of Alexo Stryker."

I groaned, rather loudly. "You made up my last name?"

"Yes, but you'll have it no longer—for obvious reasons. You're now a Wincrest."

I turned the corner and strode into the living room, eager to reach my mother. She sat on the gray couch, then stood the second she saw me.

I ran to her, meeting her in the center of the room, her arms banding tightly about me and mine around her. I hugged her hard, shaking because I'd finally reconnected with her again, the past few hours of worry settling at least a little within me.

"I'm sorry, honey." Mum's voice wobbled. "For everything. The lies. For whom Silvie and Seriah are. I can barely believe all Alexo has told me."

Dad cleared his throat. "Don't take Silvie and Seriah's involvement upon yourself. I saw the same forewarning as Carlisio did at Faith's birth, that our child would somehow have an impact on Loveria's family. I knew there would be some kind of future link, only it wasn't one I could halt, not after I returned to Dralion and found every single move I made followed so closely. I couldn't even sneeze without a warrior reporting it to my father. It wasn't an easy time."

And he'd been my age at the time, which somehow brought an element of light to things.

My mother's embrace tightened, her cream cardigan flapping to her knees. "I should never have withheld my knowledge of your father from you. He clearly loves you, only I never knew." She released a deep breath and her hands shook. "I'll do everything in my power to keep you safe. Even if that means living in Dralion and acting as his wife."

My heart squeezed. "Did you say acting?"

"Yes."

Dad grimaced. "That is her decision, and I will be content

with it for now."

My mother crossed her arms. "That's right—you will."

Dad let out a rush of air, took Mum by the shoulders, his gaze softening with her. "You need to relax around me. I'm certain Donaldo will be distracted by Faith, but no one must think you're not fully committed to us being back together, and that includes around my sister, Goldwyn, for she has the sight of a hawk and misses next to nothing.

I frowned. "I have an aunt? Are there other family there as well?"

Dad turned to me. "I have only the one sibling. Goldie was my parents' late surprise, and at nineteen, she is only a year older than you. Although Goldie comes and goes from Dralion."

"And where does she come and go to?"

"Goldie's chaperoning Hope in Australia, although Hope hardly considers it chaperoning. She's eighteen and an absolute delight."

My mother's brows rose. "You haven't mentioned Hope before. Who's she?"

His jaw clenched. "We'll speak of Hope another time, when we're not dealing with quite so much, but she is family. Now, we are deviating, and I must speak to Donaldo and prepare him for what's to come. We'll leave this Mount apartment once I've notified him." Walking into the adjacent kitchen, he began his communication.

Releasing a sigh, my mother moved to the couch. "He's hiding something, but right now, sit. I need to know about Davio Loveria. Your father told me who he truly is, a prince of Peacio."

"He's also my mate." Sitting, I clasped my hands in my lap. "The bond builds between us fast, and he has the same feelings for me that I have for him."

"Then I'm doing the right thing?" She cast a glance across the room at Dad.

I nodded. "I don't see there being any other choice."

"Donaldo's expecting us."

Those three words from my father made me freeze.

And in that instant, my life changed forever.

I stood, my heart pounding. "I need to use my forethought to collect the image of the dome room, and before we go."

"Yes. Take it from my mind." He didn't question my request.

I connected and pulled the image, my eyes widening. "Truly? That's the dome room?"

It was dark and dungeon-like. There were no doors, just four gloomy walls constructed of a gray-black brick with slabs of floor-stones in a dull gray-green. Aged cracks in the floor's surface oozed with slimy green moss. So repulsive.

"Ick. Does no one care to clean the place up?"

"It must remain the way it is. No one would ever imagine such an image as the secured point in and out of Dralion, and that in itself adds a level of safety we require."

"Does anyone guard it? Should I expect someone to jump out at me when I arrive?"

"No. It's completely blocked off and well below ground level. You see the walls?"

I returned to the image. "Yes, but what of that old well in the center. Does that not lead somewhere?" The yucky green stuff trailed over the blackened brick edging of the well.

"The well is deep and we've never found the end of it. The energy within that well is what the enchanter, Gilles Moyer, tapped into. He spelled the dome into existence using his skill."

I screwed up my forehead. "Where to from there?"

"We'll move quickly since the dome room smells as bad as it appears. We'll meet Donaldo at my personal apartments on the eastern third floor. The palace is a large residence with over four-hundred rooms. It's a fortress and has stood the test of time for hundreds of centuries."

My mouth popped open. I should have expected this, yet

because I hadn't seen it, I hadn't truly comprehended it. Now I did.

"We are running out of time. Donaldo has never been a patient man and knowing whom I bring, makes him even more so." My father tapped his head. "I see him pacing the receiving room." He took my mother's arm and looked at me. "The last image you'll need is the main reception room of my apartments."

He flicked up the image and I gasped. So beautiful. Stunning white and blue diagonal floor tiles captivated with a central motif of a massive "W." The area was ballroom like in size. Elegant sitting chairs covered in a white-gold detailed fabric, the legs and arms a polished golden wood, were tucked against the walls in sets of four, at least twenty separate sets in total around the perimeter of the room. Separating each set, a white marble arch framed double doors which led away from the area in varying directions.

I blinked, taking it all in. A high ceiling rose maybe twenty feet, with twelve brilliantly lit crystal chandeliers, six each side, both lines running parallel to each other. Beautiful, not to mention light beamed from them over striking scenes of hand-painted artwork displaying battles, much like in the Sistine Chapel here on Earth.

"Wow. When you said you lived in a palace, you truly meant it."

"It's now yours and your mother's home too. Do not forget that."

My mother cleared her throat. "Let's just go."

Dad tipped his head to me. "You have the images, and I will move ahead of you and see you in the receiving room."

"You will, right after I speak to Belle. I don't have a telepathic link with my mate and he needs me to check in. You two go on ahead." He blinked away, taking my mother with him, and I pulled open my link with Belle.

"I'm leaving. I have the image."

"Of the dome room?"
"Yes, of everything I need."
"I'll tell Davio. Take care. I'll speak to you soon."
I took a deep breath. *"Later."*
I closed the link.
No more waiting. It was time.

Chapter 11

I flashed through the dome room, sucked in only one breath for the taste of mold in the air coated my tongue in that mere moment. Then I was there, arms lifting as I balanced on the slippery and shiny blue and white floor tiles of the receiving room.

It was as I'd seen, only now included in the room were my parents, along with four men, three clothed in heavy combat gear surrounding the one who could be no other than Donaldo Wincrest, my grandfather and the ruler of Dralion.

His violet eyes cut directly to me, moved over every inch of my face.

I froze, even though I hadn't been moving.

With his bearing stiff and proud, he appeared a clear leader, a man with thick brown hair and a full, dark beard, one giving him the appearance of an age greater than the youthful one of the others of this world. Then he adjusted his shoulders and stepped forward in leather boots. He wore an impeccable red shirt with silver buttons, his long legs encased in black leather pants.

Dad stepped up to him, and Donaldo raised his arms, seized Dad to him in a firm, forearm embrace, his thumbs adorned with two large gold insignia rings.

They released each other and Dad lifted a hand, indicating my mother. "Father, meet my wife, Kate Wincrest."

Donaldo's gaze darkened to a striking hue as he inclined his head at Mum. "If my son says you are wed, then you are welcome here. I can see your daughter is Alexo's." Another spearing glance at me.

Dad beckoned me forward. "Come here and meet your grandfather."

I cleared my throat and pushed one foot in front of the other, shoved my shaky hands behind my back and tried to keep my composure. Not easy.

Donaldo crooked his head, raising his hands to me. "Don't be wary of me, child." His eyes crinkled at the corners. "I wish to meet my granddaughter. It's a shame Goldwyn and Hope aren't here. This is a moment none of the Wincrests should miss."

My heart pounded as Donaldo embraced me and kissed both my cheeks.

"You are in your rightful place, and my gratitude now goes to your mother for keeping you safe since your birth. I will accept her for she gives you to us."

"You mean that? No harm will ever come to my mother?"

He nodded. "It shall not. The mated bond has prevailed and given me a skilled granddaughter. It has not been an easy afternoon with your father missing, but his arrival with you now sets me at ease. We shall spend as much time together as we can in the coming days."

He released me, turning his gaze on my father. "I hope you understand. Guy Moyer will be called to see to your wife's confinement here. As an Earthling, she can't be permitted to leave through the dome room. Faith may, since I have no intention of revoking her use as one of our direct blood."

Alexo glanced at Kate. "You'll be spellbound to Dralion by Guy, a warrior enchanter. Guy is the nineteen-year-old grandson of Gilles Moyer, the warrior who first enchanted the dome energy field over Dralion forty years ago. What his family line spells, remains in place. Do you agree?"

With her hands straight at her sides, she nodded. "As you wish. I'm not leaving."

He set his hand at her waist. "Then it shall be done."

"Good," Donaldo boomed. "It pleases me well that your intent is to ensure your wife stays bound to Dralion and to you. Your marriage will be one of fruitful means, and by that, I expect from this woman more grandchildren."

My mother turned a startling shade of white, and I cringed. What had I gotten my mother—no, she was strong. I shouldn't question her decision to come. She would hold her own footing with my father and grandfather.

Donaldo looked over his shoulder. "Michael, collect Guy. He'll be in the warriors' barracks."

I shuffled from foot to foot, but within half a minute, the warrior returned with another. This man was young with unruly, coal-black hair and pale blue eyes. When he stared at me, silver came to life and swirled about the edges.

"Your Majesty, you called." His hand tightened over his side-buckled sword.

Donaldo faced him. "I want you to enchant Alexo's wife. She is not permitted to travel through the dome room and outside of Dralion. He has brought her here from Earth. Ensure your spell holds firm and can't be undone."

"I need her full name for the spell. And that one"—Guy's gaze returned to me—"looks like Hope. Who is she?"

I opened my mouth, but halted as Alexo took one menacing step toward him.

"Mind how you speak, Guy. This is my daughter, Faith, and she is permitted full rights to travel where she pleases, within our land and beyond." He motioned toward my mother. "My wife's name is Kate, and they both take my last name."

Donaldo crossed his arms, eyeing Guy. "What's bothering you? Your frustration is clear to see. If you need to talk, do so."

Guy inclined his head. "I apologize. Our warrior spy was captured days ago in Peacio, and my own father two years past. I thought we were close to finding their steel containment cells and now we've lost a vital chance to do so. Send me to Peacio. No one will work harder than I at finding our imprisoned warriors."

A deep inhale. "I can't send you. Your father is contained somewhere beyond our reach and there isn't a chance I'll lose you in the same manner. You're only a year into your skills, and I'm already working on a replacement for the warrior who was unearthed. Your father and the others warriors captured over the years will be found, but this all takes time." Donaldo scraped a hand across his dark brown beard. "Now, spell my son's wife so we may all get some rest this night."

Guy spoke a precise verse over my mother. A half minute later he was done, bowing to Donaldo. "She can't leave, sire." He flashed away without another word.

"Excellent." Donaldo nodded at Alexo. "I will see you all in the morning. I have much to see to after this disruptive day. Rest and recover. Goodnight." Then he vanished without waiting for a response, the warriors who'd stood around him leaving the second he did.

I shook my head. My mother was now powerless to leave Dralion, unquestionably giving up her freedom.

Alexo's brow creased, and he lifted a finger to his mouth in a shushing motion at me. "I know what you're thinking, but there are staff about. We'll talk more in the morning. For now, you'll find your chambers down that passageway." He pointed since there were several exits. "The fifth door on the right."

"Tomorrow." I hugged him.

"I'll send Jilly to you. She's the head of this wing."

I hugged Mum too. "Will you be all right?"

"I'll find you in the morning, and we'll talk as Alexo said." She cupped my cheek, kissed my forehead. "Sleep well."

"I'll try." Mum had made up her mind. She was here and not leaving. Neither could I for now.

I turned and headed toward my room.

The passageway was wide, yet dimly lit with wall sconces holding candle-like bulbs. I didn't slow since all the doors were closed, but at the fifth, I halted. The curved, ornate brass knob chilled my palm as I pushed the door open.

I did a double take. Wow. This room was three times the size of what I had back home, with a ginormous bed I'd likely get lost in.

Across the polished wooden flooring, I walked and gripped one of the four carved hardwood posts rising high above the bed. A canopy of sheer lace netting swished down each post and I pushed one corner of the lace aside and ran my fingers over the violet silk bedcovers. So pretty, with detailed stitching in mauve and golden thread.

I scratched my ear. This would take some getting used to.

Double glass doors sat to one side of the room, partially hidden by the softest snow-white curtaining. I bounced across to the door, pushed back the curtaining and gasped.

This was Dralion.

The moon, full and high, and at first glance far larger and more orange than Earth's moon, hung within a black blanket spread across the sky. Millions of diamond-like stars glittered and twinkled.

Below my window, the moon's glow shimmered over a high rocky cliff face, the cliff dropping swiftly down to meet the ocean. The Great Orbiting Ocean, from Davio's lesson on the beach.

I pinched myself, swung both balcony doors wide and stepped outside. Ornate inky-gray pillared railing and gray tiles completed the space, along with two chairs in the corner tucked under a round latticework table.

Hands on the railing, I brought the image of the cliff top

fully into my mind and 'ported. On the craggy precipice, I stood, the ocean so eerily beautiful below, almost beyond magnificent in its violent splendor, the waves rolling in hard and spraying high with a silvery mist.

Whipping around, I grinned at the sight of the palace spread out before me. The wind whisked my hair about my face as I took in my new home. Four majestic floors in height, all built in gray-black stone, and from each of the many corners, a slender tower rose to double the height of the palace, at least a dozen towers in all. This residence was a fortress, although a stunning one with light shining from behind stained glass windows along the lower floor.

I shivered as the wind picked up, bringing with it a chill to the air. Along the far property line, iron gates enclosed the property, and beyond those an array of darkened outbuildings rose. The forest swayed in the distance, this land so vast and stunning.

I wrapped my arms around my waist as the ocean spray drifted over me.

Since I couldn't travel any farther this night and had no desire to, not when I needed to remain close to Mum, I flashed back to my balcony.

Discovering more about this land would have to wait until another day.

Certainly, this new world was part of my heritage. My father had been born here, and the depth of that knowledge had never rung so greatly through me until this very moment.

I stepped inside, gently closed the double doors and tucked the snow white curtaining back in place.

"Excuse me, milady."

I swung around.

A woman stood in the doorway with a tray in hand. She popped a quick curtsey, her full-length blue skirts touching the ground as she did. "May I come in?"

"Of course."

"Milady, I've brought you a supper tray with tea and biscuits. My name is Jilly, and I'm the head of the eastern wing staff." She set the silver tray on the hardwood bedside table, and adjusted the white apron tied at her waist.

"It's nice to meet you, Jilly."

"As it is to meet you." She smiled. "May I be of any assistance?"

I nibbled on my lower lip. "You're so young." Oops. I clapped a hand over my mouth. "I'm sorry. This aging thing still catches me off guard."

Her eyes brightened. "Prince Alexo said you were raised on Earth, but I am a full generation older than you. I have two grown daughters and two teenage sons, and nothing catches me off guard. Speak to me as you wish. I'm here to aid you however you might need it."

"Then I could use some help. I have no clothes for tomorrow. I seem to be turning up all over the place without them."

"I'll see to that immediately. Simply tell me what you prefer to wear." Curls of mousy-brown bounced around her pixie face as she searched an apron pocket. She pulled out a notepad and pencil. "I'll jot down what you'd like."

I raised a brow. "Okay, um, low-cut jeans and I wear t-shirts of any color. I like skirts and blouses and summer dresses."

She scribbled down my requirements.

"Also training pants and sports shirts. I run daily and like to get my exercise in."

"Shoes, milady?"

"Yes, size seven, please. Is it truly appropriate to send someone to Earth for such purchases?"

"Yes. You'll wear what you desire. I'll have one of our warriors, a young woman by the name of Alexxis, go shopping at one of your malls on Earth. Alexxis loves to shop, and for local clothing, we have a tailor. I'll send him to you whenever it is necessary for specialty items."

"Thank you."

"If you will, allow me to show you your amenities." She spun around, headed toward one of the two side doors and I followed her. "This is your bathroom, and everything you should need will be stocked within the vanity, but if you have any particular requirements, let me know."

A deep white porcelain bath sat against one wall and a shower next to it. A mirror hung the entire length of one wall and thick white towels sat on top the vanity's counter. I opened the cupboards and drawers and found it fully stocked. "This is wonderful."

"Lovely. Follow me, if you will."

"Coming." I dashed out after her.

She opened a second door beside my bathroom, flicked on a light and illuminated a dressing room that was way too big for what I'd ever need. "This is where your clothing shall be hung once Alexxis returns with it. I'll instruct her not to disturb your sleep should you be resting when she returns."

"That's all right. I sleep deep. I doubt she'll be able to wake me even if she tried."

"As you wish. Do you have any questions?" She headed toward the tray she'd brought in and poured a cup of tea, passed it to me with a smile and waited.

"Ah, is there a training room in the palace where I can run in the morning? I'm not keen on heading out into any unfamiliar territory just yet."

"Yes. There's a training facility on the ground floor."

I tapped my head. "Could you show me the image?" At her confused look, I added, "I have forethought."

Her mouth opened. "You mean like Prince Alexo. Oh, that's wonderful. The prince said you were his daughter, but I wasn't aware you held the rare skill of forethought." Jilly clapped her hands. "This is exactly what our people need. The image is in my mind. Take it."

Her exuberance had me smiling, and I connected and gathered the image. Talk about another wow moment. What a training room. Gear galore, including cross-trainers, treadmills and weights, all so very similar to what one would find at any local gym back home. A lap pool too, three lanes wide and indecently long sat beyond the glass banking of windows separating the two divisions of the training area.

"I see the Wincrest family like my home world's conveniences."

"They do, and why not since travel is open to them. The warriors' facilities outside the main gates is also as well-equipped."

I sipped and set the pretty teacup down, snagged two biscuits—chocolate coated toffee pops of all things. "Does Alexxis shop the supermarkets on Earth too?"

"Yes." Laughing, Jilly retrieved the empty tray. "There are certain foods like chocolate which your family adores."

I stopped mid-bite. My family. She'd said my family. I now had a family, and far more than just my mother and me.

I tingled all over. There were others, the aunt named Goldwyn whom Dad had spoken of, and another person named Hope, whoever Hope was. I couldn't wait to meet both of them too.

"If that is all, I'll see you in the morning." Jilly backed away toward the door. "Goodnight."

"Yes, goodnight to you too."

The door clicked shut behind her, and I smiled as I returned to the balcony doors looking out over Dralion. Some of my uncertainties melted away. Mum and I would make this work.

"*Faith.*"

I groaned and I mean I truly groaned. It was just as well

Belle was the only Peacian I'd created a telepathic link with.

"*It's late, Belle.*" And it wasn't that I didn't wish to speak to her, it was that I didn't wish to have anyone intrude on this special moment.

"*How are you?*"

"*I'm good. How's Davio?*"

"*He requires an update.*"

"*Is he with you?*"

"*Yes. We're in the castle's recreational room, and he's pacing a hole in the floor. This rec room is where we relax, but not right now. No one will retire for the night. He's so agitated. Silas is ready to knock him out, just so we can all get some rest.*" A very loud sigh came through. "*So, if you don't mind, an update. Davio needs to know of Donaldo.*"

A shiver chased down my spine. "*I can't speak of him. It doesn't feel right.*"

"*Just a second. Davio is tapping on my shoulder and I need to be the intermediary between you both.*"

I waited, counting as twenty-two seconds passed.

"*Okay, let me remind you that these aren't my words, but his.*"

And then it came.

"*You will speak of Donaldo. I need to know what occurred on your arrival, what has happened every minute since, and I want it word for word.*"

Now, it would take a genius not to know that those words hadn't come from my mate, but still I snarled. "*You can tell my mate that my mother has sacrificed her freedom for mine. She is now bound to Dralion.*"

I flicked the lock on the balcony's doors and crossed to my bed.

"*Sacrificed what freedom?*" Belle's tone rose with the question.

"*My mother is spellbound to Dralion. She can't leave.*

Ever."

"Why would Wincrest do that when she is from Earth? Argh, Davio is breathing down my neck. Give me a second to pass on what you've said."

Pulling off my jeans, I gritted my teeth, then left my t-shirt on as a makeshift nightie and tucked myself into bed.

Twenty-eight seconds later, she was back.

"You can still move about freely?" Asked in a tightly controlled tone.

"Yes, but I will not be leaving my mother. This place is new for me, as it is for her. Give me a couple of days. We both need to settle in."

She gasped. *"Can you not come now? Even for a few minutes?"*

"No." I hadn't forgotten that my mate had kidnap on his mind earlier. *"I'm sorry, but I have to say goodnight."* As far as I was concerned this conversation was at an end. *"Tell Davio to stop pacing and to sleep tight."* Then I closed down the link and for a moment considered blocking it, only I didn't. It seemed I couldn't go that far.

* * * *

I stretched as the first rays of dawn warmed my face. Again, I needed to run, my legs throbbing. Throwing back the violet silk bedspread, I opened my eyes to the sight of clothing. Piles and piles of clothing draped across the richly upholstered settee at the end of my bed. What had happened to a few new pieces of clothing? The contents of an entire clothing store lay in heaps before me, not just the odd item.

I crawled down the mattress and sat near the largest pile. Carefully, I pulled new and very expensively labeled pieces across my lap. Wow, these were mine. I slowed my inspection and grinned. Leather jackets and pants and cute cable-knit sweaters were bunched in and around jeans of every color, as well as t-shirts and blouses, skirts and dresses. Enough for all the seasons. I would have to sincerely thank Alexxis. She surely knew what she was about in the shopping department.

"You're up." Jilly halted on her tiptoes as she walked out of my dressing room. "Alexxis needed assistance with hanging your clothing, but she had to dash off to do the same for your mother. She too requires a wardrobe now she's here."

"Thank you, and pass along my gratitude to Alexxis." I whipped up onto my feet, searched and found some training clothes within the piles and pulled them free. "I don't mean to be rude and run, but I have to head to the training room. Excess energy and all."

"I understand." She motioned toward the dressing room. "If there's anything missing, let me know."

"I will." I jumped to it, changing and 'porting off to the gym.

I skipped straight to the closest treadmill of which three stood side by side. I turned up the speed and elevated the slope, humming under my breath. Arms pumping—so good.

"Faith." Mum stood at the entrance to the training room, her gaze wide on me.

"I'm coming." I jabbed the stop button and hopped off the platform, then caught her up in a hug as she met me halfway. "How'd you know I was here?"

"Alexo gave me a tour. I asked him to leave me alone to speak with you for a few minutes. Get back on the treadmill," she said as she shooed me toward it. "Your father explained you have to run each morning to deal with your excess energy."

I scrunched up my face, but did as she bid. "You worry too much."

"It's a recreational hazard of being a mother." She rocked back onto her heels as she eyed the increase in my speed. "That's really fast, and you can keep that up for two hours?"

"Yes, now tell me how you're feeling?" My words were a demand. I didn't wish to wait to hear how she was.

"Well." She exhaled loudly. "Your father is such a stranger to me, and it's not easy being in such close proximity to him again."

"Is there even a little love? You were once mates."

"No, honey, I don't love him anymore. How can I when he left me and never thought I was strong enough to handle the slightest of explanations?" She rested one hand on the side bar closest to me. "I pined for him for years. I was lost and lonely, and I vowed never to let another man into my heart who would hurt me in that way again. I'm afraid I can't ever allow your father back into my heart. Suffering that pain once was enough."

"Where are you sleeping? 'Cause my bed is big enough to fit ten people in it, in case you want to bunk down with me." We'd done that often with each other over the years, bunked down together, either her bed or mine.

"I've got my own suite of rooms next to Alexo's, and for obvious reasons, I need to stay there." She gave my arm a quick squeeze. "What I need is for you to resume your studies. I can see you'll have to live two lives, one on Earth where you'll need to complete your education, and one here in Dralion where there's your future to embrace."

"Good morning." Alexo strode into the room, the large double doors swishing shut behind him. "I've spoken to Donaldo. He's aware of your upcoming exams, of your need to return to school. You may return as soon as you're ready, Faith."

"Hey, Dad. Where is he now?" I kept moving on the belt, not once breaking my stride.

"He's in a meeting." He lowered his voice. "Yours are unusual circumstances. You have lived on Earth your entire life, unlike any other Wincrest before you. Donaldo will need to see you accept your heritage and your country here as well, but I'm sure you can do both with ease."

"Of course I can." I'd try my hardest for certain.

Dad caught Mum's hand and settled it into the crook of his

elbow. "And you need to adopt Dralion too. So let's finish your tour."

Flashing away, they left in a blink, and I picked up my speed.

Oh, my father was in trouble because I knew my mother hadn't finished talking to me. I laughed as I imagined him getting an earful, one that was usually reserved for me.

As my giggles subsided, I centered my mind.

It was probably best I not think about Silvie, who'd surely be dressing for school about now, or Belle who hadn't as yet contacted me this morning, and certainly not Davio, in case I felt the need to go to him. Nope, I would not use my forethought on them this morning, not when it was Donaldo who intrigued me the most right now.

I focused on him and his image shimmered into my mind. He sat on a golden-threaded regal chair at the top end of an elevated stage within a meeting hall. Men, women and children of all ages lined the outside perimeter of the public room, some standing and some sitting on wooden benches.

Donaldo's personal guards stood evenly spaced out in a half circle behind him. A man dressed in dark cotton pants and a clean shirt approached from amongst the people. The newcomer asked a question and Donaldo answered. He offered advice to the man and then asked for the next person to come forward.

I stayed with him, intent on the discussions at hand, those between him and his people as he oversaw issues that had arisen within his land.

Time passed.

Two hours later the door thumped open, and I jumped, my vision dissolving.

In single file, six men and two warrior women entered the room. The man at the front of the pack was colossal in size, with oily black hair hanging down over his shoulders, a vest of gray leather flapping open across his chest. Fire-breathing dragon tattoos curled one over the other on his muscular chest and arms. Sharp silver spikes were pressed into every inch of his leather belt which held a roughened metal mallet dangling from one side.

I gulped. Oh no, this could not be good.

His dark brows drew together. "My name is Killian. To my right is Abelard, next is Frey, then, Hiram, Laidley and Nicolas. The warrior women to my left are Xrnina and Leoda." Blunt and to the point.

I glanced at the women. They looked scary. One had half her head shaved on either side, giving her a mohawk of bright red. A piece of coiled silver pierced one nostril and round silver hoops looped through both her eyebrows. Tight leathers showed off a toned and strong body.

"Nice to meet you." I rubbed my chin, although kept my hands to myself.

The second woman cleared her throat. Little less than a strip of black leather contained her breasts and black leather pants hugged her hips. The exposed skin from her waist up was painted in a dark camouflaging mud, and she held a bloodied dagger in one hand. "Welcome, Princess." A firm nod of her head.

I tensed, jabbed the treadmill's stop button and halted. "Thank you for the welcome."

The man beside Killian stepped forward, the one named Abelard. "We are the leading eight of the warriors and should you have any need of our services then our king has stipulated you ask." Brown scraggly hair fell forward to cover one half of his face, and he had a singular spiked piercing in one ear. Biceps bulging, his fists balled around not one, but two bloodied swords.

I cleared my throat and found my voice once more. "I appreciate the introduction."

One by one, they snapped a severe bow, then promptly left

the exact way they'd come.

I shivered. That was intimidating.

"*Faith.*" My father speaking in my head. "*I see the leading eight visited. Do not worry about them. You only ever have to call on me, and I will come. Donaldo's intention would be to ensure they knew you held a strong position, which is why he asked them to introduce themselves to you. It is his way.*"

"*You could have told me that was going to happen.*" I teleported back to my room and sat on the end of my bed and unlaced my sneakers.

"*I could have, but you need to stand strong on your own two feet now, particularly when your rising is so close.*"

"*Ah, what's a rising?*" I seemed to recall Belle using that word at one time.

"*A rising occurs around a month following a Magioling's eighteenth. It signifies the conclusion of your skills coming in.*"

"*Can you give me more?*"

"*Of course. As this rising is reached, you'll feel an overpowering assault on all your senses. The adrenaline pumping through your body causes an all-time high and your moods will swing. Also, when your rising begins, you'll need those closest to you to aid you in draining the excess energy. I'm speaking of your strength levels rising, to three times the strength they currently are.*"

I couldn't imagine that. "*I'll have three-times my normal strength and my hormones will be raging? Is that what you're saying will happen during this rising?*"

"*Yes, but thankfully a rising only occurs once. Still, you'll have to take care not to hurt anyone as you go through your rising. Allow others to aid you, because it will take two or more people to match your strength and the moods that link it.*"

"*Why am I only hearing about this rising now?*"

"*You are new to Magio. There is much you don't have the knowledge of, but all will be known in time. I'll teach you all you need to know.*"

"*Thank you, and while we're chatting, is there anything else you'd like to enlighten me about?*" So many new surprises likely awaited me.

"*As I said, prepare for a difficult few days.*"

"*Lately I've been inundated with difficult days. I can handle a few more.*"

"*If you'd like to go and visit Loveria, take the time now while you can.*"

"*No. I'm not leaving Mum. Not this soon. Thanks for the offer though.*" I cut the link, rolled my shoulders. Mum was here and now bound to Dralion for no other reason, other than me. She needed my support, and I intended on giving it to her.

I lobbed my training clothes into the bathroom's hamper and showered. I could handle a rising, just like I could handle having Davio for a mate.

Chapter 12

I could not handle a rising.

Two shaky days passed, days where my emotions spiked, the levels going up and down and all over the place, but still my rising had not yet come to pass. I also had school to consider. I really couldn't afford to take any more time off, or else I'd get too far behind.

"Oh, look, miladies," Jilly said, one hand flat on the sitting room windowsill as she gazed outside.

Mum rose from the imperial corner chair and joined Jilly at the window. "What is it?"

Jilly pointed to the west. "King Donaldo and Prince Alexo are about to ride. Have you been to the stables yet?"

In two short days, I'd become reliant on Jilly's presence. She cared for us in a way I couldn't have done without. Not only was she the head of this wing, but quickly becoming a friend, particularly to Mum. The two were the same age and got along famously.

"No, but I've always loved horses." Mum smiled. "When I was a child, the local stables sponsored four of us from the orphanage for a season. I was only thirteen, but I was fortunate enough to have riding lessons for two weeks." Her smile grew.

"Where are they going?" I asked as I moved in beside Mum.

Jilly glanced at me. "The four-day tribal summit which is being held half a day's journey from here. King Donaldo is going, and Prince Alexo is traveling as far as the village of Herring. He'll be back in a couple of hours." Her brow quirked. "It was mentioned yesterday."

"I remember now." I rubbed my head at the familiar ache as it began, the one which meant I needed Davio and to cement our merge. It seemed I couldn't go three days without needed to fuse my mind with his.

"Why don't they simply, you know"—Kate clicked her fingers—"do that flashing thing they do instead of traveling by horseback?"

I listened as Jilly explained how Donaldo preferred riding on horseback at times. How he liked to travel through the villages and see the countryside.

"Faith? You there?"

"Hey, Belle. I'm coming soon." I'd told her I would return to school today, especially in light of my mother's settling in. *"Where's Davio?"*

"The training hall. He's venting his frustrations on Silas again. How far away is soon?"

"Not long."

I crossed the room to the ornate coffee table, collected my textbook and scooped up my sandals from the floor. "Mum, it's almost nine, and I'm supposed to be at school."

She eyed the book in my hands. "Yes, you should go." She turned to Jilly. "You'll stay with me?"

"Yes, and I'll ask a stable hand to saddle two of the smaller mares. We'll take them for a ride. There's a beautiful path right along the edge of the forest."

I hugged Jilly who jumped. "Mum will love that. What a great idea."

She patted my back. "Um, certainly."

Stepping back, I grinned at her blush as I gave Mum a hug.

"You two have a fabulous day."

Bless Jilly—I officially loved her.

Summoning the image of the dome room, I flashed through it to the training hall, of which I'd already locked down the image from when Silas had taken Davio there the other day.

I arrived in the blink of an eye, curled my toes into the cold slate flooring and lugged in a breath of air tainted with the clear scent of sweat. All around me, men battled in pairs, their swords clashing and steel ringing loud.

I fell back a step, hit the brick wall at my back and scraped my shoulders.

In all the times I'd watched Davio in this room over the past two days, I'd never once seen it filled with protectors in this way. I'd presumed only Davio and his nearest used the space located in his grandfather's castle.

So where was he?

I reached out with my mind and searched for him. The connection always came with ease when he was close, only he wasn't here amongst these men. Not as Belle had said.

"Do. Not. Move." One of the men pressed a very sharp blade to my neck, the prick drawing blood, which meant he was in trouble should Davio learn about this. "Now, who exactly have we got here, boys? Looks like a pretty blonde who's not where she's supposed to be," the man gloated as he moved directly in front of me, his sword scraping around to the front, a bitter slant to his lips and his chest bared and drenched in a river of sweat. "Only protectors are permitted within the castle's indoor training hall and you are not one of us."

Another man swept in beside the first, poked his blade into my arm, his eyes all gleaming and bright. "Drop what's in your hands."

Gah, why hadn't I considered the possibility of this? If only my forewarning worked on me.

I opened my fingers, and my textbook and sandals fell to

the floor with a *thump*. I raised a brow, my overly aggressive emotions once again rising due to the other "rising" I still awaited. "Huh, now that's handy them being on the ground where I'll just have to pick them back up again."

He snorted. "We have a smart aleck, eh?"

"I'll admit to being a touch moody lately. A girl has to go through her rising and all—apparently." I clenched my fists and glared at the giant before me. Black hair was plastered wet to his scalp, his neck almost as thick as his head, and his shoulders were so wide he could easily carry a full grown man over each side. So enormous, and I should probably keep my mouth shut. "If you don't mind, I'm after Davio Loveria."

"No," said the first one, narrowing his gaze and holding me firm. "The fine for teleporters sneaking into the castle is a week in the cesspit. The cesspit is not a pretty place. I'm Derick, and the one with the other blade is Warrick. He'll be taking you to the cesspit for your upcoming stay."

"He's right." Warrick twisted me around in a move so fast and jarring, everything blackened. "Anyone who turns up unexpectedly like you have, would know that this is not the way to gain an audience with our prince."

In a flash, we were gone.

He released me, the first drag of air I pulled into my lungs so rotten my stomach heaved. So dark. Only a wall-mounted lantern cast a small glow down the passageway of gray bricks on each side. Warrick shoved me from behind. "Now, along a little farther are our steel lined cells for those lovelies like yourself, who can clearly teleport to wherever they wish."

"No." My heart thumped. "My name is Faith. Your prince is my mate." I didn't hold back, not when it appeared my life might very well be on the line. I couldn't be contained within a steel lined cell, not when should I go missing, Dad wouldn't hesitate to search for me here. A war would likely ensue, something I didn't want to have happen.

The monster only laughed with deep grunting noises that boomed and hurt my ears. "So says you and every other little pretty who wants the prince as theirs. I've heard it all before so why don't you shut up. You've got some time to learn this isn't to happen again." He pulled open a steel door.

Oh hell. I was out of time. "*Belle.*"

"*I'm here. When are you coming?*" Same opening words as always, only this time I loved the sound of them.

Warrick shoved me into the cell and I crashed to my knees. "*Warrick. Some kind of—*"

The door slammed shut.

My connection with her cut off.

I squeezed my eyes shut.

Nothing.

The steel that lined this cell finished me.

Inhaling, I coughed at the reek of sludge all around.

I stayed still in the dark where I'd fallen, the sludge covering the floor seeping into the knees of my jeans. No more. I pushed to my feet and slimy muck oozed between my toes.

Gagging, my movement only stirred up the stench beneath me until it clogged my airways. Oh boy, this really was the pits.

"Davio!" I screamed his name. "Where the hell are you?"

Peering through the pitch black toward the door, I slipped through the muck and slammed my fists against the cold metal. The dull thud of each hit reverberated all around.

"I mean it, Davio. Get me out of here!"

"Hell, Warrick."

I sagged against the door as Davio's voice echoed on the other side. "Davio!"

"I'm coming."

The steel door cranked open, and I grabbed my head at the sharpness of my mind flying toward my mate's. Such a piercing need to connect, one I couldn't hold back.

His answering grunt sounded as I made the merge and

snuggled into my special spot in his mind, then a beam of light hit my eyes and he caught me tight. "Silas, take the lantern." Davio's voice rumbled over my head.

"Got it." Silas stepped forward into the light and took it.

Davio's arms firmed around me. "This should never have happened."

"Trust me, you don't want to hear what I have to say about the way your protectors protect, but let me enlighten you anyway." I drew in a deep breath as he led me out of the cell "That one." I pointed at Warrick who stood in the flickering lamp's glow. "Needs to die."

"I'm sure he does." Davio scooped me into his arms. "But first, let me take you out of here. I can't stand seeing you in this place."

And he did, zapping us straight into an outcropping of trees which edged a roaring river. The instant change of location, the bright vivid colors and the shock of morning sunlight beaming through the dense foliage, had me pinching my eyes shut.

I took a moment, slowly opened them again and when I did, Silas appeared before me. "No," I bellowed and jammed a finger at him, "you have to go back and kill Warrick."

He crossed his arms. "Before I do that I have to make certain you don't take your anger out on my cousin."

I huffed as Davio set me gently on my feet and gripped my shoulders. "I can't believe you're here. You should have told Belle you were coming. We would have been on the alert. There's always certain security in place, particularly within the castle. Until I've introduced you around to those in my closest circle, you'll need to take all care."

"Then alert this," I snapped. "Warrick. Dead. Now."

Silas sighed. "How about I go and see to Warrick. I'll return once I'm done with him, and I'll bring something back with me that'll take that awful stinky smell away." Frowning, he slanted his head at me. "And sadly I didn't mean you."

I scowled, hating all things Silas. "Go."

He wavered and disappeared.

"We'll clean this muck off you in no time. The river's deep enough in the center, and it's not too cold." Davio shucked off his boots and taking my arm, steered me down the bank and into the river.

"I'll do anything to get rid of this stink." The water rose past my knees, then my hips as I walked in deeper. I rubbed my arms as the chilly water covered me. "Grrr, this is freezing."

I stopped, lowered down into the water's fast flow until I'd covered my shoulders.

"Hey." Silas was back and far too soon. "Catch." He tossed a large bottle from his position on the bank and Davio caught it midair. "I'll give you two a few minutes to clean up."

"Thanks, and bring Viv back with you when you return," Davio called back over the rushing river water. Lowering down in front of me, he squirted out a glob from the bottle and raised his brow. "Dunk, love."

I didn't argue, went under the frigid water and after it closed over my head, I popped back up to a new kind of goop landing on my head.

With the cold water flowing briskly past us, Davio scrubbed my hair until I smelled lavender sweet instead of icky and foul. Shadows darkened his eyes, his worry and lack of sleep clear to see.

"I'm sorry." I touched his cheek with my palm. "I couldn't come any earlier. Mum needed me."

"I understand. How is she?"

I traced along his jaw, the two-day stubble raspy on my fingertip. "Have you slept at all?" I searched his mind, but he was blocked. There was nothing.

"Your mother," he insisted.

"She's handling things. Although I need to be home by the time school finishes this afternoon."

"Why so soon?" His jaw tightened. "It's Thursday and you've been gone since Monday night. The weekend is coming. You're sleeping in the enemy's territory, and I don't know from one minute to the next whether I'll ever see you again."

The tumbling water sucked at my clothing. "Don't go getting mad at me. I'm unstable at the moment as it is." I meant with my rising since it still hadn't quite taken full form and begun. The delay had my emotions tossing up and down in a stormy mess. All that additional strength, three times as much, which would soon be upon me. I stamped my feet in place, trying to keep my circulation going. "As nice as this river is, I need a warm shower."

He took my arms and lowered us further into the water where the current whipped my hair into a tangle around his neck. "You didn't answer me."

"Ah, freezing my butt off here. I've got to get out. That's all the answer you're going to get for now."

His gaze darkened. "Then I'll have your answer after you've showered. I'll meet you in the recreational room. Take the image from my mind so I know you'll always have a safe place to arrive."

An image of where he said flashed into his mind, and I stored it. Next came an image right on the cuff of that, one that showed a very exclusive male bedroom.

"This is my private domain. Which means, I expect to see you."

I gritted my teeth. "One day at a time."

A low growl rumbled from his throat. "That's all I've heard through your link with Belle these past few days. I need to see you."

"Ah-hem." Silas stood on the bank, Viv at his side.

She took one look at me and held out a towel. "Come out of there. You're turning blue."

I pushed my way toward her, shaking more as the cold wind

hit me. I accepted the white towel she held out and wrapped it around me. "How fast can you move?"

"I've got you covered." She wrapped her hand around my wrist and we zipped from the chilly river to a brightly lit yellow bathroom.

"Oh, this is perfect. Now, where am I?"

"Silvie's quarters. This is her bathroom." She pointed to the yellow vanity top where Silvie's hairbrush lay with strands of red-gold hair twisted in the bristles. Beside the brush, her favorite gold clips sat.

My heart panged. I missed her.

"Silvie's at school. I'm sure you two have shared clothing before, and she'd want you to help yourself. Her bedroom adjoins this bathroom."

"Thanks."

Viv backed up. "After you're done, come to the rec room. We'll be waiting for you."

I stood alone after she 'ported away, and because I couldn't help myself, I focused on Davio.

He remained on the sandy edge of the riverbank, a matching towel to mine covering his shoulders. "Faith will not commit, Silas. I haven't seen her in days and she's already said she's leaving this afternoon."

Silas raised his hands. "Hey, I'm the last person who'll ever understand her."

"Well, this I do understand. The longer my mate remains with Wincrest, the stronger her blood-bond with him grows."

My fists bunched, for I couldn't be everywhere and all at once. How could he not see that?

I unclenched and switched my forethought to Silvie. She sat in our Physics class, where I should be, only not while I dripped water all over her bathroom floor.

I shut down the visual and flipped the shower's lever to piping hot. With her favorite lilac soap, I scrubbed my skin until it glowed red.

In her castle bedroom, I pulled open drawers, found a red button-down blouse that was mine, which she'd borrowed an eon ago. I teamed it with a pair of her dark blue jeans, and because I wanted to feel a touch glam, added her three-inch fire-red heels.

Refreshed, and with my hair dry and tucked behind one ear, I 'ported directly to the rec room. Such a massive space, fifty to sixty feet long and just as wide. Divided into two noticeable areas, the half where I stood had polished wooden flooring, a table tennis platform and a pool table. Behind me pool cues stood slotted in a wooden frame against the wall, and next to them a game board hung to keep markings.

On the eastern wall, square cut, wooden edged windows with soft draperies of caramel-cream tied back, overlooked a green garden with tall hedges.

At the other end of the rec room, four separate white leather couches faced each other and Zac and Viv sat on one, Silas and Belle the other, and Davio opposite them. He stood and I met his gaze and soaked in the sight of him. His custom-fit black jeans hugged his tight rear and a paneled black and white shirt lay loose and untucked. Damp hair hung to his shoulders. He'd clearly showered too. "How are you feeling?" he asked me.

"Much better."

"Come and show me." He held out his hand.

I zapped straight to him, my mind merging solidly with his. I should probably warn him about my coming rising, which was clearly already doing a number on me, because it was either that or I was losing myself. "I hope you didn't have Warrick killed, and I hope I smell better."

He inhaled as he leaned over me. "You smell like lilacs, and Warrick still lives."

I sighed. "I heard what you said to Silas at the river, so I should warn you right now my rising is close, and my emotions are swinging back and forth. I'm just waiting for the tripling of my strength, which sounds real swell." I rolled my eyes. "Jeez, I can't believe there's a rising. I'm sure looking forward to when I completely lose it."

Silas laughed. "And here I thought you were always this emotional and annoying."

"I am not normally this way." I snapped around and glared at him. "Much."

Davio took my arms and backed me up toward the couch. "Clearly your rising's close. Which means you'll be staying here since you'll need those closest to you to get through it." He settled one hand over my mouth. "Don't argue that point with me either. I won't have you go through your rising anywhere else but with me."

I tugged his hand away. "I have school."

He sat, pulled me down with him onto his lap. "Your need to attack others will become uncontrollable. What you have is me."

"No, what you have is me." My heart raced and I leaned in, because in that instant, my mood jackknifed and I very much wanted him.

He clearly caught my change in mood and nabbed my wrists. "This is what we call uncontrollable."

I brushed my nose against his nose. "I want to drag you behind this couch and show you what I call uncontrollable."

He let out a slow, stuttering breath. "There are others in the room so no, you won't. Your increasing anger and desire are all part of your rising."

"Kiss me and prove it."

"As much as I'd like to, I can't now you've enlightened me as to what is coming."

I looked at his lips and licked my own. "You want to explain exactly why."

"As your rising escalates, the full force of it will hit you. Giving into you now will only make things more difficult at the end. If it helps, during my rising I used to count. By around thirty, you'll find yourself able to breathe the tension away."

Zac piped up. "Counting aided me as well. During Viv's rising, she experienced the same physical pull as to what you're displaying. It's worse if there's been some length of time apart, and you two can't deny you've had that."

I glanced at Viv. "You really controlled it?"

"I did, not that I cared for keeping my hands off my mate."

I yanked my hands free of Davio's and wrapped them around his neck. "It seems I don't care for keeping my hands of you either." I leaned in and kissed him, actually devoured would be the more appropriate word since I wasn't prepared to stop.

And it was perfect, until my craving for him surged yet again.

I retreated a bit, breathing fast. "We need—"

Silas grabbed me, and in a heartbeat, lifted me away from the one I wanted. As he did, the most feral sound gained momentum in my chest until it rose up as a hissing spit. I kicked out at Silas and swiped my hand at him, nails drawing blood.

"Calm down. You can't control yourself, so this is the new way I'm going to insert some control." Biting words in my ear.

"I really hate you, Silas. It hurts not to touch him." It truly did, for the gulf Silas enforced had me slamming my elbows into his stomach.

He grunted, his hold tightening as he pulled me even farther away. "I'm doing this for your own good."

"I double hate you."

"That's okay. The feeling's mutual." He hauled me to the wall at the far end of the room.

I was too far away from Davio, my mind-merge shattering. I sobbed, grabbed my head between my hands as pain lanced through. "Let go of me. I'll leave if I'm not wanted here."

Davio growled, low and menacing from across the room. "You're wanted. It has to be this way until you can think more clearly."

I ground my teeth together, my vision darkening.

A blackness smothered my sight.

I shut my eyes, my forewarning activating in the midst of such turmoil.

Guy Moyer's image crystalized, his midnight black hair and pale, silver-blue swirling eyes, unmistakable. He traipsed through some kind of communal dining hall where dining protectors sat at low wooden benches around wooden-slatted tables. With a sword belted at his side, and a sharp dagger sheathed at his wrist, he blended in with his battle leathers.

"Forewarning." I shoved my eyes open and eyed Belle. "Is there a dining hall nearby? I see a lot of protectors eating together, maybe two-hundred of them."

"Yes, in the village, five miles from here."

"Oh hell." I grabbed both of Silas's forearms. "I have to go and I swear no one can follow me. Don't let it happen. My forewarning doesn't include any of you." It didn't include me either, but someone had to stop Guy from walking amongst his enemy. Death would come to him fairly fast otherwise.

Davio was a blur, his legs flying as he sprang toward me. "You're not going anywhere."

I dived behind the pool table and rolled clear, pulled the image of the communal dining hall from my forewarning and zapped straight to it.

Such a hive of activity, but Guy was there. He patrolled, moving about the room with grace and purpose toward the table with the greatest number of protectors.

What he was doing here? Was he on a suicide mission?

Chapter 13

Behind me the air stirred—they had all come—and Davio bolted toward me. He whipped his right arm around my waist, hooked me back against him then breathed down my neck, "You need to cease leaving me."

I wriggled against him, edging closer and not farther away as I should. "You were forced from me first." I tried to find Guy through the crowd.

Dralion's enchanter halted, his gaze catching on mine. He let out a low snarl. *"I'm here for Loveria, and I know you can hear me through your forethought."* His thoughts flew freely, easy to catch.

Which meant Guy wanted this. He wanted his own demise, and I couldn't let him have the one he was after.

"Who is that man?" Davio ground out.

I had to make a decision and fast.

"Wait for me somewhere and we'll speak," I yelled to Guy.

He lifted his middle finger and shoved it at Davio, then stepped in behind another protector in the crowd and disappeared from my sight. He flashed away, fast.

"Obviously he's not one of yours."

Davio swung me around until I faced him. "You knew the warrior was here. Give me his name."

"He's gone." Only he hadn't gone as far as I'd hoped, or so

my forethought showed me. Guy waited in a field of green grass, and behind him, high on a steep rise, Loveria Castle sat.

Which meant I had to go to him since I had no idea how long my order would stick.

Davio gripped my shoulders and shook me. "Answer me."

I fisted my hands deep in his fine black and white shirt and dragged him to me. I kissed him until my skin heated and so did his. I pulled back, breathing deeply. "I don't have time for an argument right now." I pushed him away and dropped, then swept one leg out and tumbled him in a move that had my mouth opening. Oh, this had to be the start of my tripling in strength. I should not have been able to take him down.

I brushed my hands off and 'ported out of the room, then arrived in the center of the frigidly cold river I'd already over-acquainted myself with today, but a necessary visit in order to mask my 'porting airstream. I'd have to thank Dad at some point for telling me earlier how that was done.

Shouts resounded behind me, and holding my breath I dived deep, nipping straight to the field where Guy waited.

Water flooded to my feet in the lush grass.

"About time." Guy's jaw clenched. "What the hell are you doing with Loveria? Does Donaldo allow his own family members to consort with our enemy now?"

"No, he doesn't, but Alexo does." Knowing lies would only dig me into a deeper hole, I chose the truth. "You know I'm Alexo's daughter and that he brought me here from Earth. Loveria's cousin, Silvie, was schooled in the same town as me. We're best friends and I met Davio through her, or it was something close to that. Davio and I are mated—that whole soul-bond thing."

He eased one foot forward. "Damn, not good. What did Alexo say about this?"

I wiped my damp face with my wet sleeve, hoping I didn't look so much like a drowned rat, but rather like someone who knew what she was talking about.

"That Donaldo can't know. Alexo reveres the mated bond and accepts I'm here with Davio. But if you wish, I'll work hard on finding your father and our other imprisoned warriors, provided you promise not to breathe a word of what you've now learnt, not to anyone."

His eyebrows pinched together, and then slowly flattened out. "You would keep your word?"

"Yes. None of our warrior men should have to be caged behind steel. Although I need time, and I need you to give me sufficient space to find them and see them freed. Do we have a deal?"

He sauntered closer. "I'll give you that time and keep your secret, but I want updates." He halted, his gaze moving over my head. "That castle up on the hill is a stronghold that must fall. We don't imprison their protectors, not as they do with our warriors."

I followed his line of sight. Blue sky reigned over a stunning castle of gray-stone with turrets and flags flying, a castle that would compare to any of England's finest residences. "Davio is my mate and this war isn't mine, but I fully agree there should be no prisoners."

He withdrew his sword from his scabbard and pressed it into my hands. "Then this is for you. You're Dralion's princess and I will not leave you unarmed, mated to Davio Loveria or not. Make sure you find my father. If you need my aid, just ask."

I took his blade, curled my fingers around the burnished hilt as Guy blinked away.

My fingers and toes tingled, and I closed my eyes. The lightest of hums rumbled through my very soul. I smiled, stroking the hilt, over and over. Such a sweet song, as if it were in my very blood and it resonated directly from the blade.

Around me the air moved, chilling my moist skin.

I lifted my sword arm and held the blade steady.

Davio appeared and beside him Silas, who held onto Belle.

"Damn it. Who told you about using a water source?" Davio was dripping wet, from head to toe.

Slowly, I turned the blade in my hands over and it shimmered so beautifully in the sunlight. "My father." I tracked a finger carefully down its length and whistled in appreciation. "I take it Carlisio told you where I was?"

"Yes, and where is the dark-haired warrior he saw you with?"

"He returned home." I pulled my gaze from the weapon, looked my mate straight in the eyes. "Guy holds the skill of enchantment and is the grandson of Gilles Moyer, the warrior who first spelled the dome containment field." I offered the information because Davio could never get to Guy, and it didn't matter that he now knew.

Davio fisted his hands at his side. "What are you doing with that sword?"

I spun the piece around and balanced it over my two index fingers, one each end of the smooth metal.

My heart pounded. "Guy gave it to me." I pulled it back and clutched it to my chest. "I think you might have some competition. I swear I'm about to fall for this blade."

He flicked his fingers, motioning to Silas to move around me. "Merge your mind with mine, Faith. We don't need you getting any more aggressive with what you have in your hand. Obviously, your strength is increasing. Silas brought Belle to help calm you down."

"No." I straightened to attention, taking the hilt and gripping it in the palm of my hand. My brow rose as I stared at it. "Okay, I seriously love holding this weapon."

He groaned. "It's the battle skill taking you. It comes into being once one fully touches a blade."

Silas whistled as he edged closer. "Yeah, it feels good, doesn't it? Like the blade in your hand is singing to you."

I twirled around and swung the blade in a deadly arc, aiming it directly at Silas's head. "I wouldn't come any closer if I were you. We've already gotten off to a bad start, and you're not getting this pretty thing from me."

"Hell." Davio pushed a hand deep into his hair, tossing up the wet mess. "I should have guessed this would happen. Every Wincrest I know holds the battle skill. Why should you be any different?"

"It appears I'm not."

"Hand the sword over." Belle stepped forward, her gaze on me. "I'll keep your weapon safe for you. You'll need instruction on how to wield it, but with a blunted sword, and not that one."

I narrowed my gaze, pointing it now at her, but she was right. I didn't like it, although I understood that was the truth. Instruction with a blunted sword would be needed.

Taking my time, I lowered the weapon and pressed the tip a few inches into the soil. Pulling my hand away, I sighed as the hilt swayed back and forth.

Best to walk away quickly.

I left Guy's sword behind and merged my mind with Davio's as I advanced on him. "You are in a whole lot of trouble right now. I have to have my hands on something, and it's going to be you."

His chest rose. "Take it easy. We'll compromise."

I pressed my hands flat to his chest as I knocked into him. "What kind of compromise?"

"You need to train in the battle skill so you can move fully through your rising. I'll give you Warrick and Derick to battle with, but it'll happen under strict guard. You'll have triple the strength, and it'll take both of them to wear you out."

"Oooh." I taped his chest with my finger. "You are such a flirt." I wanted nothing more than to come face to face with the two men who'd taunted and imprisoned me when I'd first arrived here.

He eased a hand around my waist. "Those are your increased emotions talking."

"I like it, and I like you."

"I can see." He glanced over my head, but I was too late to react.

Silas snagged my arms from behind. "There should be dangerous pay now we have a Wincrest in our midst."

I scowled over my shoulder at Silas, who I really wanted to kill. "You take all the fun out of being mated, Silas Carver."

He cocked a brow. "Does it look like I care? No." To Davio, he said, "I'll look after your mate and call Warrick and Derick. I can see this is going to be a long day."

"I'll see you in the training hall. I'll have Zac and Viv meet us there." Davio reached for Belle who nabbed Guy's sword. He took her with him as he flashed away.

Silas came around in front of me. "Look, a word of warning. Davio watching over your battle training is not the best idea, particularly when these men will be raising weapons against you." He hooked a finger into his belt. "You understand what I'm saying?"

I mimicked his pose, lifting my chin. "Yeah, that I need to take care."

He glared. "You are worse than Silvie. Now four minutes remain. Go and see what you can find in her drawers."

I didn't stick around.

I nipped straight to Silvie's room and searched through her drawers. I found a pair of sky-blue shorts and two singlet tops in white and gray. I shook out the dust and dressed, tightened the string on the shorts and double layered both tops. I laced up sneakers and pulled my hair into a tight ponytail. In the training hall, Warrick and Derick were ready and waiting as I returned, both dressed in full black ninja-like gear. They even had strips of black cloth tied around their foreheads. At over six feet in height and twice my size, I should have sensed some form of unease, but I didn't. The sight of them had me grinning, my blood racing through my veins at double the speed.

I wanted this. Particularly vengeance at the way Warrick had treated me. Idiot.

"Are you ready?" Silas asked, extending his hand toward the rack of blunted training swords.

"Like you wouldn't believe."

"The others have arrived."

They had. Zac and Viv wore their battle leathers, the same as I'd seen that first day. Belle rushed through the double doors and waited at the edge of the room.

Silas gripped my shoulder. "One's battle training is marked with honor, although because of who you are, we can't afford to train you in the arena before your peers."

I shook off his hand. "Your protectors are not my peers."

Davio shimmered into the room and my attention zoomed straight in on him. He wore midnight-black pants and a billowy white shirt, his sword belted at his side and boy, did he look hot and incredibly delicious. My mind scrambled fast to bridge the gap and merge.

He looked at me, then right past me, his sight zeroing in on Warrick and Derick as they selected their blades. He marched toward them. "I'm warning you both, inflict one unnecessary nick or scratch on my mate, then I'll go for your blood. Keep her training clean and professional." He glared at Silas. "You arbitrate."

To the others in the room, his voice boomed as he said, "Zac, you take the southern wall. Viv, the eastern. Belle, you're on the western by the doors and I'll take the windows. All eyes alert and make sure no one enters and disturbs these proceedings."

They all took their positions.

I frowned, and Silas pointed to the rack. "The safety measures are necessary. Now choose your weapon."

Walking along the line, I reached for the one which I sensed the energy humming from the strongest. A beautiful long and perfectly aligned blade, yet as I wrapped my fingers around the hilt, chills raced down my spine. I focused, a dark vision curling around the edges of my mind. A forewarning, and these I couldn't control.

I gripped the sword tighter, pushed for more and a face emerged from the shadows. Derick's. He battled, and out of the fog, a blade punched forward, slicing deep into his stomach. He staggered, blood spurting as a man shrouded in red snatched at the gold chain at Derick's throat and ripped it free. I gasped as the vision slid away.

Never had I witnessed such a dark forewarning.

I stormed across toward Derick. "Someone harms you, by use of this blade." I tossed it to him hilt first. "Do you fast-heal?"

Smirking, he caught it and held it up. "Yes. We train with these blades. Getting hurt happens even though they're blunted."

Warrick clapped a hand to his back and laughed. "Ha, I believe I've cut you with that one before." Derick grinned back at him and the two jostled shoulders together.

No, they weren't listening and this was what my skill was about. "You have to hear me, Derick. I had forewarning. What I saw is real."

Silas came forward and took the sword from Derick. He ran his thumb over the engraving on the hilt. "This one is favored by Davio." Lifting his head, he scrutinized me. "We'll remove it today if it brings such harm as you speak. Will that do?"

I nodded. "Yes. Get rid of it."

He tossed the weapon to Zac, and the protector flashed away with the sword then reappeared seconds later without it. I sighed.

Silas placed a hand on my shoulder. "When one trains, you must use a blade that perfectly aligns to your grip." He returned to the rack and withdrew another. "This one fits a woman's hand to perfection. It's Viv's baby."

"Thank you." I accepted it, and the metal warmed in my hands. No forewarning. This one was good. "It's perfect."

Near the wide bank of windows, Davio tapped his fingers restlessly on the windowsill he leaned against. "Keep your eye on Derick. He approaches."

"Of course." I whipped around.

"Let's begin this showdown. One rising about to be dispelled." Derick tapped his sword against mine, looked past me to Warrick closing in on my rear and instructed, "We'll train in turns. I'll guide her on movement and balance, and you can instruct on finding an opponent's weaknesses and benefiting from them." To me, he gritted out, "Copy my moves."

He sliced a figure eight in the air and swung at me.

I twisted and just in time threw up my arm, our swords meeting with a ringing crash dead center. I eyeballed him as I breathed rough. "Oh, you did so not want to go there." Then I grinned, my heartbeat racing. "Show me that again."

"I said keep it clean." Davio paced, fists clenching.

"Ignore my mate." My Wincrest blood fired. "Push as hard as you like. Davio told me I'd be able to whip your butt today with this additional strength, and I'm going to since it'll be the only time I can." Yeah, these two men better watch out. Earth woman were smart and crafty. "You've been warned."

Derick rocked from side to side. "I believe I might like you."

"Like is a strong word, but by all means, try and prove it."

"As you wish." Derick struck again and I met the blow.

My lesson had well and truly begun.

For the next three hours, my adrenaline continued to surge, the euphoria almost overwhelming in its intensity. Wow, I loved this battle skill.

The rush brought such clarity forth between my mind and body, and the torrent of energy which I let loose invigorated me.

I fought against both Derick and Warrick, the men far exceeding my experience, yet even though I didn't have their skill, I still had more energy from my wonderful rising and was able to hold my own.

Hours passed, and at times I lost my footing, but I was back up within seconds and rearing for more.

"Wait up." Silas stepped into the fray, coming up right between Derick and me, and once we'd lowered our swords, he marched across to Davio and the two spoke. "Your mate has moved into the full strength of her rising. Do you agree?"

"Yes, she should start to tire soon."

Tire? Ha. Tired was the last thing I felt. I could barely stand still as I waited for Silas to give me the all-clear to continue.

Hands to his knees, Derick puffed loudly. "I might bow out for a bit, and let Warrick take over in full."

"Feel free to rest as you need to," Silas said to Derick as he returned, his gaze cutting to Warrick. "If you need me to jump in, yell out."

A quick nod from Warrick.

I rushed forward and swung. Warrick caught the strike, his eyes glinting with appreciation. We battled, hard.

The fourth hour came and went. Then the fifth. The sixth.

I was having the best time.

Davio groaned, swearing as the eighth hour approached. He pushed off the wall and circled Warrick and me. "You're not slowing down. Tell me how you feel."

"Like I'm on fire, and I hate the thought that this rising won't last much longer." Warrick's attention diverted and I took advantage, cut my sword over his left side. He barely caught the hit, stumbling as he did. Sweeping in behind him, I kicked the back of his knees. It was a dirty trick, but he toppled forward, and I dropped on top of him, mushed his cheek into the cold stone floor and bit out in his ear, "So sorry about this, Warrick, but a girl has to go through her rising and all."

"I'll get you back." He groaned. "I never forget."

Derick rose from his sidelined position, and headed toward me. "It's my turn again."

Davio flashed directly in front of me, and slammed a hand into Derick's chest. "You may leave and take Warrick with you. I'll drag the rest of my mate's rising out of her another way. That's an order."

"Yes, Your Highness." Derick nodded, bent and helped Warrick to his feet then cast me a sly look. "Until the next time we meet." It was a promise I didn't want to wait for, not with my emotions spiking.

I pushed against Davio's back, tried to get past him to nail Derick with another strike. "Hey, come back here," I taunted as he walked toward the door. "Can't you ignore one order? Don't be a wuss. Come and fight me."

Davio blocked me, his frown fierce.

I tried to dodge past him, but he whipped out an arm and kept me in place. Damn, he was being obstinate, and completely immoveable.

With a snigger, Derick shut the door behind him and Warrick. Drat. I'd lost my chance for more payback.

"I've told you your strength is three-times what it should be. Calm down." Davio pulled me up tight against him, burrowed his nose against my neck and breathed deep. "I need to consider your next move," he murmured in my ear.

"You and Silas fight me. Or send for more protectors." I slipped out of his hold and skipped in place. "Oh yeah, do that. Send for more. Lots more protectors."

A ragged sigh. "I can't. We've already seen this morning how a warrior can infiltrate the village and right now, I can only allow those who I implicitly trust near you. Derick and Warrick are amongst those I trust." He grabbed my hand, worked his fingers underneath mine and dragged the weapon free. He tossed it to Silas.

"Hey, give that back."

Silas grinned and backed away with the sword toward the rack.

"Listen to me, Faith." Davio gripped my jumpy hands. "By my count, the first three hours was about your battle skill training, and the following five have seen you moving through your rising. My rising was six hours, and you're still going strong. We need to up the ante and drag this out of you with speed."

"With speed?" I still wanted my blade back, only Silas slid it into the weaponry rack. I moaned and tried to push forward. "Let go. My fingers itch for that weapon."

He continued to block me. "Look at me."

I did, and he quirked a brow. "The speed I'm talking about is a hard run. The castle's meadow will make the safest place. I can give you Silas to run with if you like."

A groan from Silas, and his back sagging. Clearly he didn't like the idea of running with me.

"Super. I'd love that." Anything I could do to annoy Silas would be perfect. I rubbed my hands together, brought the image of the meadow into view and holding Davio's hands, zipped us straight there.

Silas shimmered in beside us, clearly following my 'porting airstream.

"It's almost dark." The sun hovered on the horizon across the other side of the rolling fields of lush grass, streaks of vivid red spearing into the darkening sky. "My mother." I clasped a hand to my mouth. "I've left her alone for the entire day."

"Check in with Wincrest if you wish to find out how she is, but he would have told her what was happening, that you're going through your rising."

"You're right." My feet tingled, and I jogged in place. "I can't go anyway." I gave him a wink. "Sure you don't want to run with me? I can make it fun."

He tweaked my nose. "We both know I can't be left alone with you right now. You have no self-control left, and I'm only holding onto mine by a thread." He slid his gaze to my lips. "I want to hold onto you and never let you go."

"Oh, that I'd love." Oooh, yes, give me my mate now.

"Which means it's time for us to go." Silas swept in between us, pushed me back and motioned to the track rimming the large field. "We have this spot all to ourselves. Do your worst. If you can."

Oh, his gibe was exactly what I needed to divert my attention from Davio. There was nothing I liked more than competition. I headed out, my pace fast and Silas ran in beside me. Together we rounded the field. Again and again. Hour after hour.

Another three hours passed, the moon having risen high overhead and glowing a stunning orange, its light bathing the field in a golden shimmer.

Silas dragged back and coughed, his breathing labored as he lost his ability to keep pace with me.

I felt for him…

What?

I double-checked. That couldn't be right. I felt compassion for Silas?

I slowed and ran backwards while he stumbled in pursuit of me. "Guess what?" I sing-songed.

He whimpered. "You're a pest?"

I laughed, then gasped, caught a hand to my chest and suddenly panted. It was as if I was winded. Surely not.

"Damn, what's that I hear?" Silas tapped his hands to his ears. "Are you short of breath?"

Each lungful of air I breathed became harder to drag in. My rising was almost done, a staggering length of time. With my last burst of energy, I ran and did a full cartwheel then with a grin, dropped to the ground.

I lay on my back, the twinkling sky a glittering array of diamonds overhead.

Silas flopped down beside me and let out a long moan. "You've no idea how painful that run was. Silvie will not believe me when I tell her about the feat I just managed."

"You mean I managed." I lifted my heavy arm and dropped it down hard on his chest. "I'd beat you up right now, but that's about all I can manage."

"There's always tomorrow." He chuckled, actually chuckled. "I'd like to see you beat me up when you're not going through your rising. Betcha I'd win the fight."

The air swirled around us, and I merged my mind with Davio's as he knelt at my side. "That's unbelievable. Eight full hours for your rising." He reached over and clapped Silas's shoulder. "My gratitude knows no bounds."

Silas groused, "I'm sleeping in, and don't think to wake me. Not for anything. Remember that no bounds in my books means unlimited days of sleep-ins."

A laugh in answer, and Davio ran his hand over my brow. "I'm so proud of you."

I stared into his gorgeous eyes. "I might be whacked out, but for some reason you still seem hot."

He slid an arm underneath me and scooped me up. "Let's get you off this damp grass."

I snuggled closer, laying my head against his shoulder. "Can you show me to a bed? I'm not up for a water escape before slip and sliding all over the dome room floor before I finally make it to my own bed in Dralion."

"One second." He flashed us both away, the cool night air gone as we made it to his bedroom. Yep, definitely his bedroom. It looked identical to the image he'd given me this morning.

A royal blue comforter covered his king-size bed, which dominated the room. Square-cut wooden windows with heavy drapery tied back at the sides, faced the meadow we'd just come from, while across the other side of the room, three doors led elsewhere. One was partially open, showing a glimpse of a blue and cream tiled bathroom beyond.

"Do you have a bath? Can I take one before I go to bed?"

"You can." He brushed a kiss against my forehead and carried me into his bathroom. Gently, he set me down on a white wicker chair beside the bath, plugged the hole and lifted the silver lever to run the water. It gushed out, all steamy and hot. "Your clothing should have been purchased and hung by now. I'll fetch it. I won't be a moment."

"Take your time. I'm not going anywhere." He walked out the door and since my head felt like a rock, I rested it back against the chair's headrest, my eyelids sliding shut. Wait. I jerked back upright. My clothing should have been purchased and hung by now? "Davio," I yelled out, "what clothing?"

He strode back into the room with a small bundle in one hand and laid a pair of brushed cotton pajama shorts and a lemon singlet-tee on the vanity's smooth marble countertop. "After you had to borrow Silvie's clothing earlier, I contacted Seriah. She took Silvie with her after school and the two of them purchased some items you might need and then passed them onto Crossley. He hung your new belongings in my wardrobe."

"Who's Crossley?"

"My personal assistant and he's very discreet. No other staff member enters my private rooms other than him. He takes care of all my needs and oversees my schedule. You'll meet him. He flits about as necessary." Davio tipped a bottle of bubble bath into the running water, and as it streamed out, the scent of lilac perfumed the air.

"I see, and how long has this Crossley been around?"

He cast me a glance. "Since I was a small child. It's important I have a trusted man around. He doesn't speak of his duties to any other, will certainly never mention when you're here and in my bed." Opening the vanity door, he returned the bubble bath. "My parents and grandfather have their own wings elsewhere in the castle. You won't come across them. These rooms on this wing are exclusively mine."

A mountain of bubbles foamed. "Did Crossley leave that here for me too?"

"Yes." He pulled me to my feet. "I loved the way you smelled earlier. Crossley stocked the shelves. You'll find a toothbrush and everything you might need there as well."

"Okay." He'd done all this for me, ensured I had clothing and the necessary items so staying with him was no issue. My heart lifted, his care of me so comforting. I looked into his eyes, desperately wanting to express those words.

"I know," he whispered and touched his lips to mine.

"You make a great boyfriend."

"I want to be more than your boyfriend. I want to be your world, just as you're already mine."

"You're lucky I'm so tired right now, otherwise I'd be all over you."

Smiling, he lifted my hand to his lips, gently pressed a kiss to my palm, his eyes so seductively beautiful. "Have your bath. We'll speak once you're out."

"Sure. I won't take long."

"You better not." He left and shut the bathroom door with a soft click.

I missed him already. I shucked my sweaty clothes off and sank into the blessedly warm water. Such bliss. I stretched and soaked, the ache of my sore muscles slowly receding. Thank heavens for fast-healing, although unfortunately that skill didn't ease my exhaustion. Only sleep would do that.

I dunked my head, washed my hair and rinsed the bubbles out, then rested my head on the rim and drifted.

"Faith." A knock on the door. "I hope you're not falling asleep in there."

I slid down into the water, grabbed the sides and heaved

back up. "Not at all. I'm coming."

I dried, dressed and dragged the door open.

Davio was there, and I merged my mind with his.

"Let's get you into bed. You look ready to drop." He set a hand at my waist, guided me to his monstrous bed and pulled back the covers.

I slipped between the sheets and he tucked me in.

In tan silk pajama pants and his mouthwatering chest on display, he walked around the bed, extinguished the lamp on his side table and shuffled in beside me.

With his drapes remaining open, moonlight shimmered in and lit his beautiful brown eyes speckled with gold. He inched closer, ducked his head to my neck, his warm breath tickling my skin. "I don't sleep well without you."

"This bond grows so deep and strong."

"And it'll only continue growing deeper and stronger with the passing of each day." His voice was a husky murmur as he stroked a hand down my arm, then he rose up over top of me and I caught my breath.

"There's no Belle or Silas here to separate us at the moment."

"Which sounds perfect to me." His lips brushed mine. "Sometimes their company isn't desired, or needed."

"I'm in perfect agreement with that." I wrapped my arms around his neck, twined my fingers deep into his golden-brown hair curling onto his shoulders.

"I need to kiss you, like really kiss you." His gaze moved over my face, his eyes filled with that need. "Say yes."

"Yes."

Then he kissed me exactly as I'd longed for all day, his mouth capturing mine as he shared his breath and his deep desire. He was my rock, the one man who wanted me by his side and never wanted me to leave. This was the mated bond. This was what I wanted with all my heart, to know I'd always have him, no matter he was a Loveria and I was a Wincrest. Maybe we could be the ones to halt the fighting between our countries. It would certainly be a dream come true if we could.

All too soon, he pulled back, his breathing rough as he rolled to his side and tucked me in beside him. "You're exhausted and need to rest. Go to sleep."

"One day, you're going to stop ordering me about. I can't wait for that day to arrive."

"I doubt it ever will, so don't bet on it." A light chuckle.

"We'll see." I closed my eyes on a sigh, every last ounce of my energy now sapped, and since I had none left even to argue with him, I slowly drifted and allowed the night to take me under its heavenly wing, my mate exactly where I needed him to be.

Chapter 14

"Are you dressed?" The clomp of Davio's heavy step on the other side of his dressing room door had me scowling.

"No, I'm not dressed yet." Hands on my hips, I eyed the racks of clothing he'd had Silvie and Seriah purchase for me, my shock and anger rising. Last night I'd thought his gesture was so sweet. This morning was a different story, particularly when I'd entered his walk-in wardrobe and discovered that he'd purchased even more clothes than what Alexxis had. "Would you give me some space for a change? You're too close and it's making me madder."

He knocked on the door. "Tell me what's wrong."

My shoulders stiffened. "I'm feeling a touch more pressure in the clear light of day."

"It's noon and Crossley's delivered brunch. I want to take you on a guided tour of the castle and show you my home. I want you to meet my parents and Carlisio. And Silas will be up shortly."

"You realize I actually have a home, and it won't be here. I'm a visitor at the moment." I clenched my fists. "And why on earth would you think I'd wish to meet any of the men in your family? Have you forgotten the battle of our blood? Mine fights against a Loveria's, meaning I'm going to hate your father and grandfather at first sight. I'll only want to grump and grizzle at them, which is not a good look right now."

"You're worrying about things you shouldn't. They'll love you, simply because you and I have formed a soul bond with each other. That's what all our people desire." The door rattled. "I'm coming in."

"I'm still in my nightwear."

Then he was there, appearing out of nowhere as he flashed in and grasped my hands.

"You're annoying." I glared at him. "And don't look at me like that."

"Like what?" He leaned in and rubbed his cheek against mine.

"Like you're about to get away with buying a department store of clothing for me, and without listening to a word I've even said."

"I see." He picked up a length of my hair and wrapped it around his finger. "If what was purchased doesn't suit you, then I'll have the items returned and changed."

I rolled my eyes.

"I want you here." He tugged on my hair, drew me even closer. "I've no intention of living without you."

"I live in Dralion now. You can't keep me from my new family and country. I have an obligation to them, one I can't turn away from."

"I'm well aware." He heaved a sigh and flipped through the racks of clothing. He selected a short white skirt and violet tank top. From a drawer, he pulled out a one-piece white swimsuit, then pressed it all into my hands. "Put the swimsuit on underneath your clothing and we'll forego the family meeting. Instead, I'll take you to the cave on our property for some more bonding time. There's a private underground cavern with a natural pool. I'll ask the others to join us so your bonds strengthen with them as well."

"Which others?"

"Zac, Viv, Belle, and Silas."

"What about Silvie?"

"Silvie's at school and taking notes for you, but she'll be ready to collect at three this afternoon. She can join us once Silas brings her."

"Well, that's where I should be." I checked my watch. "I have Calculus and PE after lunch, and Silvie will be grumping the entire time if I'm not there. She seriously hates Calculus, not to mention any form of physical activity. The two combined always put her in a foul mood."

"Right, then we'll head to school first for those two classes. Afterwards I'll bring you back here for a swim. How's that for a concession?"

"A concession wasn't what I was after." Although what he'd offered was immensely helpful. "Let me offer my own options. How about I head to school, and you do what you normally do here, like aiding your father and grandfather in running this country. I'm not in hiding anymore. I even know the dreaded Donaldo Wincrest, so there's so much less for you to worry about."

"I'll worry regardless." His gaze narrowed. "I'm also grateful that you realize he's dreaded."

"Get out of here so I can get changed." I smacked his arm. "You're completely impossible sometimes."

"Yes, but I'm your impossible. I'll be in the sitting room off my bedroom." He kissed the top of my head, reversed and disappeared out the door.

Two minutes later, I walked out of the dressing room. His voice traveled to me through the open door leading into his sitting room. "That might be a problem. I'll deal with it, Crossley. Thank you."

I waited a moment, until the man dressed in dark pants and a crisp white shirt—who must be Crossley—had closed the door on the far side of the sitting room. Only when all was clear, did I step into the spacious and private abode.

A cozy arrangement of padded chairs and a sofa in a blue pinstripe sat underneath the windows overlooking the front meadow, while brunch was set out on an oak dining table in the corner. An impressively tall oak bookshelf with a myriad of leather bound tomes lined the far wall, while a gold figurine of two men in battle sat on a polished corner stand.

I lifted my chin and scratched my throat. "Nice digs."

From behind a sizeable writing desk with a leather swivel chair tucked behind it, Davio stood and smiled. "Come here."

I crossed the deep blue carpet, so lush and thick, while he walked around his desk and perched his butt on the front edge. I slowed, my gaze on his, then as I joined him, he pulled me into the V between his leather-clad legs.

Gently, I rested my cheek on his shoulder and gasped at the stunning picture hanging in pride of place on the wall behind his desk. The large portrait showed a woman who could only be his mother, seated on a red velvet imperial chair, her delicate and young features framed by hair the same gorgeous color as Davio's, but where his hair was short, hers swept down over her shoulders in lush waves of brown with glimmering shades of gold woven within. In an elegant cream-beaded gown, she gazed at the three suited men surrounding her rather than at the photographer's lens. Davio stood to the right, his father in the center with one hand on his wife's shoulder, and his grandfather to the far left. All three men bore striking resemblance to each other, from their wide brows to their patrician noses and cleft prominent in their chins. So much love encapsulated them all, and it stretched forth from the image to me. "You look like your father and grandfather. When was this photograph taken?"

"The day following my rising. A huge celebration ensued in the ballroom." He threaded his fingers through mine. "My mother longs to meet you, and since she's not a direct Loveria descendent, her blood won't battle with yours."

"I'd like to meet her too, but another day." I lifted a hand and traced a finger along his lower lip. "I seem to be building a fascination for your smart mouth."

"As I have a fascination for yours, although right now it's to do with feeding you. I need to ensure your wellbeing. When did you last eat?"

"Breakfast, yesterday, and I haven't exactly had time to eat since." Although the heavenly scent of bacon escaping from underneath one of the steel domes covering a plate in the center of the table wafted toward me and made my mouth water.

"Then let me feed my mate." Davio swept me across to the small table and pulled out a chair. I sat and he eased into the chair across from mine, stretched out a leg and hooked it around my legs, making the skin-to-skin contact I needed to ease my boiling blood. "Begin wherever you like." He turned his palm out in offering, the sleeves of his impeccably pressed sky-blue shirt rolled to the elbow.

"Thank you." I lifted the domed lid closest to me and uncovered bacon strips and a mound of scrambled eggs. Golden hash browns sat to one side, along with several plump gourmet sausages. "Ah, now that's surely going to replenish my energy." Far better than my usual tub of yogurt on the run. I lifted the second serving lid and grinned as fresh bread, still warm from the ovens, delighted my senses. "Now that's what I'm after."

Davio removed the domed lid on the third plate and exposed a prized treasure of pancakes stacked at least ten high with layers of banana and warm maple syrup oozing out from between them.

I couldn't wait for a taste of that. I tracked my finger through the top scoop of fresh cream, and my taste buds tripped over themselves for a proper bite. I pulled the entire plate closer and knife and fork in hand, cut into the delicious layers. "Do you eat this way every day?" I moaned as I chewed my first mouthful.

"I would if you promised to join me." He ran his thumb over my lower lip, swiped a trace of cream and licked it from his thumb.

"You've so got a deal."

He arched a brow, stabbed his fork into the tower of delight and scooped a mouthful for himself. "I believe this will be our first seated meal together, that's if we get right through it."

He was right. "I'm game to make it through this meal if you are."

"Deal."

Together, we ate, until we were full to bursting.

Patting my stuffed belly, I closed my eyes and settled back.

"You look content." His voice was husky.

I cracked one eye open, then the other. "I am, but I really should go soon. I shouldn't be frittering my day away with you when there's school. Exams are just around the corner."

"I'm well aware, and I understand your need to leave." Pushing back from the table, he stood and took my hand. "Silas will appreciate that I'm staying, as will my father and grandfather. I won't have to miss the meeting they wished to have, or to aid Silas out at Dunbarn." He brushed his fingers along my cheek. "I'll be there after school to collect you."

I leaned in and gave him a quick kiss. "Sure, you meet me there, just in case I've forgotten where Peacio is and all." I winked and stepped back. "Go and slay some actual dragons."

I left to the giddy sound of his chuckle and zipped straight to my mother's home, the only home I'd ever known until just a few days ago. I searched my bedroom for my backpack. I was down a textbook, but I tossed the rest of what I needed for Calculus and PE into my bag and flashed to school.

Oh yeah, I truly loved that I could 'port like this.

The afternoon bell shrilled and students trekked to their classes.

I jogged across the field from the tree I'd emerged behind

and in my Calculus class, I searched amongst the students for Silvie.

"Hey, here!" Silvie waved from the back of the room.

I dropped into the seat beside hers. "Hey back at ya. Where's the teacher?"

"Sick. There's a substitute coming." She crossed her arms and arched a brow at me. "You've missed almost a week of school, and don't go using your record-breaking rising as an excuse with me. What's been happening to keep you away?"

"A whole new family." I set my refill and pen on the desktop. "Who told you about my rising?"

"Mum gave me an update this morning. She got the news straight from Aunt Genevy who popped in to see us."

In front of us, two classmates, Jensen and Rua, shuffled on their seats and leaned closer. "Yo, what's a ris-ing?" Jensen slurred disgustingly as he bumped shoulders with Rua. "Anything that rises in the morning is in-ter-est-ing."

Silvie rolled her eyes and harrumphed. "Obviously it's not the kind of rising you're thinking about. Get a life and go and listen in on someone else's private conversation."

Jensen went to kick Silvie's chair, but she slammed her foot down on his ankle and ground down hard.

"Damn, Silvie." Pulling his ankle free, he shook his head. "You're lucky you're a girl."

"Look the other way." She gave them a fierce frown, which seemed to do the trick. Grunting, they turned their attention back to the front of class. Silvie tucked her head closer to mine. "Sorry about that," she whispered. "I can't believe your rising took eight hours. Carlisio's took seven and that was a major. Why'd it take you so long?"

"You're asking me?" Baffled, I shrugged. "I've no idea."

"I guess it's because you're a Wincrest." She squeezed my arm. "Which reminds me. How's your mother? I can't imagine what she's going through with all these changes."

I gasped. "I haven't had time to check."

"Do it now. Whip up a visual. You've got forethought so you might as well use it."

Silvie was right, and now was as good a time as any.

Channeling my vision through the dome room as Alexo had taught me, I focused. What came to me was an indefinable image, one blurred beyond recognition. I'd never seen such a thing. I focused instead on Dad, and the same blurred image reappeared. He and Mum must be together, had to be since the blurred images were identical.

I frowned, scratching my head. Now, provided I centered on the dome room first, I could see those within Dralion. I'd watched Davio in reverse plenty of times during the three days I'd been with Dad.

"What's wrong?" Silvie bumped her shoulder against mine.

"Um, all I'm getting is a blurred impression."

Silvie's eyes widened, and she clicked her fingers. "Oh, one time my curiosity got the better of me." She spoke fast. "I asked Carlisio what happened when his forethought showed him something he shouldn't be looking at. He said he saw blurred images."

My lips titled to the corner as I considered what I shouldn't be looking at.

They were together and... Dropping my head into my upturned palms, I groaned. "Ew, but they're my parents, and they're not supposed to be getting back together. Mum said she'd need to act her way through being with Dad."

"She's clearly changed her mind about him." She rubbed my back. "They're mates who've been separated for a long time. Even my mother struggles when she's away from my father during the days we're here in Te Puke. I'm sure you miss Davio when you're away from him?"

I looked up. "I try not to think about it."

"But you do?"

I ran a hand over my forehead. Yes, I understood the mated bond. Even now, I wanted to talk to Davio, but without a telepathic link, I couldn't. Just thinking about him had that need escalating though. I opened my forethought and brought his image forth. He stood in a navy and gold decorated stateroom. Silas stood beside him, Carlisio and Everio within their group too. I cranked up the volume.

"Faith's with Silvie in class. The image is grainy, but I'd know Silvie's profile anywhere." Carlisio scrubbed his roughened jaw as he spoke to Davio. "There aren't any problems that I can see."

Hold on. Carlisio was watching me while I watched him.

Spooky.

Davio set a hand to his chest. "I just needed to know she was safe and where she should be."

Carlisio laid a hand on his shoulder, his lips thinning. "I know how troubled you've been, but she's fine. We should speak more about her Wincrest blood."

I probably shouldn't listen in on their private conversation, but since it was about me, I stayed with them.

Carlisio continued, "There isn't a doubt we're all in agreement about Alexo Wincrest. With his daughter falling into our lap, we mustn't allow this opportunity of seizing him to pass us by. She must be contained, then used to lure him out."

"You mean contained, as in 'holding cell' contained?" Silas interrupted. "With the other warriors we've captured, or just on her own?"

The hairs on the back of my neck lifted. This couldn't be happening. Davio would stand up in a second and fiercely disagree to any such containment, or that I be used to lure my father out of Dralion and directly into their lair. He had to.

I waited.

Slowly, he nodded. "I'll do it."

"Good." Carlisio's eyes brightened, the vivid golden-brown

of his eyes matching the honeyed color of his suit jacket. "For the people of Peacio." His words were a cheer.

Everio folded his arms over his red silk shirt buttoned under his flapping black leather vest, not looking nearly as certain as Carlisio. "She's your mate, Davio. Are you sure you can do this? You'll need to use her to hand her father over to us."

Standing taller, Davio let out a long breath. "I'm sure, Father. Alexo will come to her aid should he see what is about to unfold. Hopefully, she doesn't even make it into the cells, although I understand the need for Donaldo's son to be captured and contained. We'll hold the upper hand for once in this long and drawn out war if we can nab him. He is the one with forethought, the most valuable of skills."

I gritted my teeth, worked my jaw from side to side.

How could Davio sell me out this way? I wouldn't let him.

I closed my forethought down and turned on Silvie. "Your family seriously sucks." I stopped as abruptly as I'd begun. Jeez, I couldn't speak to her about this. She'd likely inform them of what I'd heard when I needed to sort this out myself.

"It's all right. Mates struggle when parted from each other. I understand that." She got my angry comment wrong, and I didn't correct her. "We only have PE after this and then we leave. You'll see Davio soon enough."

I would and we'd be speaking. When I'd hid at my father's apartment after first finding out about Silvie's deceit and been gone for days before returning, he'd said in the future we needed to address our problems. That if we had an issue, we'd talk about it. Well, right now I had an issue. A very big one. There would be no containing me, or capturing my father by doing so.

Never would I place myself in such a position of vulnerability, and I'd certainly never accept him doing it either. Not happening, ever.

* * * *

"The boys are here." Silvie slung her bag over her shoulder

as we exited the PE girls' changing room, the last to leave.

"Perfect." I took a deep breath as Davio strode toward me within the stillness of the gym, Silas beside him.

"You two took your time in there." He caught my hand, and my mind *thunked* into his—so annoying.

"Did you have a good afternoon?" In small circles, he stroked my palm with his thumb and because I couldn't help myself, I swayed into him. Damn it. Where was my focus? He'd spoken of imprisonment.

"No, I didn't." I held my ground.

"You want to talk about it?"

"Yes, but alone." I shot Silvie a look, one she thankfully understood.

"I'll see you in the cavern once I'm changed." She linked arms with Silas and the two of them flashed away.

Davio pulled me closer. "Let's go." He zipped us there, so fast.

My feet sank into soft sand, the air warm and the entire cavern filled with a light steam which rose from a large crystal clear pool of water a few feet away. Dark rocks lined every side of the underground pool other than for this beach area, while muted light tunneled in from an entrance to the side.

With a finger under my chin, he tipped it up. "You seem to be out of sorts. Did Belle tell you of the rumor?"

"No, what rumor is that?"

He sighed. "There was a serving maid in the communal dining hall who saw us together. She leaked word that I've found my mate." He paused, a muscle in his jaw ticking. "I had no choice. I had to confirm the news. People are referring to you as my Halfling mate, that you come from Earth."

"You told all your people about me?" How dare he. I didn't mind him telling his closest, but allowing all his people to know would place me in a great deal of danger. I mean, how many Halflings were there in Peacio? There was certainly only one

Halfling who now resided in Dralion, and that was me. I gritted my teeth. "You don't think the next warrior spy sent here might check out this leaked news? You don't think they'd be curious to see who Davio Loveria was mated to? That they might wonder if your newly found mate might also be my father's newly found daughter? How many other Halflings are there in Peacio, other than me?"

He went to open his mouth, only I butted in. "I listened in on your conversation with your father and grandfather. You intend on using me as a pawn to capture my father. You want to lock me away in the very cells you not long rescued me from."

"You shouldn't have listened in, and your father will never permit you to be locked away. With his forewarning, he'll come and that's what we're after. Now we've spread the word about your mixed heritage, he'll be here soon. I've no doubt about that."

"How dare you." I broke my mind-merge with him, the sharp pain of loss slicing through me. "I would never use you like this, Davio. Ever. You're my mate, and I'd never hand you, your parents, or your grandfather over to Donaldo, yet here you are wanting to do exactly that with me."

"You'll never come to any harm when all we're after is Alexo's capture."

"Why must you capture him at all?" Distressed and so hurt, I backed away from him.

"Too many of your warriors are infiltrating our shores and taking what isn't theirs. An attack at one of our largest diamond mines occurred three days ago. Seven lives were lost and Alexo was behind it, as is Donaldo who pulls the strings."

"You can't assume that."

"Yes, I can. It was a methodical attack by a team of eight, of which they're called the leading eight in Dralion. Donaldo hates all things Peacian, and this reeked of Alexo's forethought in how well it was run and carried out. Your father and grandfather work together. They know exactly what they do when they send their bloodthirsty warriors out."

Warriors—yes. Bloodthirsty? A memory surged forth. That first morning while I'd been running on the treadmill, the leading eight had introduced themselves, with bloodied weapons in hand.

But no, my father had been with my mother at that time, taking her on a guided tour. He hadn't been a part of that strike, and I'd never concede to laying the blame at his feet. "So where does this leave us? I won't allow you to capture my father through me."

"Alexo must be taken."

"No, you must change your mind."

"I'll never side with the enemy."

I met his intense gaze with one of my own. "You would do everything in your power to keep your family safe. You can't expect any different from me."

"What are you saying?" Gaze narrowed, he thumped one foot on the ground.

"That I'll never allow you to use me in the way you intend to. My father goes out of his way to ensure I have free choice. He allows me to come to you, and you want to do what? Lock him away and kill him."

A second. Two.

"His death would not be sought. His confinement would."

I shook from head to toe. "I can't allow that to happen. Don't do this to us."

"This is not about us, but my people. Their safety must come first, and yours will never be in question."

"Of course it's in question. You do this, and I can never roam freely on your land. You have to take back my Halfling status and let it be known it was only gossip. You have to insist I am from Peacio. Make something up, but you have to do it, and before word spreads too far."

He shook his head. "Your warriors took seven lives this

week. Two hundred and thirty-eight lives this year. They are killers with only one purpose. They take what they want."

"So, you've made your decision?"

"Yes."

A rush of wind. Silas arrived with Silvie and he bellowed with laughter as he threw her out into the water. Silvie went down, then with bubbles rising, she resurfaced and blew out a fountain of water. "That does not get any funnier, no matter how many times you do it, Silas. You're supposed to leave me on the edge of the pool, not throw me in it. You are such a pain in the neck." She cupped her hand and sprayed water at him.

This was how I should be living. I should be free and having fun. I was eighteen, yet living the life of someone who had the weight of the world on her shoulders.

I couldn't do this anymore.

And it was clearly too dangerous for me to stay here.

I would never give Davio an opening to take me.

The crystal clear water beckoned.

My water source.

My way out.

Chapter 15

Davio hadn't seen it coming. I had dived in fully clothed and flashed back to Dralion before he'd even registered my intent. But it had been the only way.

From the quiet sanctuary of my room, I watched him through my forethought. He was more agitated than I'd ever seen him. He hadn't spoken to anyone after I left. He'd returned to his private quarters and that's where he'd been holed up for the past four hours.

Silas entered his room, and joined him. "You have to speak sooner or later. I realize your mate's gone." He sat opposite Davio on the blue pinstripe sofa, concern radiating across his face.

Pressing his elbows to his knees, Davio stared at the wall. "She wants me to choose her, but there is no choice. All I can think about is the hundreds of families who've suffered a great loss this year, and I can lower those numbers if we eliminate Alexo. The only right decision is the one I've made."

"Yet there will always be Peacian deaths at the hands of Dralion's warriors," Silas pointed out.

"Not that high. We need to be given a fighting chance to defend ourselves. You and I both know how fast and precise their attacks are."

I touched a hand to my chest. Of course I didn't agree with

the loss of lives, would never condone an innocent man or woman's killing, but this war wasn't my doing, and it would never end with the capture of one man. Not when that man was my father. I couldn't lose him, not now I'd finally found him.

Silas sighed. "What about you? This isn't like you to use an innocent to gain the outcome you want. There must be a way to make this right."

Davio scrubbed both hands over his face. "There is no other way." He shot to his feet and stormed to his desk. "Faith will not leave Dralion now, not if she hopes to protect Alexo and herself." He picked up a framed photograph from his desk and stared at it. "She is the one I want, and I can't have her."

Silas crossed the room and squeezed Davio's shoulder. "So how are we better off? She'll be on her guard, as will Alexo. This argument and the loss of your mate will have all been for nothing."

The photograph in Davio's hands was the one I kept on my bedside stand, the one of Silvie and me as we'd celebrated my last birthday at Pier's Restaurant. He must have snuck back and pinched it.

Davio set the frame back on his desk. "She will have alerted him. She left before I could prevent her, and before I was supposed to have taken her to the holding cell. I should have done as Carlisio bid and made it quick, only I wanted more time with her. This is my fault she escaped."

Tears slipping free, I closed my eyes. I missed him, no matter what he'd done. I rubbed my temple, the familiar ache of being denied our connection rolling through me. Three days was all I'd ever lasted in being kept from forming the merge of the mind with him. I doubted I could go much longer than that and be able to sustain the pain. Already it had begun to build.

"Faith." Mum peered around my bedroom door.

"Come in."

She smiled, all blushy and pink and glowing, which had me

recalling exactly what she'd been up to earlier that day. "You and Dad are together again, huh?" I rolled my shoulders.

"How did you"—she coughed, clearing her throat—"ah, no, please don't tell me how you know that. The things you and Alexo can do are almost criminal."

"Trust me, I wish I didn't know." I patted the bed beside me. "Sit. We need to talk."

"About?"

"My mind-merge."

She eased in beside me, tilting her head. "Go for it."

"Dad first said my mind-merge was an extension of my forethought, that I'd activated it because of my warring blood with Davio. What I do is merge my mind with his and with touch, skin-to-skin, I no longer experience pain. Yet if Dad had this ability to bed down in your mind, warring blood or not, he would discover there is no choice—he would have to mind-merge with you." I looked into her eyes intently. "I can go a few days without the merge, but when I'm not with Davio, my mind cries out for his. He's not affected at all like I am, but then he can't mind-merge. I'm the one who has the skill—not him. So, I'm certain this is a separate ability. Entirely."

"Which means?"

I sighed, finally giving into the knowledge which resonated deep in my heart and soul. "I can't go more than three days without him. I need to reconnect to his mind to restore the balance of the merge. I don't know if anyone else has this skill. Everyone's presumed it's part of my forethought, and we all know how rare that skill is. Maybe this mind-merge skill is a rare one too."

"I see."

I shook my head. "No, you don't see. A Magioling's strength skills are passed down through their DNA. I didn't receive this skill of mind-merge from my father or from the Wincrest family line. I had to have received this skill from you, from your family line. You are thirty-six and you could pass for my sister. You are an orphan with no known family. You are also mated to Alexo Wincrest when there has never been any other mating between an Earthling and one of theirs before. Now there is Davio and me. There are too many variables. You can't be of Earth. Don't you see it?"

"Faith, no. I don't have any strength skills." She twisted her fingers together.

"Not all Magiolings do." I laid my hand over hers. "Please, you have to know something which could help me. This is so important. Already my head aches, and I can't go to him."

Her brow creased. "You fast-heal. Why can't you go to him?"

"My fast-healing skill doesn't aid me in this."

It had not relieved the symptoms for me on the mountaintop when I'd needed it so desperately. Only reconnecting to Davio's mind had completed the healing.

I heaved a sigh. "I can't go to him now, not after he's chosen to use me as leverage to capture Dad." Mum's eyes widened, her hands shaking under mine. "It just happened today, Mum. I'm sorry to have to tell you like this."

"Sol," she stated. "You know my maiden name is Sol, and that I was just a baby, around three days old, when I was orphaned. What I haven't told you is that the nuns who ran the home said my mother's name was Katerin and that she came alone. My mother left me there." The truth came tumbling out, and she grimaced. "It hurts to know she never returned. She promised the nuns she would, but she never did. Because of that there was no option for adoption."

"Katerin Sol," I repeated.

"The nuns named me after my mother. They weren't sure what else to do."

I repeated the name again, that of my grandmother's name. "It's a start. Is there anything else?"

In his dark leathers, Dad entered the room, a glow to his cheeks similar to my mother's. "I've been watching your conversation. My apologies. It's a bad habit." He clenched his jaw. "In the future, everything you two discuss of this kind of importance, you will discuss with me present. We are a family."

I pressed my fingers to my temples. "We have a name. Katerin Sol. Now where do you suggest we go from there?"

He planted his feet wide. "We start by backdating Kate's age. Thirty-six years ago, Dralion's dome had been intact for four years. If Katerin Sol was from Dralion, she would've been a female warrior for that's the only way she could've gotten out."

I bounded to my feet. "Are you saying that's a possibility?"

He pressed a finger to his chin. "No, there have been no Sols as warriors until two years past when Maslin Sol joined the ranks, and he is the first from within his family line." He looked at me. "The skill of mind-merge has never been recorded in our land, which is why I believed it must be an extension to my forethought."

"What do you think now?"

"I agree with your assessment. It's a separate skill and quite possibly rare. We need to seek more information."

Mum rose and crossed to Dad's side. "How do we do that? What of Katerin Sol?"

He took her hands. "It is far more likely she came from Peacio where there are no restrictions on their people's travels." Glancing at me, he said, "Which means you'll need to have Loveria search his history books. We have to be certain. He must hold the information we're after."

"I'll contact Belle now."

"Before you do, understand that I would never fall for any of the Loveria family's tactics. It hasn't happened in the past, and it won't in the future. If you were locked up, I would find a way to get you out without being captured. I have forethought for a reason." He wrapped an arm around Mum's waist. "We'll leave you alone to make that call." They flashed away.

In the silence, I paced, shaking out my hands as I crossed from one side of my room to the other. This upcoming conversation wouldn't be easy.

Taking a deep, steadying breath, I opened the link.

"Belle, can we talk? I need you to be the go-between again between Davio and I since I don't have a—"

"Of course. No telepathic link yet. Silvie told me why you left. If it helps, I don't agree with what's gone down. It's not right that he's using you in this way, to capture your father."

"Yeah, but I have another problem. A big problem." I opened my forethought and she shimmered into view. She sat in the rec room thumbing through a leather tome. *"Could you call Davio to you? I need to see for myself what he says."*

I didn't have to wait long.

"He's here."

And he was. He'd 'ported to the rec room, bringing Silas with him.

I rubbed my forehead, outlining every detail as it had gone down with my mother and father. I studied Davio's reaction during the telling.

He stormed to the windows, his fists clenching and unclenching. "Faith is lying," he bit out. "This must be a trick. Sol is a common family name, as is the given name of Katerin. With our form of record-keeping it would be impossible for us to locate a woman who's not been seen for thirty-six years."

Silas joined him at the windows. "I agree. This sounds too convenient."

"What it is," Davio continued in a snarl, "is Wincrest's strategy to circumvent what we've done. His wife is of Earth and Faith is a Halfling. All along Wincrest has said he won't allow any warrior spies to know of his daughter's connection to me." He crossed his arms. "This battle is between him and us, and I'm certain he'll turn up here to halt what we've done—the spreading of the truth, that I'm mated to a Halfling. I don't see he'll have any other choice if he wants to keep Faith safe."

Great. It appeared Davio didn't believe me.

"*Belle, what of my ability to mind-merge? Has anyone ever heard of what I can do?*"

"*No. If this has nothing to do with your forethought as you've said, then you're the first I've heard of, but let me check.*"

She asked Davio my question, and he snapped his answer. "If I'd known about it, I would have said so before now. It's damn convenient Wincrest says it has nothing to do with forethought or his family's line of skills."

I sat in silence. How could Davio ignore the facts? When I found my voice, I murmured, "*Belle, I'm starting to believe this skill isn't known because it's a lost one. A skill that is so rare it no longer exists.*"

"*Explain why you believe that.*" She repeated what I'd said to Davio.

Once she had, I laid down and rested my head on my pillow, the canopy sweeping overhead. "*I mean a deadly one. There is no one known who seems to have held this ability. I can't forget that time on the mountain. I had no use of my limbs and was barely with it. I also can't imagine trying to survive past that point, if Davio hadn't turned up.*"

She was quiet.

"*And then there's my mother. She told me she was left with the nuns when she was three days old.*"

She repeated every word to Davio, and he ground his heel into the floor. "I don't believe this. Now she thinks to hold her safety over my head? No. This ruse will not work against me. Belle, can you feel her pain through your link?"

She shook her head. "There's no pain, just a slight headache and I'm not surprised by that."

Davio gritted his teeth. "Then to believe her words, I demand she come here and see me. The only way to tell she speaks the truth is to see her eye to eye."

And I couldn't do that, not until he'd promised to revoke all he'd done, as well as to take back his decision to imprison me.

"No. I won't come. I'll never allow him to hold me captive, either by his decision to use me as a pawn, or to lock me up within a steel cell."

Belle told him.

"Then it's a lie," he gritted out.

I groaned. We were getting nowhere.

"Belle, perhaps if you could try and research the matter for me, I'd appreciate it."

"And what will you do?"

"Stay put."

"For how long?"

I looked at my mate where he stood. I wanted to go to him and ease his pain, yet instead, I took a deep breath and held firm. *"On the mountain, I couldn't have helped myself. I needed you and Davio then, as I need you both now."*

Belle repeated my words, and Davio plowed a fist into the wall. "Damn it, she is a Wincrest through and through. She plays with my emotions. There is no skill on this planet which ultimately kills. If there had been, we'd have heard about it before now." He stormed from the room.

"Let him go," I told her. *"But contact me if you have any information."*

There was nothing more to be done for now.

Chapter 16

I pushed back the sweaty strands of my hair stuck to my forehead. Dad pushed me in the empty arena, distracting me from my pain. His blade cut across mine and made me groan at the impact.

"Dad," I whimpered as I tried to hold my stance. "You have to give me a break. This session is killing me. You know I'm hitting the three-day mark away from Davio." My training clothes were saturated, my feet so wet I slipped within my own socks.

He twirled around and came at me from the behind, his white shirt billowing. "Another two minutes. You can't arrive there too soon."

"I won't arrive there at all, at this rate, and why are you working me so brutally hard?"

Now in front. "You need to perfect this move. Every second counts." He sidestepped and crossed his blade in a beautiful line, bringing it right up under my nose.

I slammed my blade down, cutting him off in the nick of time. "Hey, okay, that's enough," I muttered. "I happen to need my nose." Why did he keep changing positions? One moment he was in front, the next behind, to the side—it was endless.

Mum called out from the sidelines, her arms crossed and pressed to the top of the safety railing. "Alexo, her nose is bleeding, and she's so flushed."

I wiped my nose, the back of my hand now coated in blood. I'd never had nosebleeds before. I dropped my sword because I hurt. Everywhere. "Okay, so what exactly was your forewarning all about? You never did elaborate."

He took my elbow as I stumbled to the side of the outdoor arena. "I can't elaborate, not when I have no wish to alter my forewarning's course. You've practiced these battle moves, and now the field of play is far more even."

Huh, and Davio thought my father wasn't fair. He was too damn fair. "My time's almost up. I can't do anymore."

"I know." He cupped my cheek. "You can go to him now. The time is right. Loveria will be in the training hall where he works out with Silas. Here, take this." He lifted a very new and gleaming sword from a bag lying on the bench, and passed it to me with a smile. "It's yours. I had it crafted for you by our sword smithy. Consider it a belated eighteenth birthday gift."

So gorgeous. The most beautiful blade. I held it up, balancing it horizontally across the tips of my two index fingers. Perfect. I flipped the blade and the fine hilt slid snugly into my palm. "Thank you." I glanced at Mum, who nibbled on her lower lip.

"Hey." I hugged her. "I'll be back."

"You better be. I didn't spend the last eighteen years watching you grow for no reason."

"Agreed." I 'ported to my room, splashed water on my face and changed into a figure hugging black cat-suit. I belted my sword at my side and it blended with ease into the brassy strip that ran down the side of the clingy suit.

Stretching, I ran my shaky hands over both legs.

I was going in to fight, and I wouldn't be backing down.

With another two painkillers popped into my mouth, I gulped water. I'd taken meds this morning, primarily out of habit, and particularly since my fast-healing didn't work at all on this pain. I'm not sure the meds helped, but they certainly couldn't have hurt.

I opened my link with Belle and fanned my face. *"Do you have anything yet?"*

"No, still nothing. It is as Davio said. There's no record of a skill like yours."

The failure in her tone increased my pain. *"Hey, you tried, and I'm most grateful you did."*

"I won't stop looking, but you need to return. Please, Davio is in the training hall, going at it with Silas again."

I flashed straight there. My father had said the time was right, and no more would I delay.

"I'm here."

"I'm coming," she rushed out.

I turned about within the training hall. Davio puffed as he stared out the large bank of windows in form-fitting black jeans and a black t-shirt, the grassy meadow and rolling hills spread out into the distance. Silas stood beside him, heaving deep breaths as well from their workout.

I closed my eyes, each breath becoming more difficult to draw in. Right now, I had to maintain my focus, because for certain I needed to withhold the mind-merge, no matter what. It would be my only leverage, provided he could see the pain I was in.

Opening my eyes, I set my gaze on him. "Davio."

He spun around, his hand on his sword hilt belted at his side. "You're back." Dark shadows under his eyes showed he'd had very little sleep of late, and with them being so deep and dark, I wanted to cry.

Silas gripped his shoulder. "She's here. It's not your imagination."

Davio's gaze traveled over me. "Your skin is flushed, but apart from that you look fine."

"I'm a Wincrest. We try not to show our pain." Fighting

words as the pressure of the merge I withheld magnified and pressed out within my skull. He stepped forward, breaching the five feet mark, and it all went to custard. I grabbed my head. "No. Don't come any closer."

I had to ensure my safety and my father's first. There would be no mind-merge.

I stumbled back, trying to gather more distance between us, only he flashed in behind me and I thumped into his chest.

Gripping my shoulders, he turned me around, his lips flattened into a tight line. "Your heartbeat is racing out of control because you're not mind-merged with me. Do it. Now."

I wheezed. "Only if you revoke what you've done." I had to stick to my plan. "Inform your people I'm not a Halfling, and then promise me you'll never lock me away in order to capture my father."

"I can't. My people's safety comes first."

"Then give me some breathing space. It hurts too much with you this close."

He clasped my face in his hands, looked deep into my eyes. "Merge and the pain will be gone."

"No." I wiped my bleeding nose.

His eyes darkened, and he let out a low growl. "You walk a dangerous line with your actions. I'll give you a minute and no more." He walked away, boots thumping across the hard floor.

"Faith." Belle flew into the room, the double doors crashing open. Zac, Viv and Silvie were hot on her heels. "See," she said, breathing fast. "I told you she was back."

I staggered to the wall, braced a hand on it as Davio paced a parallel line five strides from me. "She may be back, but she is more stubborn than ever." He glared at Belle. "See what you can do."

Belle eyed me, her hand extended. "I can alleviate some of the pain. Let me touch you. It's bad. I can feel it."

As she advanced, I withdrew my sword. "Don't you dare

tap into me as you did the last time." I drew in a breath, and it rattled around in my chest. "This fight is between Davio and me. I need him in every way, not just physically, but mentally and emotionally." I faced him. "Please. You can't lock me up or use me as leverage against those I love. Just days ago you said no skill could kill. So that means in your eyes, it can't be necessary for me to merge. You also said I'm a Halfling, but I say that's not true. Open your eyes and see that I hold a skill given to me by my mother's line. You have to revoke what you've said." More blood dribbled from my nose.

He grimaced. "When did your nose start bleeding?"

"I've been working out with my father, too hard obviously." More drips, a steady stream, and far more than I expected. I pinched my nose, but the blood continued to flow.

"Then merge." His knuckles turned white as he fisted his hands.

"Why is it you want me to merge so badly? You don't think this skill can kill. In your estimation I'll be fine just like this." My vision wavered, and I blinked to bring it back into focus. "Being near you and withholding is accelerating my death. I can feel it."

"Enough. You aren't dying, not when you can fast-heal. Zac, Silas. Disarm her, but do it gently. Viv head in behind." He glared at me. "You stand there, and I can't do a damn thing."

I lifted my sword against Zac and Silas's divided approach. Zac came at me from the front and Silas from the side. Viv was right behind them. "You do what you need to, and I'll do what I need to."

I met Zac head on, using Alexo's fast move to spin and dodge. I dealt with him then caught Viv's strike. Silas thrust his blade at me, and I met his advance next, our swords clashing.

For the barest moment, my heart soared, and in the next, a hot burn tore through my lungs. I held up a hand, bent half over and grabbed for air. "Cease."

I shuddered as liquid filled my lungs, slammed a hand to my chest and heaved. Blood gushed from my mouth and splattered the floor.

"She's bleeding internally," Zac bellowed, kneeling in front of me.

Viv pulled the sword from my hand, and Silas gripped my arms.

Silvie screamed, but I barely heard her. I shoved against Silas, swept my leg low and kicked him.

Then everything blurred and my own heart stuttered within my chest. I dropped to my knees.

Silas caught me around the waist from behind and jerked me back up. Bending over me, his hands fisted into my stomach, he wrenched. "Cough it out. All of it."

He shoved his fist in hard again, and a racking spasm took me. More blood.

"Now merge with Davio before you die," he growled in my ear.

I lifted my chin, found Davio. He stood, his face ghostly white. "There's so much blood." He stared at the floor. "Too much blood."

"There will also be death before capture. I promise you that."

He dropped to one knee, not breaching the mark which would end my life, the stricken look in his eyes showing he now believed too. "You have a strength skill passed onto you through your mother's line, and it's a deadly one. You are a full-blooded Magioling and everyone here has heard me. Silas will spread the word."

"And you promise not to imprison me?" I needed his promise. Everything hindered on it. "My father will not fall for any future ploy. You know I don't"—I scraped in air—"lie."

Pleading, he shoved out one hand. "Merge with me and it will be as you ask."

I closed my eyes and allowed my mind its release.

From darkness to light.

I fell into him.

He held me tight

Such strong arms.

So warm.

"You truly are the most difficult mate ever." Hoarse words, and they seemed so far away. "I swear you will never do this to me again, Faith. Do you hear me? You're my mate, always mine."

I couldn't lift my heavy eyelids.

* * * *

"How does she feel to you?"

A voice echoed in my head.

"If you let her go for a second, maybe I could tell."

Was that Belle?

A rocking motion, lips pressed to my brow. "It's been hours, Belle."

"Yes, but she no longer bleeds, and I need to clean her up. Faith will not want to wake up this way. You can still feel her mind-merge?"

"Yes."

The voices drifted away.

And the dark welcomed me again.

Water splashed. A soft cloth brushed my face, my arms and my chest. Warm and soothing, water flowed over my body.

The dark still clutched ahold of me, but it was receding.

"I'll carry her." A deep voice. Davio's. I'd never mistake his tone for another. "Wake up, love. If you don't stir soon, you'll leave me with no choice. I'll have to go after your father."

That wasn't happening. I wouldn't allow it.

"Silvie is threatening to pull me apart, limb from limb for what I've made you go through. She said she'd make it hurt."

I smiled for Silvie surely would.

A finger brushed over my lips. "That's it, wake up for me."

I pushed the receding dark fully away and blinked my eyes open. Brown eyes flecked with gold searched mine. Davio. There'd been so much blood, and pain. The battle for my own life and Dad's had been fought, and I'd won. "You almost left it too late," I rasped, touching a hand to my throat.

He lifted me higher in his lap where he sat on a couch in the rec room. "It'll never happen again." Two tears slid free of his eyes and streaked down his cheeks. "I love you. I never want to go through a day like this again. Losing you would have killed me."

With a shaky hand, I wiped his tears away. "And your mind is open, not blocked at all as it usually is. Are you feeling all right?"

He caught my hand and pressed my palm against his cheek. "I had hoped to shock you awake by remaining unblocked, but it didn't work." He blocked quickly, and I couldn't help but smile.

At least I could always trust in the knowledge that he would.

From the side table, he nabbed a glass and held it to my lips. "Your throat's dry. Drink."

I sipped then gasped as I caught my now changed state. Someone had removed my cat-suit and clothed me in a pair of blue jeans and a thick white sweater. "I seem to remember water." I edged up a little on his lap and did a quick search of the rec room for anyone else, although we remained alone. "Who aided me?"

"Belle and Silvie gave you a bath."

He took the glass from my shaky fingers. "You're still healing, so lie still."

Footsteps echoed and Silvie breezed through the door. Shaking her head at me as she approached, she muttered, "So, finally you're awake. Three days of worry and sleeplessness and page turning with Belle, just to find out you have a lost skill that can kill." She stopped in front of me and flicked my leg with her finger. "You're a full-blooded Magioling. It's no wonder your rising took so long. The signs were all there."

Yes, they had been.

Davio groaned, his lips pursed in a grim line. "Hell, it's all my fault. I should have listened to you. You're mine to care for, and never will I make the mistake of putting your life on the line again."

"You mean that?"

"You are my first priority."

I soaked in the sight of him, for I couldn't get enough. "Then I love you too."

His gaze softened. "You are more precious to me than you can imagine."

I grinned. "I think this is where we kiss and make up. You wanna get to that now?"

"No kissing." Silas strode in, and halted beside Silvie.

I sent him a daggered look. "For goodness sake. You have the worst possible timing."

He crossed his arms. "If you go pulling that kind of stunt again, I won't be held responsible for my actions." He eyed Davio. "Have her swear her allegiance to you, so none of this damn nonsense ever goes down again."

Davio laughed. "Get out of here. I was just about to do that."

"Gladly." He took Silvie's arm and blinked away.

Davio pulled me closer. "Right, now repeat after me."

I clapped a hand over his mouth. "Don't even go there. There will be no swearing of allegiance."

Because Dralion was my home and my relationship with Davio wasn't only about the two of us. No. The scope was much broader.

There was Guy Moyer's lost warrior father to locate and many others. And I was a full-blooded Wincrest, one who had the chance to right a very bad wrong.

Davio's arms tensed, his hold tightening on me. "Okay, what are you thinking right now? Because I can tell by the look on your face it's entirely wrong."

I hooked my fingers into the front of his shirt and held on. "Just that loving you is going to be a wild ride. Are you ready for it?"

He took my face between his hands and kissed me, so urgently that a wild ride began. "I'll deal," he murmured between kisses. "Somehow."

Love these characters and want more?

Don't miss the rest of this spell-binding series from a *New York Times* and *USA Today* Bestselling Author.

To love and protect…across worlds.

Princesses of Myth

Protector, Book One

Warrior, Book Two

Hunter, (Novella – Book 2.5)

Enchanter, Book Three

Healer, Book Four

Chaser, Book Five

JOANNE WADSWORTH

WARRIOR

Hope and Silas's Story, Book Two

JOANNE WADSWORTH

ENCHANTER

Silvie's Story, Book Three

HEALER

Belle's Story, Book Four

CHASER

Goldie's Story, Book Five

HUNTER

Lieska's Story, Book 2.5 (Novella)

JOANNE WADSWORTH

Joanne Wadsworth is a *New York Times* and *USA Today* Bestselling Author who adores getting lost in the world of romance, no matter what era in time that might be. Hot alpha Highlanders hound her, demanding their stories are told and she's devoted to ensuring they meet their match, whether that be with a feisty lass from the present or far in the past.

Living on a tiny island at the bottom of the world, she calls New Zealand home. Big-dreamer, hoarder of chocolate, and addicted to juicy watermelons since the age of five, she chases after her four energetic children and has her own hunky hubby on the side.

So come and join in all the fun, because this kiwi girl promises to give you her "Hot-Highlander" oath, to bring you a heart-pounding, sexy adventure from the moment you turn the first page. This is where romance meets fantasy and adventure…

To learn more about Joanne and her works, visit:
Website and Blog
http://www.joannewadsworth.com

www.ingramcontent.com/pod-product-compliance
Lightning Source LLC
Chambersburg PA
CBHW031630200726